Praise for **The Gloaming**

"A paean to a magical continent of silent forests, slow, dark rivers, wild green mangroves; a world populated by child ghosts, haunted whites, and AK-47-toting rebels. It is through this heart of darkness, a landscape rich in possibilities, that Pilgrim stumbles towards the light."
New Zealand Herald

"A thought-provoking novel… deftly set in a world of mercenaries, philanthropists, and witch doctors in polyester suits, the book asks how one atones for atrocity."
Tatler

"Full of empathy and intelli̶ ̶ ̶ ̶ ̶ ̶ ̶ ̶ ̶ ̶ ̶ ̶ly
optimistic and very moving."
Sydney Morning Herald

"Compelling."
The Australian

"I rarely get as invested in the outcome of a novel as I did reading *The Gloaming*, but the empathies that Melanie Finn evokes in this powerful and unpredictable book are not casual; these traumas could be our own. These characters could be us. And so, the themes are familiar and unyielding: Pain. The past. That flyspeck point of convergence where they meet. The regrettable inevitability of everything that passes after that. And shame. Her prose is hypnotic and knife-precise and at times so beautiful it's unnerving. I didn't read this book so much as I experienced it and it will haunt me for a very, very long time."
Jill Alexander Essbaum

THE
Gloaming

a novel by MELANIE FINN

Two Dollar Radio
Books too loud to Ignore

TWO DOLLAR RADIO is a family-run outfit founded in 2005 with the mission to reaffirm the cultural and artistic spirit of the publishing industry.

We aim to do this by presenting bold works of literary merit, each book, individually and collectively, providing a sonic progression that we believe to be too loud to ignore.

COLUMBUS, OHIO
For more information visit us here:
TwoDollarRadio.com

The Gloaming by Melanie Finn was published in slightly different form as *Shame*, in 2015 in Great Britian by Weidenfeld & Nicolson, an imprint of the Orion Publishing Group, an Hachette UK Company.

Author photograph: Britta Jaschinki
Cover image: from *Ladies' Home Journal*, 1889, Newell Convers Wyeth

Printed in Canada

For Matthew

THE
Gloaming

The Summer Before

We were living in Geneva, the high, light apartment on Rue Saint-Léger. We had just come back from two years in East Timor, and we reveled in the cleanliness of Europe, how easy it was to buy what you wanted: a certain kind of shampoo, books, fresh asparagus, Italian shoes. We went for weekends to Paris or Amsterdam or Berlin or to the country house of some new, interesting friends.

At such a house we met Elise. I've considered that it's possible we met her before but she was simply so forgettable that I didn't remember. Even this particular time, I recall only certain details.

It was early June, a heat wave. The house was on the far side of Lac Léman, right on the water. Tom and I had the attic bedroom and we jokingly called it Manila, it was so hot and humid in the small room.

Elise wasn't staying at the house, she only came for lunch on the Sunday. She was an odd, little mouse of a person with sharp, almost twitchy, movements. She didn't say much. But she was sitting next to Tom at the table, and he spoke to her, engaged her, as he did everyone. Even a little mouse.

After lunch, Tom and I napped, and, waking bathed in sweat,

took a cold shower. We made love. It was reflex, turning our bodies without thought or premeditation, the way I might twist my hair into a chignon or Tom would button his shirt. I took for granted that sexual ease, believed it sufficient. 'Let me look at you,' he said, taking. 'Love, love, love,' he whispered, and the holding, and how it always felt, the slow belonging to.

When we came downstairs, the host suggested a walk. About seven of us went. Along the lake edge, a well-worn path, the day still high with solstice heat and bright summer light. It was too hot to hold hands so I let go of Tom. I walked ahead by myself for a short while. I'd had enough conversation, and I wanted to watch a flotilla of sculls and their lovely rhythm, the oars pawing the sun-tinted water.

The group was behind me, not far, so that I was aware of their murmuring and bouts of laughter. I looked back. Tom was talking again with Elise, bending slightly to hear her, for she was not only a small person, but she spoke softly. The breathless air held everything in place, like a still life; any movement seemed amplified, impulsive: a swallow dipping against the water, a shiver in the long grass of an unknowable creature. Elise's hands fluttering up to her face as she laughed at something Tom said.

Magulu, April 27

The sound of it, metal squealing, torquing: the sound of it pounces.

The glass, tinkling: the sound snow might make, and how it fell with just that grace and beauty.

Even with my eyes open. Even in daylight. Even in another country. A faraway country where nothing is the same, not the light, not the faces. The trees, even, are a different green.

I force myself to look at the trees.

Baobabs, figs, acacias.

We pass a man in a pink shirt on a bicycle. He wobbles slightly, for the road is narrow and uncertain. The road lacks confidence. It changes tack, only to veer back again; it widens and then contracts. Should it be here? Or over there?

A woman with a red bucket balanced on her head turns down a path and instantly disappears into the bush. Thick bush, a tangled, knitted green stretching over the earth, a hot wool itching with insects, snakes and birds.

I look at the green. The leaves are stitched together with sunlight.

'Jack, you gotta stop,' says Bob. His wife, Melinda, has her hand over her mouth. Her eyes are panicky. Jackson stops. Melinda opens the door, leans out, retches. She's been vomiting for the last two hours. When she sits back, I hand her a bottle of water.

We are in the car driving to Magulu where there is a government clinic. The hotel manager suggested Melinda call in the flying doctor. But she told him her eldest brother died at Dunkirk. Her mother is 101. If the government clinic is good enough for Tanzanians, then it's good enough for her.

Melinda was horrified by the beggars in Arusha, by everything since—the huts people live in, the scabby dogs, the waiters at the hotel who make less in one month than she and Bob have spent for one night in the room. She's talked a lot to—at—Jackson about civil rights in America. Which he knows nothing about. He's never even heard of Martin Luther King.

Bob says, 'It must have been the fruit salad. Everything else we had was the same.'

I say, 'I had the fruit salad.'

Bob glances at me. He's secretly annoyed. He likes to be right. But it's also very important to him to be polite. And protective, paternal in an old-fashioned, vaguely chauvinistic way. He insists on buying me a cocktail every evening. On holding open every door. He's probably my father's age, but nothing like him.

This was supposed to be a private safari, just Bob and Melinda, touring the Tanzanian bush. But at the last minute I arrived and the safari company added me. Melinda made Bob agree because it cut their cost by a third. She's very conscious about money—about the guilt she feels in having more in her wallet than any black person out the window has in a lifetime. I think Bob is just an old-fashioned cheapskate.

In the buffet queue at the last hotel in Serengeti, I overheard him grumbling to Melinda about Jackson's expectation of a tip, as politely suggested by the tour company. Haven't we paid enough for the safari, Bob asked. Isn't it the company's responsibility to pay their employees sufficiently? It's just a show of appreciation from us to him personally, countered Melinda, you know, for the extra effort he's put in. Oh, said Bob, and just what would that be? Slowing to fifty so we can catch a glimpse of a lion? Apparently, he went on, we should have stayed home and watched the Discovery Channel if we actually wanted to see the animals as anything other than a blur.

Melinda is slim and fit for her age—late sixtyish, and neatly attired in a khaki ensemble. I imagine her speedwalking around her neighborhood in Chapel Hill, North Carolina. In her tanned and weathered hands she will hold little weights, and these she will swing vigorously to tone her upper arms.

Bob has the expensive teeth of a much younger man. He tries to keep pace with Melinda, who is relentless in her forward momentum. Even standing she tilts forward by degrees. I'm sure she senses the decay that awaits Bob, who does not exercise and eats and drinks too much. It will be a stroke, a heart attack or cancer. In only a few years, Melinda knows, she will become a caretaker, ferrying Bob to a series of specialists, keeping track of his oxygen intake, counting out his pills.

Contained in a car for six hours a day, Melinda maintains checklists of birds and animals. She asks Jackson about trees, grasses, the weather, geology. His answers are usually vague, even plainly wrong, and I often see impatience glance across her face; for the money they're paying she expects more. But this is always replaced by genuine sympathy—and perhaps the strong desire for Bob not to be right about the tipping issue. It isn't Jackson's fault he's black and uneducated and born in Africa. He must be so grateful for this job. She's read that the average employed Tanzanian supports forty unemployed relatives.

I am being unkind in how I describe them. Tom hated my sarcasm. 'Poor man's wit,' he called it. But I never had another kind of wit. And Bob and Melinda's Americanness comforts me. They are familiar. I can understand them, not just the words but the motivation and the culture behind them. I have been away from America for so long. I like that Melinda isn't afraid to ask questions. She doesn't worry that her curiosity will be taken as ignorance. As an envoy of her country, she wants to be kind and strong: give me your poor, your unwashed. And even Bob, when we finally stopped to watch a leopard sleeping in a tree, sat very still and whispered unashamed as a child: 'Goddamn, that's a beautiful cat.'

There are more huts, closer together, and gardens containing crops. Children in rags scatter and cluck like chickens, waving at the car or running from it.

'So many children,' Melinda says. She has statistics for this too. Seventy-five percent of the population is under fourteen.

A boy runs right at the car, banging it with his hand. I feel my stomach lurch. Is that what it sounds like—a child hitting a car? The sharp, sudden thud, the quick release of the sound?

The car, so large, absorbs the impact and continues on, effortlessly. I turn to look over my shoulder at the little boy. He's chasing after the car, laughing, and then he vanishes in the dust. Eclipsed, as if he was never there at all.

Then I correct myself: the sound I'm trying to place isn't a child hitting a car. But a car hitting a child. Hitting *children*. Smashing into them. Children who didn't run away, laughing. They broke open. They stained the asphalt.

'These children,' Jackson says. 'They are very bad.' These children, these children. I move my head on its axis, casually, slowly toward Jackson. I appear completely normal.

'What kind of a future are they gonna have?' Bob shakes his head sadly, angrily. 'No land, no jobs. No Serengeti, that's for damn sure.'

'Are we any better off?' Melinda valiantly battles her nausea to score a point. 'Texas has the highest rate of child poverty in America. And some of the richest people.'

Bob scowls, 'You read too much.'

How does she stand him?

Jackson doesn't participate in these conversations. Either he genuinely has nothing to say about the current state and future of his country, any other country, the entire world; or he doesn't want to express his opinions. I get the feeling Jackson is like a train on a single track—one of those airport monorails. He goes around and around, the doors opening and closing, people he doesn't know and doesn't care to know getting in and getting out. He drives the same routes, Manyara, Ngorongoro, Serengeti, stays at the same hotels, answers the same questions, points out the same lions, turns around, drives back, gives the same smile whatever the tip.

Now he grips the wheel, as usual driving too fast, hunched forward. Is he even looking at the road? Or at the end of it? To the bustling capital of Arusha where he lives: the bar, the girlfriend, the blessed silence or the loud music—anything but the ceaseless chatter from the back seat, what's that, what's this, does an elephant, does a giraffe, where is, how is, when is, what, what, where, how, *I specifically asked for the vegetarian lunchbox.*

'Oh, God,' says Melinda, and this time she just pukes out the window.

Bob says, 'This is no joke, sweetie. We should be going to a real hospital. Not some quack shack in the middle of Tanzania.'

A grand roundabout heralds a town. A town of sorts. The cement structure at the juncture of two dirt roads comprises a series of flying arcs. But I'm unable to interpret the artist's vision as a large section has crumbled, revealing a rusting rebar skeleton. Perhaps there was supposed to be a fountain, but the cement floor has cracked wide open. Instead of sparkling, glittering water, the roundabout holds all manner of trash, which is picked over by chickens and children.

'Where are we?'

Jackson slows momentarily to avoid a goat. 'Magulu.'

'Magulu, Christ.' Bob peers out the window. 'It's goddamn Splinterville.'

'What comes after Magulu?' I ask Jackson.

'Nothing.'

'It's a dead end?'

'Yes,' he says. 'It is a fully dead end.'

'For God's sake, sweetie.' With his bandana, Bob pats away the spittle on Melinda's face, 'We have good insurance, we're fully covered for evacuation.'

Low-slung breeze-block buildings extend beyond the roundabout. Small side streets drift off between these buildings to mud-and-wattle shacks. But beyond them, Magulu loses interest in itself. The thick, knobby bush resumes, relentless, interminable, muttering on until the sky. The rolling geography of the land means the horizon could be anywhere. Am I seeing a hundred miles or twenty?

There's a bar with four breeze-block walls and blue UN tarpaulin for a roof. Inside I can just make out a pool table, red plastic chairs, men peering at us. Outside, a duck with a broken wing pecks at an old corn cob.

Jackson stops in front of what must be the clinic. The whitewash is fresh, the door marked with a painted pale blue cross. Perhaps this is a good sign: someone, after all, cares.

Three women and their babies sit on a wooden bench under the overhang of the tin roof.

Bob swats at a fly. 'We should just turn around and go back to the hotel. Get the flying ambulance like the manager said.'

'We've come all this way,' says Melinda. 'At least let's see if this doctor can help.'

When Jackson is out of the car, walking up the steps, Bob says, 'You know Africa is where all the pharmaceutical companies dump their out-of-date stock and all the crap they can't get past the FDA.'

'For goodness sake, Bob, dear, let's just see.'

Jackson comes out of the clinic with a small, odd woman. She wears a beige polyester trouser suit, high heels and a badly fitting wig. The wig is cut in a pageboy style, black with garish blonde highlights. It's the kind of wig a prostitute might choose. Yet, she is wearing a white lab coat. The overall effect is confusing, and I wonder for a brief moment if she's a tiny transvestite. I'm certain she's a woman, but that's the feeling: of disparity, of pieces that don't quite fit. She is oddly and overly dressed, yet her features are neat, naked of makeup, and her dark brown eyes are quick and clever.

'Hello.' Her gaze moves from one to the other of us in the car. She smiles. 'I am Doctor Dorothea. I am here to help you.' She speaks with the faintest of lisps.

'It's Mrs Phillips,' Jackson gestures to Melinda. 'She's very sick.'

Doctor Dorothea's eyes widen and she follows Jackson's look to focus on Melinda. 'Oh, I am so sorry. Mrs Phillips, please. Let us go inside.'

Melinda gets out. She wobbles slightly and Jackson catches her arm. 'I'm all right,' she snaps.

'No, you're not,' Bob says, taking her other arm. 'I'm coming with you.'

'Of course,' replies Doctor Dorothea. 'We must all come.'

Jackson now looks at me. 'You come, also. You cannot wait here at the car.' He then waves an arm in a general way. 'These people are not good.'

'Yes, yes,' Dorothea says. 'There is room inside.'

A small crowd has gathered to watch us.

Dorothea turns and stage-whispers, 'These people are all thieves. They stole my stethoscope. Can you imagine? For what? What are they going to do with a stethoscope? It's just to steal, that's all.' She shakes her head and makes a little snort.

We reach the door and she pushes it open. The coolness inside is a dark, calm well in the heat. But the room is too small and there aren't enough chairs. I tell them I'll wait outside. Melinda looks as if she's about to be sick again. Bob turns to me, 'Yes, you wait outside.'

There is space on the edge of the bench, next to the women with the babies. I sit and shut my eyes against the sun. I can feel it through the red tissue of my eyelids. The sun holds me, I hover in the heat. I am encased by warmth. Still. I can allow myself this, can't I? Not peace, merely stillness.

I can hear Dorothea talking quietly inside the clinic, the calm and sure tone of her voice, Melinda's grateful murmur. Bob says something about fake drugs from India. Dorothea reassures him.

When Bob and Melinda and Jackson come back out I tell Jackson I won't be joining them for the rest of the trip. I'm slightly surprised to hear myself say this so definitively because the thought has only just surfaced. But maybe that's why: I haven't had time to consider the consequences.

I don't choose Magulu; simply, I can't go back. I can barely bring myself to summon the image of Arnau and its Swiss chocolate quaintness, the faux chalets, the geranium window boxes. Within the coil of its streets, people whisper: *Kindermörderin.*

'Are you also ill?' Jackson squints at me.

'No,' I say. 'I'm not ill.'

'But,' he insists, 'it's not possible.'

'What's not possible?'

'For you to stay here.'

'Is there a law?'

'There is no law. No law. But nothing, look, look! There is nothing here.' His voice begins to rise, almost to a squeak, like a teenage boy. 'There is nothing here! A bus once a week! Not even mobile service! Nothing!'

I give him a hundred bucks. 'It's all right, I take full responsibility.'

He takes the money and gets in the car.

Melinda is in the back, lying down. Dorothea has put her on a drip and given her a full complement of antibiotics.

'Don't be ridiculous,' Bob says to me. 'You can't stay here.'

'You are my witness,' Jackson turns to Bob. 'I don't want to be accused.'

Bob looks me over. I sense in him the shades of menace, what he hides even from Melinda. How he hopes bad things happen to people. He is familiar with the soothing pleasure of spite. 'Don't expect us to sort out the mess you're gonna find yourself in.'

I try to look calm and resolved. 'Thank you for your concern, Bob. I hope Melinda feels better soon.'

'Foolish,' he mutters.

Foolishness is the least of it, I feel like telling him. If you found out about Arnau, I would watch your face transform with disgust; and even Melinda would shrink back as if from a foul smell.

'You are my witness!' Jackson announces in his falsetto, this time stabbing the air, then wagging his finger at Bob. 'It is not my responsibility!'

This moment of my transgression will bond them, I think. They will talk for hours about my foolishness. They will discuss all the signs that I was trouble, all the ways I was difficult on the trip. How he and Melinda hadn't wanted me along anyway. I just showed up, a party crasher, with a small suitcase and no safari clothes or sunscreen—not even binoculars or a camera! Odd, yes, there was something odd about me from the beginning. Bob will end up giving Jackson a good tip and calling him 'pal.' Back in Chapel Hill, he'll talk about his pal, Jackson. 'What a stand-up guy.'

As they drive off, Bob glances back. I wave, a quick ticktock of my wrist. He turns away.

I sit quietly, listening to the sound of the car recede. I feel a touch on my shoulder. Doctor Dorothea. I'm sure she's going to ask me what's the matter, why have I been left by my friends— why I am here. But instead she asks if I need somewhere to stay.

Magulu, April 28

She doesn't speak any English, but somehow we communicate. Gladness is proud of the Goodnight Bar and Inn. It seems to be her own business. When she shows me the room, she walks around it pointing out its many features in loud Swahili. But it is the gestures and the enthusiasm I understand: Look, the windows have bars on them, the bed has a net without holes, the cupboards are roomy. Here is a small sink and mirror. Here are the towels. And a complimentary pair of green rubber flip-flops. Down the hall are the bathroom and the shower. *Baridi*, she says, turning the knob so that water trickles out. I check my Swahili-English dictionary: cold. She picks up an empty bucket, '*Moto*.' Hot. The hot water comes only in a bucket.

She does the cleaning herself. I watch her in the bar area, bent double so that her torso is almost perfectly parallel to her legs, dragging a damp rag over the floor. She wipes down the plastic table cloths and the plastic chairs. She polishes the glasses behind the bar. She waters the plants on the veranda. Her industry stands in contrast to the sloth of her customers. They lean back in the plastic chairs and stare at the television and drink beer after beer. The TV is on mute, while a radio plays African rap and whiney Swahili gospel. 'Mwanza *fresh*!' the announcer burbles. 'Mwanza *poa*!'

Mwanza, I remember the name. Melinda was looking at the map with her endless questions and pointed to one of its larger dots. 'Mwanza. What happens in Mwanza?'

Jackson shook his head disconsolately. 'A bad place. Mwanza. The people there burn old women as witches.'

'How awful,' Melinda gasped. 'Do they really?'

'They see the red eyes of the old women and they say they are witches, and they lock them in their huts and set the huts on fire.' He tapped his head. 'The Sukuma people are very superstitious. But me, luckily, I am Christian.'

Melinda wanted to know more about witches and about black magic, but Jackson quickly became reticent. I think he was ashamed, insulted even.

Now I'm sitting with a Coke on the veranda. The local police-man appears, PC James Kessy. His uniform is immaculate. He speaks very good English, and this makes me think that like Doctor Dorothea he comes from somewhere else. He says he needs my name and passport number. I produce the document. He peers at my passport photo.

'This is you, Mrs Pilgrim Lankester?'

I think to correct him. Not Mrs. Not Lankester. Anymore. Yet, the truth, that versatile palimpsest, will lead to more questions, will unravel Arnau. 'Yes,' I say, instead. 'That is me.'

'You have traveled a lot.'

'Yes.'

'Ethiopia. What were you doing in Ethiopia?'

'My husband was working there.'

'East Timor?'

'My husband was working there.'

'He is UN?'

'International Red Cross.'

Kessy nods in a knowing way. 'There is always a war. Refugees. Famine. Always employment.'

Yes, I think. Always a large report documenting what humans can do to each other. Always a case file marked *Atrocity*.

'And where is he now?'

'Switzerland.'

'But he did not come with you?'

'No.'

'Why?'

Why? An image of Elise flashes in my mind, her frizzy, badly cut hair, her small, sharp features. Her nose is slightly red, as if she has a cold. She is holding her baby. Their baby. Tom and Elise and the baby, like an image on a greetings card. 'He is busy with work.'

'What are you doing here?'

'I am on holiday.'

'Holiday?' he laughs. 'Without your husband? In Magulu?'

'Yes.'

'I think you are confused. Maybe you want to go to Zanzibar or Ngorongoro.' He looks closer at me. 'No beaches here. No wild animals.'

'I don't want those things.' I can see how badly he wants to ask but doesn't: What could you possibly want in this forsaken place?

He hands me back my passport. 'How long will you stay?'

'A week.'

'Then you will return to your husband?'

I nod vaguely, the best I can do. Perhaps he thinks I'm one of those women looking for a young African man, a Masai warrior, a hunky tour guide. Indeed, PC Kessy keeps his eyes on mine, discerning. Half of the truth is part of a lie. But which half? He's not quite sure.

'I hear these NGOs have very good benefits,' he says. Then he walks past me, and takes a seat inside at the bar.

★

In my room, I wash my face at the sink. The water is cold and I imagine the dark walls of the well and the smell of the damp stone encasement. The bed is too short so I have to lie at an angle, from corner to corner. I turn out the light, but the room is not dark. Light from the hallway shines over the top of the doorway. There is no ceiling above the rooms, only the pitch of the roof. So the walls are no more than privacy screens. Light and noise breach the walls with ease. It is impossible to sleep as I can hear the men drinking in the bar, low banter and laughter and the loud wah-wah of the radio.

Then, about ten, the generator cuts out. The darkness is sudden and complete. The radio stops and the voices mute and an entirely new layer of sound surfaces. The wind shaking the leaves of the bougainvillea bushes outside my window. The scuffing of feet and chair legs on the floor in the bar. A cough from one of the other rooms I didn't know was occupied.

After a while, the men in the bar finish their drinks and wander out into the street. I can hear them talking as they walk away and the conversations fade or end one by one as they diverge into the night. 'Exactly,' someone is saying in forced English, 'that is my point exactly.'

There is a brief hiatus of silence, then a dog barks. And a faint, rhythmic squeak begins, as if off stage. It grows louder, approaching, and I know it's a bicycle. I have in my mind that it is the man in the pink shirt whom I saw on the way here. I get out of bed and go to the window. But he has passed and there is only the empty street and the long, deep shadows of the moon upon the dirt road that goes nowhere, to nothing.

Magulu, April 29

Gladness is sweeping. The dust particles tremble in the sun-beams. I am eating breakfast: tea and a greasy chapatti. Even though the menu is extensive, Gladness admits only the chapattis are available.

'Not even a blood-pressure cuff,' Dorothea says, sitting down. Today her wig is a red pageboy and she wears a black-and-white harlequin trouser suit. She orders Gladness to bring her a Coke, and I note Gladness's hesitation. There's something in the doctor's tone she resents. A touch of superiority? But she obeys.

As Gladness puts down the Coke, Dorothea announces, 'Everyone here has an STD.' Gladness accidentally spills the Coke, grabbing it before it tips all over Dorothea—who continues regardless: 'Gonorrhoea, syphilis, genital warts. They are all infested. They are all having unprotected sex. I don't know about AIDS. What is the point of testing? There are no retrovirals available.'

Dorothea is so small that her feet, in worn-down kitten heels, barely touch the floor below her chair. The silky red strands of her wig sway in opposition to her almost continuous movement. She cannot sit still.

I turn my head toward her. This is encouragement enough. I learned through my years with Tom—dinners, cocktails, luncheons, barbeques, embassy functions, speeches, gatherings, get-togethers, Christmas parties—that most people require only the slightest response to believe you are listening. The flicker of a pulse, really, is sufficient.

'Do you know I chose to come here? I chose it! Yes! I believed it was my duty. All the others in my year, they wanted postings in the cities, in big hospitals. Me, I said, "It is my duty, it is my responsibility to provide medical care to the poor people in the countryside." Do you know our first president? Julius Nyerere? *Mwalimu*. Teacher. He was a teacher, a humble man and he wanted a nation of humble people. He sent people from the cities, he forced them to go and live in the country so they would not think they were superior. They would know the life of a peasant. But the joke is that I have no blood-pressure cuff. Sometimes I don't even have antibiotics because there is no distribution. The government pretends we do not exist. I gave my last Ciprofloxacin to your friend.' She pauses to order another Coke from Gladness, then hurries on. 'How can I get some? Anything? Betadine. Antimalarials. There is no vehicle, not one in this town, not one for many miles, and the District Medical Officer never sends anything to me. What kind of medical care can I provide? How can I be a doctor? Can you tell me?'

I mumble the sympathy she must be expecting.

Dorothea hasn't finished: 'I cannot treat people so of course they do not come to me and they continue to go to their *mganga* and so nothing changes. We are still living in a primitive time and they believe if they take tea from this root or that tree bark it will cure venereal disease, will cure glaucoma, will make it possible to have a baby even though the woman's uterus is full of infections. Her ovaries are scarred. No eggs can come out.'

Now she sighs, leans back, and again I am struck by the physical dichotomy: her neat, doll-like features belong to those of a young girl, but her skin is slack at the jaw; she's older than I had first thought.

I realize that I'm quite glad of her company, for she apparently requires nothing of me. She doesn't want to know. She just wants to talk, to complain, and her voice is like an idling car; it gently pads the otherwise blank air. I drink my tea, tear at the chapatti and wonder where to wipe my greasy fingers.

The dust lifts from Gladness's broom, sparkles, and the stillness revolves around me and I'm in the middle of it, sitting very still. But there is something beyond it—movement, and I feel a tiny quiver at the base of my spine.

On the periphery there is the rushing.

On the periphery there is glass bursting.

Little bouquets of flowers.

Mrs Gassner trying to tie her shoelaces.

A little girl moving like a beetle on its back—

'Friend? Would you like a Coke, friend?' Dorothea says.

I wade back toward her. I see her clearly and precisely in the chair beside me, her head cocked to one side, smiling, but also with the same look of concern she had for Melinda. I feel a momentary rush of gratitude, as if she's pulled me from rough water. I want to touch her small hand to confirm she's here, I'm here. The dread in my stomach uncoils.

'Do you have a fever?' she peers from under the red pageboy. 'You look somehow unwell.'

'No, no.'

She laughs, a little snort, 'And what could I do anyway! No stethoscope. No antibiotics!'

Later, I look up the word *mganga*. It means witch doctor.

Arnau, March 12

I went out the door and down the stairs. Mrs Gassner was sitting on the hall bench, putting on her shoes. She glanced up with her watery gray eyes.

'*Grüsse*,' she said.

'*Grüsse*,' I replied, fumbling even with this basic Swiss German greeting.

'I go to the doctor,' she said, trying English now. 'My arthritis, it is true pain.' She shook her hands at her shoes.

Her shoes. Stout leather lace-ups. Swiss made. Of course.

'Look, my hands do not work.'

'Can I help?'

'Like a child. I cannot do my own shoes.' But she moved her feet toward me in request.

I bent down and pulled the laces tight, tied them in double bows.

'Is that okay?'

'*Danke*. This a bit tighter. Okay. *Danke*, thank you.'

Mrs Gassner's handbag was there beside her feet. It was slightly open, enough to reveal several white billing envelopes inside.

'It will rain in one hour,' she said, standing up, adjusting her hat. 'I feel my old bones.'

She saw me walk back upstairs to my flat. 'You forgot something?'

'My phone bill.'

'Ach, they cut you off no mercy. Watch out.'

In the flat, in the small kitchen—there it was by the toaster, the white envelope. *MAHNUNG!*

I put it in my bag.

I wondered, briefly, why I should bother to pay it at all. The phone hadn't rung since Tom left. Our friends in Geneva were Tom and Elise's friends, now. They were phoning Tom and Elise.

I went back downstairs.

Mrs Gassner was just driving off when I came out. Seeing me, she suddenly stopped and rolled down her window. 'Oh,' she said. 'I forget to inform you. My cousin, he say the land, Tom never buy it.' She gave me a little wave then jerked forward a few yards, the ancient white Fiat confused by the conflicting commands of the accelerator and brake. Mrs Gassner was a terrible driver.

I stood, quite unable to move. Stalled, not unlike Mrs Gassner's Fiat. Tom had never bought the land. Never. Bought.

Tom never bought the land.

Although we'd taken a picnic, and lain upon the green, late summer grass, still woven with daisies, the high air a-shimmer, the occasional hum of a bee. The land, *our* land. Although he'd said the words, 'This is our land now.' The mountain behind us, up a steep path and onto a knife-like granite ridge. Below us, tumbling down several thousand feet of village and road and cow meadow, Lake Thun pooled in the sun. As it was summer, the deep blue water had been dotted with boats.

And at that same time, at the exact moment when he kissed me, when he put his hand up my skirt, Elise had been in Geneva. She had been four months pregnant.

There was the story I told myself because Tom, when he left, wouldn't explain any of it. And in my story, he hadn't known about the pregnancy, not until much later, perhaps the eighth month. This made the summer and everything in it true. Coming to Arnau in August. Talking about the dream house, our plans, how many bedrooms, a bathroom with a view. Renting the flat was a temporary measure, a way to be in Arnau on the weekends and, as Tom said, 'To get a feel for the land.'

But the land had been a lie. He'd never bought it.

In September he'd suggested I stay in Arnau during the week, take German lessons in Tunn. He arranged these. He told me about yoga classes at the local school, about a hiking club. He wanted me to become part of the Arnau community, 'make connections, make friends.'

On weekends, he couldn't get enough of me, constantly taking me to bed. 'Let me look at you, let me look at you.' He'd been inside me with his lies.

I was aware of a bad taste in my mouth, as if the corruption was corporeal, like cancer. My skin smelled of it, my sweat reeked of it. I put my hand on the car door. Keep going, I said to myself. The language class in Tunn. It was a fact, like the car. It was all I had. Where I had ended up, after the world, the farthest corners of it, the clever conversations with diplomats and aid workers, after marriage, in this tiny, little life.

I got in the car, I started the engine. Keep going. Even though I'm terrible at languages, even though I could barely say 'Grüsse.'

And I was driving. Straight, straight on. Through the village. I passed the small grocery shop, the post office, the apothecary— the pin-neat commercial array which was Arnau. Around the corner, toward the recycling center. Keep going, keep going, I told myself.

And then the windshield burst open like a crazy flower.

Magulu, April 30

Evening, around five, and I decide to go for a walk. To follow the nowhere-nothing road north. I intend to go a few miles and turn around. I walk past the clinic, which is shut—no sign of Dorothea. There are then the two half-finished buildings, which precede the edge of town. Immediately after: the bush. It is a matter of feet to step between the two worlds—this awkward human outpost and the stuttering, fidgeting bush.

The road bisects the green, drawn with all the certainty of a three-year-old's crayon, wobbling, but indelible. I can't understand why it's a road at all as I never see cars, and there isn't the trace of a tire track on the earth, even where, hard packed, some imprint might remain from the rainy season. There are, however, many bicycle and livestock tracks and footprints, some bare.

I walk for about ten minutes before I see the children. They are still some distance ahead—perhaps five hundred yards. I see they are playing with a puppy on a string. I wonder where they live, for there are no huts nearby, none that can be seen, only paths that diverge abruptly into the bush. I think how much is hidden.

As I come closer, I realize the children aren't playing with the puppy, they are torturing it. One drags the puppy along the dust, the rope so tight around its neck it cannot breathe or squeal, while the other two hit it with sticks. They are so involved with their game, laughing hysterically as they hit and hit the puppy, that they don't notice me until I shout, 'Stop it!'

Immediately, they look up. Their faces express a strange and shifting mixture of emotion: fear, excitement, and something else I can't quite register. They abandon the puppy, which has urinated and shat all over itself, and rush toward me, dancing around me.

'*Mzungu*! *Mzungu*!' they scream.

'Pen, pen, pen!'

'*Mzungu*! Pen! *Mzungu*! Give me, give me!'

They circle around me, laughing, their bare feet stirring little clouds of dust. '*Mzungu*! Give! Give! Give!'

I feel sharp little fingers pulling at the pockets of my skirt. 'Give me!'

I grab the girl's hand and push it away, 'No!'

They move quickly, their dexterous little hands poking and pulling. And dancing, they laugh, so I can see their little pink tongues and sharp, white teeth. 'Pen, pen, pen!' I smell them, their unwashed clothes, the rags that pass for clothes, their filth and sourness.

'Stop,' I say again, but they do not pause or care.

One of the boys slaps the back of my thigh and screams with laughter. The other reaches over and pats the front of my skirt, my groin. I try to back away, but they move with me, patting and slapping now, pinching, dancing, laughing, chanting:

'*Mzungu, mzungu, mzungu*, give me!'

'*Mwacha!*'

An angry shout, a male voice.

In an instant they scatter, and are gone. Absorbed back into the bush.

It is PC Kessy. 'They are animals,' he says.

'They're just children,' I turn, holding the tremor in my voice. 'They don't know what they're doing.'

Kessy raises his eyebrows, 'They touch you like that and you think they don't know what they are doing?'

'They don't really know what it means.'

'And when they do know, do you think they'll stop and become civil?'

'Yes.'

Kessy laughs. 'You should not stay here.'

'Because of these animals?' I say it with a kind of challenge in my voice.

'Because you don't understand.'

'They are just children.' I repeat this as if to convince myself. Yet, I wonder: what would they have done to me if Kessy had not come?

He is silent a moment. 'Please, madam, walk back to the town with me.'

'No, I want to walk on. Not far. To the top of the rise.'

'But the view is the same from here as it is from there.'

I start to walk anyway. He shakes his head and falls in beside me.

'I don't need a police escort.'

'I am just walking this way. To the top of the hill.'

So we walk, saying nothing. And from the top of the rise I see the land rummage on. In the distance are more hills.

'That is Kenya,' Kessy says. 'Less than twenty miles.'

'And the road goes there?'

'Not officially.'

'Not officially?'

'The border is closed. People must only use designated border crossings.'

'But they cross anyway.'

'Of course. Smugglers, Masai, local people. Who is going

to stop them? Me? With my club? My flashlight?' He laughs at himself. 'My laws?'

We stand for a while in the low wind. I'm thinking about the children. The way their teeth chattered and snapped. They are a rendering of this place, of the hidden, dark huts and the weary violence that breeds there, and ends up, one day, in a report on the desk of a human rights lawyer marked *Atrocity*.

Walking back, we pass the place where they disappeared. I can make out their footprints in the dust, a fandango, and here and there the tiny paw prints of the puppy.

'What are you doing?' Kessy asks.

'Looking for the puppy.'

'It has gone. It has followed the children. Look.' He crouches, shows me the tracks.

And I'm washing my face in the sink. It is later now, after dark, and the generator has quit, so I have only a cheap candle and this wavering, narrow light. I'm washing my hands, surprised at how dirty they always are. I look at myself in the cracked mirror above the sink, push back my hair. I've lost weight, it shows in the hollow of my cheekbones. The children—of course, they are just children. Their gender and their number are a coincidence. A girl and two boys. From huts in the bush. But there, again, is the odd loosening, the wavering, and I force myself to look in the mirror. Here I am. Here. My hands on the sink. The solidity of things. Touch my face with my fingertips. Feel my skull under the skin.

Bern, March 13

I wanted Tom.

But in the same instant I knew he wouldn't be there. Knew like looking at the whole world from space, a spinning blue marble: Tom was with Elise and their new baby.

I opened my eyes and saw the rectangular lights and white ceiling.

'Mrs Lankester?'

A face loomed over me. A man, unknown. For some reason I focused on his nasal hair. 'You are okay,' he said. His voice was heavy with Swiss German. 'You are in a hospital in Bern. Everything is okay. Just a bad concussion and a few bruises. You are very lucky.'

Lucky?

I tried to speak, to form the word 'why.'

He leaned in. I could smell his aftershave, the hint of peppermint on his breath.

My tongue was burred, heavy. I labored to form a 'w.'

'Water?'

I nodded, or seemed to, or perhaps just shut my eyes. Everything began with 'w.' Why, what, who, water.

He said, 'I'll have the nurse bring you some.' Then he shone a pinhole of light into my eyes. 'Look at the light. Follow it.'

I did as he said.

'Now, my finger. Follow. Yes. Good.'

'What.' I said. 'What.'

'Water?' Briskly: 'Yes, yes, I'll ask the nurse.'

I shut my eyes, focused, my mouth forming the words clumsily. 'What. What.'

He looked at me. 'Do you have any bad headache?'

'Everything. Hurts.'

'Can you then think, please, about your head.'

I tried to feel my head like a detached object, a vase with potential cracks or chips. There was no specific pain. I told him this.

'Good, good. We shall keep you for observation for twenty-four hours and then you can be released. Unless the police—' he cut himself off, busy putting his little flashlight away.

'The police?' I grabbed at his sleeve, nipping the fabric.

He pulled away with a shocked expression, as if I was a leper or beggar. Then immediately he covered what I'm sure was disgust with a professional look of query.

'Yes?'

'Why am I here?'

'You do not remember?'

Really, I had no idea.

'It's very common. In such an incident of trauma to have memory loss. Post-Traumatic Retrograde Amnesia. Some memory may eventually return. Or it may not.' He glanced over my chart. 'CAT scan is normal. Blood? Yes, yes, all fine. But let us know if you feel any severe nausea or experience ringing of the ears or blurred vision.'

'What trauma? What police?' It was difficult for me to speak, as if there was a great distance between my brain which held the words and my mouth which should speak them. I sensed the doctor's evasiveness, but then was not sure at all. Was I just not understanding? As I struggled to speak, my mind felt sluggish.

But he didn't answer. Instead: 'Is there someone we can contact for you? A friend? A relative?'

'No,' I said. Why wouldn't he tell me what had happened?

'Are you sure?' he regarded me. 'There must be someone.' Now he flipped to another page on my chart. 'Your husband? Mr Thomas Lankester.'

'We're not married.'

'He is listed as your next of kin.'

'The divorce,' I said. 'The paperwork...'

'Ah, yes. Here it is,' he stabbed the relevant paperwork. 'I see that the police called him, but he declined to come.'

I felt a humming of humiliation in my chest. Keep going, I thought.

'And there is no one else?' He sounded incredulous.

No one. Because we always left or they always left. The projects, the tribunals, the stints—it was impossible to form attachments, friendships. We joked, Tom and I, of our 'associates.'

When I didn't answer, the doctor turned to leave. I spoke now with determination to be clear: 'I want to know what happened, why I am here.'

'The police are coming in a minute. Wait for them. It is better for them to explain.' And he left.

I lay back and considered the curiously intense image of Mrs Gassner putting on her shoes. I was helping her with the laces. I hadn't paid my phone bill.

'They cut you off no mercy,' she was saying.

MAHNUNG!

There was a knock on the door. A policewoman leaned in. 'I am Sergeant Caspary,' she said. 'May I come in?'

She entered gently. She was small and rounded, not fat, but neatly stacked in a series of orbs. She pulled a chair to the side of the bed and cleared her throat and took out a notepad. 'The doctor tells us you don't remember what has happened.'

'I'm sorry,' I said automatically.

'It must be very confusing for you.' Was she being kind? I couldn't tell. She took a small breath, 'I must inform you this is something terrible.'

I was trying to think—what? Perhaps if I squeezed my eyes shut I could find the memory. I could feel the outline of it in the dark. I considered the word 'terrible'—a bomb? Had there been a terrorist attack? I felt in my body a sudden lurching as if I'd been thrown.

'You were involved in a very tragic incident,' Sergeant Caspary said. She waited, watching me as if gauging my reaction. Like the doctor she'd carefully chosen the word. Like the doctor she was evading.

'*Incident?*'

She shifted in her seat. 'With your car.'

I waited. She waited, watching me.

Then she said, 'Three children have been killed.'

Obviously, there'd been a mistake. Someone else instead of me. Charts switched, paperwork mixed up. Even the Swiss can make mistakes. But Sergeant Caspary said right away: 'I appreciate it's difficult for you that you don't remember. It must seem very unreal.'

Only then did I feel a prick of panic: not about the children, but that I couldn't remember. The children were not real; no more real than if I'd read about their deaths in the paper. Their deaths had nothing to do with me. But the missing time—the part of me that I could not retrieve—it was like waking up with a stranger in my bed or finding a tattoo on my arm. It was like waking up and finding Tom gone from my bed, and that moment of confusion when I wondered where he was.

I should speak, I was expected to express my horror. But I could only turn inward, frantically searching for an image, even a glimpse—the corner of a memory that I could drag into the light.

'Mrs Lankester, are you all right?'

Slowly, Sergeant Caspary came back into focus. I knew what I was supposed to ask. 'Was it my fault?'

She shifted in the seat, still watching me. 'There is an investigation, of course. So at this time we cannot conclude fault definitively. Your car hit a bus stand, just outside Arnau village. Three children were waiting. Two died almost instantly, the third was taken to hospital. She died a few hours later.'

I turned away. I kept thinking it must be an elaborate mistake. But if I stepped back, wherever I stepped, the ground was unstable, there was no truth. Tom hadn't bought the land.

'We'll need a full statement from you,' she said. I heard her push the chair back and stand. 'We'll need you to be available for the duration of the investigation.'

I began to cry.

For myself. Pity for myself that I had lost hours, had lost my mind, was hurt and vulnerable and confused. I wanted my husband to fold his arms around me and tell me it would be okay, that Mrs Gassner was mistaken about the land. But he would not.

Sergeant Caspary put her hand on my shoulder. She was touched by my grief. 'Your driver's licence is suspended during the investigation.'

Magulu, May 1

A man is trying to lead a large white goat. There is a rope around the goat's neck, and the goat pulls back against this, matching the man's determination. But not quite his strength. Inch by inch, the man succeeds in pulling the goat forward.

Why is the goat so stubborn? Does it know that at the end of the journey there is a noose that will haul it upside down in seconds and a knife that will slit its throat? And if it can't know that, does it sense at least some kind of mute and awful darkness to be avoided at all costs? Is it lore among goats that when you are taken away by yourself with a rope around your neck, you will never return? Perhaps I'm expecting too much of the goat; the goat simply resists the man because it is the nature of goats to resist.

Another man comes and he pushes the goat from behind. But still the goat will not accept defeat. It turns sideways. So now the second man must steer the rear end of the goat, trying to anticipate or counter the determined veering, while the man in the front must maintain the tension on the rope.

Watching this, I'm tempted to think it's funny, and I catch myself almost smiling. I look around to check if anyone has seen me and I notice Dorothea coming from the direction of the clinic. She's dressed like a demented Tinkerbell today, a pale green satin dress and a little blonde wig.

'Friend!' she cries out and waves. 'Have you seen Mr Kessy?'

I shake my head.

'Are you free to walk with me? Perhaps we will find him at the police post.'

Beside her I feel like a giant. Glancing down, I can see the seams of her wig on the crown of her head. We walk toward the roundabout and turn north. A few shops line the road. They sell the same things: packets of soap powder, bottles of water, sodas, Tanzanian gin, cooking oil. There are little cafés, too, and these also sell the same things, fried balls of dough called *mandazis*, greasy chapattis, sweet, milky tea. I think the ubiquity isn't so much lack of innovation as lack of alternative. What else is there to sell? What else is there to cook? As Jackson said, the bus comes once a week. I've never heard another vehicle.

The police post is a shabby cement building with an office and a cell. No one is here.

'Where is this man?' Dorothea says, frowning. 'Let us wait. Are you free to wait with me?'

The late afternoon light stretches out the shadows and the air cools. We sit on the steps. Down by the roundabout I see the men with the goat resting. The goat bleats with passion, its ribcage visibly expanding and lifting. How it longs for the reassurance of another goat's answer.

'Kessy says you walked with him toward the north.'

As if we'd gone on a little hike. 'Yes. He came to help me.'

'The children, he told me. I'm sorry for your trouble. They are very bad. Little animals.'

'So Kessy said.'

She's looking up at me with a small smile. 'This word, animals, you don't like it.'

Tom and I could never trust anyone with frankness. In those high-minded, expatriate circles, a comment made even in dark humor or innocence could be twisted. To call someone 'an animal'—even one of the perpetrators—would lay you open to charges of racism. It would be a career-ender.

'Somehow it is shaming?' Dorothea presses.

'Yes.' And this makes her laugh.

'But they are without shame. Like animals. Do you see? You maybe feel shame for them, but they do not feel shame for themselves. They are strong, because their brothers and sisters who are weak have already died.' She waves her hand around, encompassing all we see. 'This is a graveyard. Here are more babies than rocks buried in the soil. It is too crowded. There is no room for shame.'

In my mind's eye, I see the three children dancing in the road—yes, shameless, weightless, and Kessy saying, 'Do you think they will become civil?' They were beating a puppy to death.

'Friend.' Dorothea touches my wrist with her fingers. 'Sometimes you're going very far away.'

Soon, I think, soon she will start asking questions. Why and how and who. So I turn to her, the party trick of my full attention. 'Tell me. Tell me about Mr Kessy.'

'You see that he doesn't belong here?'

'He doesn't belong here.' Tom called this means of deflection, lobbing. He was proud of my ability to lob our associates. For hours at any given dinner table I was able to deflect, to reveal not a single thing about myself while giving the impression of participating in the conversation.

Dorothea adjusts her wig. 'Kessy is a bad policeman but a good man. Once he was a good policeman and a bad man. He changed, you see. One day. In only one day, one hour, one minute. For the police, it is not the same in this country. They are corrupt. They must be.'

Possibly, I could say to Dorothea: You'd be surprised at what happens in my country. But which country? My country was

Tom. Instead, I simply lean forward, creasing my brow to show her my concentration.

'In this country,' she says, 'the salary of a policeman is too low and the barracks are filthy with very poor plumbing and often no running water.' The spool of her story unravels, the more she tells, the more she wants to tell.

There are seasons of corruption: twice a year, when school fees are due, and just before Christmas or Eid. The pressure on police to provide for their families is greatest during these times, so they set up roadblocks to check drivers' licences and find all kinds of things wrong with cars: a cracked mirror, a missing door handle. This is easy to do because the Traffic Act is hundreds of pages long. Even driving in flip-flops is an offense.

'We plan for these periods,' she explains. 'We make sure we never have a lot of money in our wallets, only small bills, because a policeman will accept even two thousand shillings. A policeman does this twenty times a day and he has made enough for one child's school fees for one term. That is what he must do. Even we, his victims, understand.'

Now Dorothea hesitates. She glances at me, gauging my interest. Tom said witnesses often spoke to hear their own voices. They sought to confirm their existence, and speaking gave their thoughts weight, transformed the invisible into the tangible. I see, now, Dorothea's need for definition. So I say, 'Kessy was a good policeman,' and she quickly takes up the thread.

Kessy was working a particularly lucrative stretch of road in downtown Arusha. The police drew lots to get these spots, and had to pay off their superiors with their takings. After all, just because you had been promoted and sat behind a desk in an office, why should you lose out on bribes? Kessy was standing at the roadside, stopping cars, telling the drivers, 'Oh, your side-view mirror is cracked' or 'You are missing a hubcap.' He was building a small house for his wife. They planned to have children. Only one room of the house was finished, and they lived in this. The rest was still a cinderblock shell without a roof, and in the back, there was a wooden latrine. It was, Dorothea explains, a beginning.

'We are not like you,' she says. 'We know it is maybe years before we have a roof or a sofa or running water. White people want everything, they are used to their own way. Sorry for this, but it's what I have seen. My mother was a house-girl for some British people in Dar es Salaam. It was in the eighties and there was no water in the town system. They couldn't believe this, they couldn't believe that if they turned on the tap nothing happened. They complained to the City Council. They wrote letters. Nobody wrote back. Nobody wrote to tell them, "There is no money to fix a broken pipe up the line." Nobody told them, "You will wait twenty years for that pipe." And anyway, small boys were stealing the letters. You would put your letter in the postbox and one minute later these boys come with wire and hook the letter. They look inside, perhaps there's money? If not, they just take the stamp. Even this they could sell.

'In the end, my mother's white people realized they were wasting their time with the officials, so they made my mother get water from the well down the street and carry it up onto the roof and fill the water tank so that they could take showers. She carried twenty buckets a day, along the street and up three flights of stairs.'

Dorothea smiles at me. 'But I don't think you are severe like that. Only...' she pauses, searches my face. 'Only it's difficult for you here because you have a white mind.'

'Kessy said the same thing. That I don't understand.'

'Don't worry,' she pats my arm reassuringly. 'When you understand this country, you know you cannot ever understand it.' Returning to the story of Kessy, she reaches a certain day, when he was taking bribes on the roadside and a young boy ran across the street near him. A crowd surged after the boy, shouting, 'Mwizi! Mwizi!' Thief! Thief!

Kessy knew well enough how these situations ended: the mob will catch the boy and the boy will be beaten to death. So Kessy grabbed the boy. The boy was not so strong. Tough but not strong, and anyway he saw he could be safer with Kessy. He went with Kessy to the car.

But an old woman pushed through the crowd. At first, Kessy thought she was a madwoman, and he ignored her, but she would not go. She followed him, then pecked at him with her words. Something about a girl, a young girl.

Why did Kessy go with her? He doesn't know, even now. He was a good policeman and good policemen do not go into the slums. They ate their *chai*, they got fat. It was a good job, being a good policeman. Easy. Instead, Kessy went with the old woman. They walked and walked, they turned corners, more corners. They stepped over ditches that were *choo*. Where else can people relieve themselves? Even Kessy could not believe the smell.

'At last,' Dorothea says, 'Kessy and the old woman came to a door.'

It was not locked. Kessy wondered if it was a trap. But it was too late, he had to find out. He opened the door. It was dark and there was another smell. He could not describe it, but it made him afraid. He knew he was about to see something that he could not have imagined, and that the vision would be with him forever. He would know what one person could do to another. He wanted to turn from this, to save himself. He heard the girl breathe.

'I'm here to help you,' he said.

He opened the door further and the light sliced across the darkness.

And he saw her. What was left of her.

'*He saw her, what was left of her,*' Dorothea repeats, as if the horror belongs to her as much as to Kessy.

Kessy took the girl directly to Doctor Miriam, a white doctor at the hospital in Arusha. Doctor Miriam didn't ask any questions.

She took the girl, this poor girl, and she sent her somewhere safe where she could never be found. The story was printed in a local newspaper and some important people were very embarrassed because they knew. Of course they knew about the girl. She belonged to one of them, and Kessy was the source of the whole problem. He was not being a good policeman.

Dorothea doesn't know what had been done to the girl. Kessy only ever told her one detail. Her toes had been smashed by a hammer. The rest he keeps for himself, inside his eyelids.

'So you see,' she says. 'They will forget Kessy, as they are forgetting me. And sometimes I think we are even forgetting ourselves and one day you will come back here and you will say, "Oh, Dorothea, how are you?" And I will say, "Who is Dorothea? There is no one here by that name."'

As we sit on the steps I think of her crazy outfits as a kind of armor against despair. She is defiant. And I consider what it must be like to be this clever woman, to have become a doctor without medicine, as Kessy is a policeman without laws.

Kessy does not come and dusk moves in and she asks me to help her look for him. We find him walking back along the nowhere-nothing road. Dorothea smiles when she sees him.

Of course, they are lovers. Who else would they choose?

Arnau, March 14

I thought I misheard. My brain, still thick and slow, resisted input, so that the exterior world remained remote. As a child I'd had my tonsils removed and I remembered the waking: the muffling effect of the anesthesia, the soupiness of my senses. In this way, I stood in front of the frozen foods aisle of the village store, trying to decipher the contents from the packaging. *Gemüsegerht. Huhn mit Reis.* I knew the words, but they were encrypted. I was hungry. I opened the freezer door, reached in. *Lasagne.*

Kindermörderin.

I stared at the packet, the layered pasta dripped with cheese. I turned the word over in my mind. *Kindermörderin*: was that the German word for lasagne? Surely it was just 'lasagne.' Curiously, I felt my cheeks flush, as if my body was able to process the translation before my mind. The heat in my face alerted me to the embedded word: '*kinder.*'

She was standing beside me, unnaturally close. Intimate. A middle-aged woman with short hair, unremarkable but familiar. She worked at the local hotel, may even have been a manager. Slowly, I turned toward her.

Her dark brown eyes hard as pebbles, her English heavily accented. 'I hope cancer eats your face.'

Then I became aware of the entirety, the stillness of the shop, the invisible antennae twitching in my direction. Every person in there was concentrating on me. Even as they chose laundry detergent or consulted their shopping lists, they attended to me. *Kindermörderin.*

I put the pieces together. *Mörderin.* Murderer.

Very slowly, I put the lasagne back. I wanted to do the right thing, to be seen as reacting properly. Perhaps I should cry, as I had done with Sergeant Caspary. Tears of grief. But I had the notion this wasn't what they wanted. I kept my eyes straight ahead, careful not to inadvertently catch anyone's gaze. At the door, I put my shopping basket back in the stack.

Outside, I checked for traffic as I crossed the road. I did not turn around, but I was certain they were watching me from the window, clustered like flies.

Magulu, May 2

He is white.

How shocking whiteness is. Having become accustomed to seeing only black skin, whiteness seems awkward—bleached. We were not meant to be white; it's an adaptation. The dappling of freckles, the coarse crop of his red-gold hair. His eyes are bright blue. How did we ever convince black people that whiteness was preferable, more beautiful? His eyelashes are pale, like those on a golden retriever. I realize I am staring.

He extends his hand, 'Martin Martins.'

A slight European accent, the origin difficult to discern.

'Pilgrim.' I take his hand; the surface of his palm is rough and surprisingly cold.

We are in the narrow hallway between the rooms. I stepped out and there he was, proximity forced by the small space.

'Are your parents religious?'

'Why?'

'The name.'

The name, the curious name, the cocktail party banter. 'They're hippies,' I say, as I always do. 'The Journey of Life.'

'Seriously?' He laughs. He actually laughs in a ha-ha-ha way.

I consider the comeback, something about how his parents

had no imagination and used the same name twice. But though Martin laughs, I already know he's not a humorous man.

'And here you are on your journey,' he says. 'Magulu. What a shithole, hey?'

I listen to his voice. Perhaps somewhere in the former Eastern Bloc. Poland or the Czech Republic. Possibly further east.

'Magulu's not so bad.'

'By what standard? A Nigerian jail?' Ha ha ha.

Tom spent two years writing a report on Nigerian jails. He came home from his research and interviews stinking. At first I thought it was the smell of the jail, but he said, no, it was him, how he came to smell, listening to the prisoners, seeing what he saw. It was a physical reaction to the suffering of others.

'Sure, by that standard,' I tell Martin.

He's clearly not sure how to take this flat response, and he inspects me more closely. 'Imagine the guidebook! The Rough Guide to Shitholes!'

'Imagine.'

He takes a packet of cigarettes from his shirt pocket and uses the act of offering me one to close again the space between us. The brand is Rooster, I notice, a retro design of a cockerel printed on the pack.

He lights up, turning his head to exhale the smoke. 'I love Africa. Love it. You can still smoke anywhere you want. When they are chopping each other's arms off and stealing billions in aid money, they can hardly say, "Oh, now we want to have stronger anti-smoking laws."'

Is this amusing? I'm not sure. Something I read comes back to me: 'You know, this Continent of Africa has a terrible strong sense of sarcasm.' I do not remember the book, one of Tom's. But this man has about him a feeling of dark experience, has taken the sarcasm to heart. He is not a tourist or a traveler. He has purpose and is explicitly unafraid.

'And you,' I say. 'What are you doing here?'

'Fuel pump's fucked on my Land Cruiser. I'm trying to get a message to a mate in Mwanza. No fucking mobile service so I had to hire a guy on a bike. I'm here until I can get a replacement. There's a bus or something. A week at least.'

I do not want him here.

I do not want his inevitable questions or his weird vibe or his cold North Sea eyes. I turn to move away.

'You going out?' he says.

'Yes.'

'Where?'

I look at him. 'Just out.'

'Promenading?'

'What?'

He taps ash casually onto the floor. 'Promenading. You know, walking around and about for the purpose of being around and about.'

'Yes, promenading.'

'You've come to Magulu to promenade?'

'It's in the guidebook. Page sixty-three. "The Promenades of Magulu."'

He laughs, ha ha ha, and wags his finger to let me know I've got one up on him. Then he taps on my door with his knuckle. 'This you? Number four?'

I nod.

'I'm just across the hall.' He gestures to room seven, as if I want to know.

I start to walk away. 'See you later, princess.'

Outside, I turn right, staying within the perimeter of the town. An old woman selling *mandazis* smiles and waves, and this feels like a blessing: a moment of normalcy, a simple, unguarded interaction. I wave back, but now she offers up a *mandazi* and I feel compelled to purchase one. Her smile vanishes, she's focused on the coins in my hand. She gives me the dense, fried chunk of dough wrapped in newspaper, and the grease leaks onto my hands. I can't possibly eat it, but I cannot throw it away because I keep thinking about the children, shameless and puppy beating, but certainly hungry.

So I walk on, holding the oily newspaper self-consciously. It grows heavier, and when I find myself back at the Goodnight my arm almost aches with strain.

The bar is quiet, the TV a cold, occluded eye without the generator's power. I look but don't see Martin Martins. Carefully, I walk down the narrow corridor to my room. I try to be silent, but the lack of ambient sound means every action is amplified: the key in the lock, the click of the lock, the grit on the floor scraping as I open the door. And the same in reverse as I shut the door, slicing through the still afternoon.

Sitting on my bed, the window framing a rectangle of light, I watch thunderclouds. Muscular and grand. Their shadows cast across miles, shifting the dominant tone of the landscape from green to deep purple. Almost every afternoon the clouds perform. But despite their baritone rumbles, there is no rain, only the damp and oppressive weight of expectation.

I can hear Martin Martins now. He must have been napping. Is that a real name? An anglicization of something unsayable? His bed creaks when he shifts his weight. I hear the sound of a match striking, a sigh, a page turning. I lie so still because I don't want him to hear me. I believe he is listening.

My hands are still greasy from the *mandazi*, and I wipe them on my skirt. The *mandazi* itself sits on the small corner table, nestled in its newspaper, gleaming with oil. Quickly now I grab it and throw it in the bin.

Arnau, March 15

Tom stood awkwardly in the doorway. He offered up a bouquet of peonies and delphiniums.

'Flowers?' I said, letting him in as though he were a salesman.

'I wanted to make sure you're all right.'

'You could have just called.'

'The phone has been disconnected.'

'Yes. So it has.'

'Is there a problem with money?'

'I forgot to pay the bill. That's all.'

He sat at the table, holding the flowers. I turned away from him. I didn't want him to see my swollen face, the bruises, how ugly I looked. And this appalled me. That my vanity held so fast.

'How's Elise? How's the baby?'

There was a tic in his movement as he put the flowers on the table. 'Fine. We're all fine.'

'That's good. It would be a waste if you were unhappy with each other.'

'Pilgrim,' he said, and moved to touch my hand.

'Don't.'

'If there's anything I can do.'

'You've done enough.'

He ignored this. 'What about your parents? Have you called them?'

'You know that's not possible.'

'They're still living like that?'

'Like what?' I wanted him to condescend, to sneer.

'Like—' But he stopped himself. 'Without a phone?'

'Yes. Still. It's how they live, Tom. Feral as goats, and happy.'

'You could—'

'Go and stay with them?'

He sighed, bowed his head. 'I don't know. But I'm worried about you. We're worried.'

We. I thought about this shift, made in a matter of sentences. Not years, not months, not weeks. Once—for twelve years—we had been *we*. Now we was exclusive of me. This new we he spoke of casually, yet with surgical precision. He was a lawyer, he always chose his words.

'I'm fine,' I said.

But Tom was not finished. 'Elise has the name of a great therapist.'

'You think I should see Elise's shrink?'

'Therapist. Highly qualified psychotherapist.' He spoke calmly. 'Shock. It's very insidious. I see it all the time at work. You know that.'

'And just what do you think Elise's shrink would suggest? That I start an affair with a married man and get pregnant by him so he leaves his wife?'

Tom exhaled softly. 'Jesus, you're so bitter.'

'Or did I get it the wrong way round? You got her pregnant so you could leave me.'

'It's time to move on.'

'Why? So you can feel less guilty?'

He stood and shook his head with contempt, 'Three children

are dead. Don't talk to me about guilt.' He tossed the flowers in the sink, an expensive bouquet worth several hundred Swiss Francs.

Magulu, May 3

A mob of children surrounds Kessy. He holds in his hands a box, and they are all trying to touch the box. Kessy is losing his temper, but he must hold the box with both hands as it is torn, at risk of collapse, and he cannot fend them off. Gladness's brother, Samwelli, wades out to help him. Samwelli is small and neatly formed, like Gladness—not so much bigger than the children, but he is quick and strong; he picks out the main troublemaker and pulls him roughly aside.

The ragged procession moves down the street, drawing in new members, as if Kessy is the center of gravity. The children are screeching and jumping, the adults grinning and chattering. I can feel the frantic energy of the crowd, the greed of it, not for Kessy, or even the box, but for the event itself: something is happening in Magulu!

Dorothea stands outside the clinic, ready and alert. Kessy hands her the box and turns on the crowd, his club swinging like a propeller, opening up a semicircle of space. People are shouting questions at him. One man, in a red T-shirt, shoves forward and stabs his finger at Kessy, his voice hysterical with accusation. In an instant, Kessy grabs him, flips him onto the ground, cold-cocks him. The crowd steps back in awe, as if they have seen a magic trick. Kessy places his knee on the man's back and jerks his wrists into handcuffs, one at a time.

Now, looking at the crowd, pulling the man to his feet, Kessy speaks in a low, hissing voice. They listen and seem to obey, for they back up. But I see in their eyes something base. One day, they will tear Kessy apart. One day, they will hit him until he falls on the earth and they will kick him, his face, his ribs, his stomach, his groin, until he is no longer a policeman, no longer anyone they knew, and when he is good and dead, when he is meat and dust, then they will vanish into the bush.

Am I beginning to understand?

'Friend!' Dorothea calls to me. 'Come, come here!'

Inside the clinic, she opens the box. It once contained paint and is tied with yards of sisal string. One panel is agape.

'Why is Kessy bringing me such things?'

Just as she finally succeeds in cutting away all the sisal, Kessy reappears to explain: some children found it in the roundabout.

Tentatively, with the end of her pen, Dorothea pushes back the flaps of the box. Its contents are wrapped in newspaper. She puts on latex gloves and unwraps the first item. It is about a foot long, severed at both ends. The surface is pale as milk, shriveled and dry. I think it must be some part of an animal.

Dorothea recoils. 'God bless us.'

She takes out another object, unwraps it. It looks like a large prune.

'A human kidney.'

'You are sure?' Kessy asks.

'And the first is a forearm, cut at the wrist and the elbow.'

There is also a hand, dried and shrunken, so that it seems to have belonged to a monkey; but these are all human parts: a heart; a liver; and two ears, wizened as dried apricots.

A human being can be reduced in any number of ways. I think of Tom's reports. Machetes. Kalashnikovs. Axes. The clustering of words in certain paragraphs: disemboweled, decapitated. We never spoke about any of it and he never read the reports when I was in the room. But they were always there, on a desk, in his briefcase, vibrating with detail.

'Albino,' Dorothea says. 'From the color of the skin, I can tell this was an albino person.'

Kessy shakes his head in disgust and turns to me. 'This is the magic of the Sukuma people and their superstitions. They believe albinos are spirits and ghosts. And their bodies are magic.'

'How do they get the bodies?' I ask, although I'm sure I already know because nausea is welling in my throat.

Dorothea makes her noise of disapproval: a soft snort. 'They kill them. Yes, they kill them, even children. And they then cut them into small pieces. Like this. For a lot of money. This magic is worth a lot of money.'

Perhaps Dorothea mistakes my disgust for disbelief. She looks directly at me. 'It is to put on a curse. A powerful curse.'

'What kind of curse?'

'For many things,' Kessy says. 'To get some land or some money. To kill an enemy.'

'How do you kill with this?' I gesture to the box.

Kessy smiles. 'Imagine someone hates you this much? What have you done to him? Perhaps in your heart you know you are guilty. And this magic speaks to your heart.'

A sensation comes over me, as if something is moving underneath my skin, one of those terrible worms that beds down in your flesh. For a while, no one says anything, and I realize Kessy and Dorothea are afraid. Yet they don't want me to see their fear: that they are like the people of the village or the people who would kill an albino and cut him up. They don't want me to see that a part of them believes in magic so strong.

Dorothea says to Kessy, 'You must keep this at the police station. It is not safe here.'

'But I have no place to keep it there. Only my desk. And there are no locks.'

'I'll keep it,' I say, and I see their relief, even as the worm flutters at my throat like a pulse.

I take the box and as I'm walking to my room I see Martin Martins.

'What you got there, princess? Some kind of treasure?'

Holding the box in one hand, I can't quite unlock my door. He moves in to help, taking the box before I can protest. He sniffs. 'Smells funky.'

Even with my door open, he refuses to hand back the box. 'Allow me.'

'I'm fine,' I say, reaching for it. Smiling, he hands it over and watches me put it in the cupboard.

'Glad I could help.'

'Yes, thanks.'

He reaches over and touches my cheek. 'Princess.'

I pull away. 'Why do you call me that?'

'Are you offended?'

'You mean to offend.'

Martin laughs, 'Princess: *The Princess and the Pea*. You know the story. She can't sleep because something in the bed is bothering her. It's only a pea. But she's a princess. She doesn't like discomfort.'

'Are you the handsome prince, then?'

He laughs louder, harder, making a show of it. 'I'm the dark prince. Bluebeard.' Ha ha ha.

Then he walks out.

For a long while I sit on the bed and I think about the box and whether I can throw it out. But this isn't possible. I can't just throw away parts of a person. And I think about what Kessy said: Imagine someone hates you this much. Enough to kill. What do you do with that kind of hatred? It's heavy and dense.

It must be placed in a drum and sealed, buried thousands of feet below a desert. And even then it might bubble its way to the surface.

Magulu, May 5

A woman is howling.

Gladness and I run to the front of the Goodnight. The howling comes closer. It is difficult to make out what we are seeing: a bicycle surrounded by a group of people. As they approach, we see that on the back of the bicycle is a pregnant woman. Two men push the bicycle and two others hold the woman down. Her mouth is agape, red, a trout gasping for breath.

Dorothea is already walking toward them. She speaks to the men, then runs past the clinic toward us.

'Friend,' she says. 'Do you know where is the other *mzungu?* We need his car.'

We go together and knock on the door of room seven.

'Martin?' I call out loudly over the sound of the woman screaming. 'Martin?'

He comes to the door looking calm and relaxed, a magazine in one hand, a Rooster in the other. He pushes his hair back from his forehead. 'Hey, princess, what's up?'

'Your car,' Dorothea says. 'Please help us. There is a woman in labor, her cervix will not dilate. The baby cannot come out.'

'Huh. I thought all that noise was the TV.' He lies so casually. 'Is it possible? Your car?' Dorothea presses on.

'I'm sorry. But the fuel pump. As I told the princess, it's fucked. Cruiser's no good without the fuel pump.'

'Are you sure there's nothing we can do?' I say. 'Rig something?'

'You're a mechanic?'

'No.'

Martin glances at his magazine, then back at us. 'It's a shit situation you're in. Really bad for that poor woman. But without the fuel pump there's nothing I can do.'

Dorothea looks at him severely. She is wearing the blonde Tinkerbell wig, and beads of sweat slip down her face. Abruptly, she turns and hurries down the hall. Her little kitten heels, worn down to nubs, make clippy-clops, like little hooves.

Kessy runs up the street. He and Dorothea speak, and he runs back toward the police station. 'He will try to radio Butiama, to see if they can send a car.' She shakes her head, 'But even if they can, it will be many hours. Pilgrim—' It is the first time she has used my name, 'I think this woman is going to die.'

The screaming continues for hours. Sometimes there is respite for a minute or two. I sit with Gladness who is trying to listen to her radio. Outside, it's as if Magulu has fallen under the spell of a wicked witch. People have shut their doors. They try not to think about the young woman dying, the baby dying in her. Or maybe they just can't stand the noise. Gladness tells me through our tentative pidgin that the men brought the woman from many miles away, traveling overnight. *Mbale. Mbale sana.* Far. Far away.

Kessy sits on the veranda. He radioed headquarters in Butiama but they said their only vehicle had gone to Mwanza. Kessy studies the plants that Gladness cultivates in old tins and cans. He takes a leaf between his fingers, examining the veins.

But I'm convinced she won't die.

Things will work out. The woman's cervix will dilate. Dorothea will successfully perform an emergency cesarean. Somehow. Kessy will find a car.

Women don't die like this.

I go to the clinic with a couple of Cokes. I'm not quite sure what I think I can do with two Cokes. But what else? At first I don't recognize the small native woman with her hair in tight cornrows; Dorothea has taken off her wig and shoes. She holds the dying woman's hand. I take the woman's other hand. She squeezes hard and screams again, her giant belly arcing upward. It takes all my strength to hold her down and I wonder how Dorothea has managed by herself for hours. I look at the woman's contorted face. She is not a woman, just a girl, perhaps seventeen.

'The baby is already dead,' Dorothea says.

After another hour, the girl begins to hemorrhage. Blood spews out from her vagina and splatters on the floor. My reaction is to try to clean it up. But Dorothea says, 'Wait, there is more, much more, before it finishes.'

I keep thinking, cannot let go of the alternative future—which is surely still possible: Martin will fix his car. An airplane will land on the road, the pilot has heard about the situation and flown in to help. The slouching beast still might change direction; there in its flexible ligaments, there in its joints, it might turn and walk away.

But then I feel it, like a dark, dark poem: how it enters the room. It displaces the air. I shut my eyes. Dark, dark, pressing down, invisible but moving, moving the air like hot breath. I feel sweat pricking my armpits. I'm afraid to look; to see it has an incarnation.

I know exactly what it is.

In the next moment Dorothea lets out a breath. 'She has passed from us now. She is with God.'

No—no, I insist, stubbornly, trying to scramble up a muddy bank. She is not dead. I'm sure I can hear the sound of an engine. It's still as if my wanting can make the sound real.

Dorothea cuts into the girl's belly, which is tough with layers of muscle, and lifts out the baby. She peels off the placenta, revealing a perfect boy. She puts the still, dead boy against his mother, between her breasts, which are heavy with milk. 'They can be together now. It is the local custom.'

The room is full of light, light falling like talcum powder. The beast has gone now, furled or folded and slipped under the crack of the door.

But I know I felt it. Know it had substance, breath. There is its handiwork.

They do not look peaceful, this dead mother and her dead baby. Her face holds the lines of her agony, her terror, her diminishing. And the boy is too tightly curled, as if instinctively he made himself smaller so he might fit through the narrow cervix after all. Or, as if he was trying to hide, the way children do, in corners or under the bed, so death would not find him.

After, in the too-quiet, Dorothea and I sit and drink the Cokes.

Magulu, May 7

'Tell me your story, princess,' Martin Martins says. He turns the chair around, so that he can rest his forearms on the back like a dude. He's drinking beer. I think he's a little drunk.

I look at him. I keep my distaste to myself, for I believe it would only give him pleasure. I was by myself, reading a book Dorothea lent me. She has the complete works of Danielle Steele, a writer I never imagined reading. But there is a poignant innocence at the core of the stories. The heroine always makes her choices based on love, which is beautiful and honorable. And, thus, even if she loses love, she is triumphant.

I wonder for whom the books are written. The young woman who still believes in love—for instance, a nineteen-year-old who meets a handsome stranger on a street corner. A budding human rights lawyer, perhaps. Or the wife who has been left, cast aside by the highly respected human rights lawyer, and needs some reassurance that there is, after all, something noble about her.

'Tell me about that hard little pea making you so uncomfortable,' Martin says, taking out a Rooster. He lights the match with one hand, a little party trick.

I look steadfastly at the text of *The Promise*. The resurrection of the heart, the wisdom that comes only from loss. Ha ha ha.

'Then don't talk.' Martin leans in, blows smoke into my face.

'Let me buy you a beer. Drink, look pretty. That's enough for me.'

Intent, I turn a page.

Now he laughs, 'Are you still ticked off about the other day? What did you expect me to do? What did you do? Did you save her? Did your crying and feeling oh-so-bad save her? Ha ha ha.'

It's impossible to read now. I can smell the beer on his breath, his cigarette smoke smarts my eyes. When I glance up, he yells out, 'Gladness! *Mbili*!'

She brings over two beers. She is looking at me in a way that I feel might be hostile.

'Okay, princess. I can see you are on the edge of your seat.' Martin drinks, settles in. 'It's really quite interesting, my story, from an objective point of view, if you didn't have to live it. I can see you're ready, you're fascinated. Ha ha.

'So, I was a pilot for the Ukrainian Air Force. Are you impressed? In the early nineties, the Ukraine sold off a lot of its old shit equipment to stupid African governments. Who else would take it? Only a dumb coon dictator so he can repaint it and parade it around. And, hey, the bombs still worked. As long as you could get the plane up, you could drop the bombs out the window and they would explode.

'In 1991, three mates and me, we get an offer to fly three MiG-3s to the Congo. Oh, excuse me: *Zaire*. Fucking joke. They should just deal with the issue once and for all and call it The Republic of Total Stinking Shit.

'These MiGs, let me tell you, princess, they were real pieces of crapola. Only one of us has working nav equipment, so we had to follow him, like little ducks in the sky.

'We plan to stop in Uganda, at Entebbe. An hour, just to refuel. But some busybody from the American Embassy hears about us, and before we know it the planes are embargoed, our money and our passports are confiscated by the authorities. The Ukrainian Government denies all knowledge of the planes and us. And Mobutu? President for all Eternity of the Republic of Total Stinking Shit. What's he going to do? Send us a check?

'So, first, we sell our watches, then our T-shirts, then our hats. We sleep on bits of cardboard under the planes. We get bitten to hell. We get malaria. We have to eat fucking *posho*. You've never eaten *posho*, have you, princess? We come up with stupid plans. How we're gonna steal the fuel or walk to Nairobi. We plan to hijack an airliner. It's all we do, come up with stupid plans. Viktor sells his shoes to a guy selling bananas and I take the money and go into town and make a phone call but I can't get through to Ukraine. I keep trying. I reach my cousin, he promises to send money through Western Union.

'Every day I go into Kampala to the Western Union, but there's never any money. When my shoe fund is finished, Dimitri sells his shoes to the banana guy and we try all over again with his cousin. Fucking Ukrainians are all fucking liars. The money never arrives.

'And there we are—you get the picture—we have our flight suits and one pair of shoes, and one night, this Angolan comes out to the planes. He says he's got jobs for us. The man had these black eyes, so you couldn't see the pupils. Hyena eyes. My *baburya* would have said he had the evil eye. But what do we care after three months of sleeping on fucking cardboard and shitting in the bushes and wiping our assholes with banana leaves. Ha ha ha. Three fucking months of *posho* and we are ready to lick the evil eye if it will get us the fuck out. And so, princess, we begin our lives as mercenaries in Africa. Twenty-five years now. Whatever you can imagine, whatever hell, your worst nightmare, I've seen it and I've certainly smelled it. And you know what I've come to realize, after all of it?'

He pauses now. He knows I'm listening, I can't help myself. His North Sea eyes never shift, never even blink.

I look at him, and wish I hadn't. 'What? What have you come to realize, Martin?'

'There're always more of them.' He smiles at his revelation and affects amazement, almost perplexity: 'No matter how many die or how they die. Burning, screaming, guts falling out, whatever. There're always more of them.'

I wait for a moment. 'Are you done?'

He laughs again, a belly laugh, as if I'm very, very funny. 'You're offended,' he says. 'Poor princess.' He reaches over and clinks his bottle on mine. And then he leans in, like a lover about to kiss, and whispers in my ear. 'Very easy to be offended by a little pea. But so very difficult to make anything better in this world of shit.'

I'm careful not to move.

Finally, he smiles, lingers, just so I know he's in complete control. Then he taps the book. 'I know this one. It doesn't have a happy ending.'

That night Martin Martins hires a hooker.

At least, I assume she's a hooker.

I listen to them, it's impossible not to.

Every detail of their fucking.

And when they're done, and when she's left, I hear him smoke his cigarette, smell the tang of it.

Finally, I hear his breathing downshift into sleep. And I listen to him sleep, for hours, his soft, baby breaths, he doesn't even move. I remember Tom saying that when he first started working in Rwanda he couldn't sleep. Stories and images, voices, sobbing, screaming—he couldn't clear them from his head. He told me that very few perpetrators had trouble sleeping; the same psychological mechanism that allowed them to commit terrible crimes allowed them to justify their crimes completely.

Guilt, he said, is seldom felt by the guilty.

Arnau, March 17

I found an empty cup in the kitchen sink. I had not put it there. It seemed oddly emboldened. Proud cup looking up at me with its remnant puddle of coffee. Black, no sugar. I placed the cup on the table. I supposed I should be frightened. Someone had been here.

Down the stairs, I knocked on the Gassners' door. Mrs Gassner opened it a fraction, keeping the chain on the latch as if to suggest she feared for her life. *'Kindermörderin,'* she hissed and slammed it shut. The word was everywhere, now, whispered like a mantra in the grocery store, the chemist, as I walked down the street. I was no longer sure if it was being uttered or if I was simply hearing it in expectation.

Kindermörderin.

'Mrs Gassner,' I said through the door. 'Do you know who has been in my apartment?'

There was no answer.

I knocked again, even louder, and tried my bad German. 'I know someone was there. *Haben Sie die reingelassen?*' Just in case I'd said it wrong, I added, 'Did you give them a key? That's against the law.'

She responded only by turning up the volume on the TV.

I raised my voice. 'I'm going to call the police.'

This was an empty threat. Because of course the phone was disconnected. And I had taken no measure toward its reconnection. There was no one to use it. The unpaid bill was still in my handbag. *MAHNUNG!*

I walked down the road to a phone box. In Switzerland, public phones still exist and they always work. I called Tom's mobile. Elise answered.

'How are you?' she asked. 'Poor thing. We've been so worried.'

We. That stubborn burr of a word. I contained myself, 'Is Tom there?'

'Oh honey bunny,' she murmured to a small squeal in the background. 'That's my little plumpkin, oh, yes, my baby boy baby Mummy's boy boy-joy.' Then to me, adjusting her vocal dial from saccharine to smug: 'Let me get Daddy for you.'

In the pause that followed I suddenly remembered myself with my leg up on the bathroom vanity as I slipped in my diaphragm. This act of preparation aroused Tom; he always watched, saying, 'Pilgrim, Pilgrim.'

Now, he came on the line and said my name. 'Pilgrim.' There was no difference in his voice.

'Were you here?' I tried to find my neutral tone.

'Here? Where?'

'Here in the flat in Arnau. This morning.'

'What are you talking about?'

'Was Elise here?'

There was a pause, a patient sigh, 'This is about Elise, then. Why on earth would Elise have gone to Arnau?'

Why on earth. I wanted to take the phone and smash it again and again against the metal hull of the phone box until it broke.

Even though he couldn't see me, he said, 'You need to get a hold of yourself, Pilgrim.'

I hung up and began to walk home.

Why on earth.

A car drove past and a young man honked, yelled *Mördende Hure*.

In my kitchen, I picked up the cup with a pair of cooking tongs. I had the idea that I could call the police and have it fingerprinted—that sympathetic Sergeant Caspary. But my next thought was how I might seem to her: in the wake of the tragic incident I was concerned about a mysterious coffee cup in my sink. And I'd already proven the faultiness of my memory. She'd wonder if I'd drunk the coffee myself and forgotten about it, the way I forgot to pay the phone bill. Forgot killing three children.

Killing three children.

The words made no impression. Should I carve them into my arm with a knife?

Sergeant Caspary would be sitting there, a frown afflicting her face. 'The cup is yours but the coffee isn't?'

'I don't drink coffee,' I would insist to her. 'I don't like coffee.'

How could she be sure I was telling the truth? There was coffee in the cupboard. A cup with coffee in the sink. No evidence of a break-in, nothing taken. She might conclude I was a fantasist or a liar.

And even though I *knew* I was neither, I felt a tearing, a leaking: if my memory was so unreliable, so ready to malfunction— e.g. the forgotten death of three children, the phone bill—then what else had I forgotten? Or simply misremembered?

I could count on nothing. Had Tom and I lain upon the land? Had he said, 'This is our land now'? Had we even been married? No physical trace of him remained in the flat, there was no ring upon my finger. Even photographs; there'd been so few, and these were packed away on Rue Saint-Léger. I had no proof of a twelve-year marriage, other than my impression of it.

Had I made myself a cup of coffee? Did I like coffee?

Facts slipped from my hands, swam away like eels.

But I took hold of the cup. The cool curve of the ceramic surface, the neat arch of the handle, its whiteness. And inside, yes, the unmistakable coffee dregs that I had not made.

Magulu, May 8

I haven't seen Dorothea for several days. The clinic has been closed. I ask Gladness to show me where she lives. She calls Samwelli and he nods at me. '*Njo, njo.*' Come, come. I follow him out the back door and down a narrow alley between houses. These are mud and wattle with rough thatch roofs. He turns corners, but I'm able to keep a sense of where I am, for I can see the main road through gaps, and the roundabout with goats standing in the dry fountain.

Dorothea's house is a real house: made from breeze-blocks with a tin roof and neat gutters connecting to a black plastic cistern. The door is painted the same pretty pale blue as the cross on the clinic door. Brown chickens peck at the ground. This has been swept to hard dirt, clean as a floor.

The door opens and Dorothea peers out. Her hair is undone completely, an afro arcing round her face. She is wearing pink Winnie-the-Pooh pyjamas. I think they were probably intended for a child.

She smiles in a small way, 'Friend, you have come to visit me. Come, come inside, yes.' She says something to Samwelli, finds cash in her handbag and sends Samwelli off. He comes back shortly with Cokes and sweet sponge cakes. This country runs on sugar.

The main room is packed with furniture, all of it backed against the wall, nothing placed at an angle. The positioning reminds me of my room at the Goodnight; and how, if I move the chair to a 45-degree angle, Gladness returns it to its original position, so it stands to attention, like a soldier, flush to the wall.

Dorothea has several large, heavily varnished cabinets which glower over the room. They are so big that there is barely a passage between them and the coffee table. The cabinet tops sprout vases of plastic flowers, teddy bears and other stuffed animals, a ceramic Jesus statue and a set of praying hands. The sofa and two armchairs are faux velvet, pale gray, decorated with electric-green crocheted doilies and antimacassars.

'Sit, sit,' Dorothea directs, taking out the cakes and opening the Cokes.

'I'm not disturbing you?'

She smiles, 'No, not you, I am glad you came, you are my good friend.'

'I thought you might be upset about the other day.'

'Me? Oh, I am fine. Sure. Fine, fine.'

'The way that woman died. I keep thinking about it.'

'It is why these people believe in the *mganga*. Because I cannot help.'

'But they also believe in you. They brought her to you.'

'Therefore it is worse when I fail. And I cannot help because I have no car, no radio, nothing, just a white coat.' She gives me a practical smile and pushes the cakes toward me. 'You still have the box with those terrible things?'

'Yes.'

'You know, at first I was very afraid. I thought it was for me. From my husband,' she says. 'Isaac is really full of such hate.'

Dorothea takes a dainty bite of her cake. 'I left him. He was always going with other women, even with prostitutes. So I took the boys to live with me. We were in Dar es Salaam. He was so angry. He wanted to kill me. But he did something worse.'

She gets up, and as she unlocks one of the cabinets I feel a sense of intense alarm. What will she show me? What product of hate? Will its toes be smashed, its severed ears wrapped in newspaper? Will it be in a report? *Atrocity*. But instead she brings out a framed photograph of two boys. The picture is staged with the hokey, drab background of a studio and stiff performance smiles.

'My boys,' she says. 'My lovely boys. That is Luke, the big one. He is seven. And Ezekiel, the young one, the baby. He is five.'

Bright faces, earnest smiles: they wanted to please the photographer. 'They are very handsome.'

'Yes,' she says. 'But this is an old picture.'

Again, the alarm sounds. What did Isaac do to them?

Dorothea takes the picture for herself and touches their faces with her fingertips. 'Isaac took them, he took them from me. To Kenya, to his tribal place. He is Luo, from north of here, maybe three hundred miles. I don't know the village. Isn't that strange? We were married and I never knew the name of his birth village.'

How easy it would be to nod and smile in agreement. What we don't know, what we never ask, what seems un-important. Instead, I say, 'Why did he do that?'

'Because he could.' Dorothea frowns. 'And then he laughed. Isaac called me on the phone and he laughed at me.'

Ha ha ha. He must have known the pain he was causing her. And he found this amusing. Had he always been this way and she'd just never seen deep enough? There, in his spine, in his sinews, in the liquid dark of his body, such deception and brutality.

We. A little echo: *We don't want children. We will build a house together. We are happy. We we we we all the way home.*

'I told you I came here to help the peasants. But it's not true. Not completely. Because here is close to Kenya. My best opportunity to be close to them.' Pressing the photo to her chest, she says, 'It is sentimental, of course. But I feel here we are having the same storms, the same rain or heat, and even this small connection I hold tightly.'

She puts the picture back, locks the cabinet door. She keeps the key around her neck. 'My boys, I knew their smell. Luke was different to Ezekiel. I could tell them apart in the dark, even when they were sleeping tangled together. I could move close and say, "Ah, this is Luke's hand. This is Ezekiel's shoulder."

'After they were gone, for many weeks after, I had a fever, I was shaking. I thought it was malaria. But the test said negative. I think now I was like an addict and my whole body was reacting. Every cell was shouting, "Where are the boys? Where are my boys? Where is their smell, their touch, the weight of them?"

'When that bad *uchawi* arrived I thought it was Isaac. But I discussed this with Kessy. I find it is important to think of the mind of a man because it is not the same as the mind of a woman.'

'And what does Kessy think?'

'That it is too much. Too much hate for a man who has already won. And you know, such a terrible curse is very expensive, a lot of money. Isaac likes his nice clothes and his shoes from Nigeria. Kessy is right, he wouldn't spend the money on me.'

'How much to buy such a curse?' Twenty thousand dollars, I think, thirty.

'Kessy says one thousand dollars,' Dorothea says. I hear Martin laughing, ha ha ha.

'But that's not much money, Dorothea, a person died.'

She puts her head to the side, smiles patiently, 'Friend, in this country you can pay someone ten dollars and they will go out and kill whoever you say. But Isaac would not even spend ten dollars on me.'

'Then who is the box for?'

Dorothea waves a hand, 'Someone in the village. It is probably a problem with land among relatives. Who can know what is going on out there?'

'What should I do with it?'

'Who is making their food?' Dorothea says, I think with purposeful incongruity. The box still frightens her. 'Who is cleaning their clothes? When they cry, who is there to hold them? I try many times to write to my ex-husband, to say, "Isaac, let us be reasonable. Let us think of the boys." But he enjoys his hate for me.'

'But you are their mother,' I say. 'You have a right to see them.'

She waves her hand. 'They are their father's children, they are Kenyan. He has taken them legally. He has the right.'

For a long moment she looks out the window, seeing the same light as three hundred miles north. Then in a rush: 'The box, those things. As long as they are here my babies cannot return to me.'

She sees that I don't understand. She takes my hand, looks into my eyes. 'You are a *mzungu*. You see only this world. But there is another. Please do not think I am an ignorant African. I believe in God. But there is a place where many strange things happen. People can change into animals or other people. There are ghosts and spirits. *Uchawi* is as real as water or earth. And the power of this curse, it is a shadow, and we are all in the shadow. You see, this is why that woman and her baby died. We are in the shadow.'

'I don't believe in God, Dorothea.' But even as I say this I remember the feeling of death in the clinic. The fluttering.

She nods. 'Of course, your argument will be very logical.'

I almost smile at the idea that anything out of my head or mouth might be logical. Tom believed my atheism was an affectation intended to annoy him, there was nothing logical about it. He suspected it was a reaction to my parents' spiritualism. Their earthship in the Mojave is filled with Buddhas and various Hindu gods and santos from Mexico. They appreciate the method of worship as a mechanism for connection to an unknowable, eternal Energy. '*Chakras?*' Tom muttered when he met them, when my mother insisted on going about naked and my father smoked his bong and said Tom's sacral and heart chakras were blocked. He couldn't wait to get away from the incense. Neither could I.

'What do you want me to do?' I ask Dorothea again.

She squeezes my hand. Tears roll down her cheeks and her face shines with thanks. Her hair is a halo of light. 'Take it from here. Take it far from here.'

'Where?'

'The *uchawi* will direct you.'

'I don't know what that means.'

More forcefully, she squeezes my hands: 'The *uchawi* will direct you.'

Arnau, March 18

'It is Detective Inspector Paul Strebel,' a voice said through the intercom. 'I tried to phone—'

'Yes, I'm sorry, it's disconnected. The bill. I forgot to pay it. Please come up.' I buzzed him up.

He appeared, almost too tall for the doorway, awkward, angular. In his early fifties, he was thin, with a narrow face, receding hair and quiet, dark eyes under eyebrows in need of trimming.

'Please come in,' I said. Polite, calm. 'Can I get you something?'

'Thank you, yes. But no caffeine. I'm not a good sleeper.'

'Tea? Mint? Chamomile?' Was this right? Should I be offering him herbal tea? He was here to talk about dead children and all I had was manners. As if I was hosting a cocktail party for the associates in Dili. Smile, serve exquisite canapés while wearing an elegant black dress. Anything to distract from *the atrocities* in the files.

'That's fine,' Strebel said, without specifying. He took off his gloves but not his coat. The gloves were fine-grained black leather, but they didn't suit him. He wasn't urbane. I suspected someone had bought them for him as a gift, his wife or daughter.

We sat, I poured. My hand trembled on the teapot's handle and he saw this. 'Don't worry.'

'Worry?'

'I mean, don't be afraid.'

'Of the tea?'

'No.' He ventured a smile. 'Of me.'

I put the teapot down. 'Is that it? Am I afraid of you?'

He leaned forward to sip his tea. 'I expect so. You don't know what to tell me. You don't know what I know.'

When I said nothing, he went on. 'Or perhaps it's more a generalized fear. It can be frightening to lose control.'

Would he know about that? I glanced at his kind, tired face and tried to imagine him losing control, shouting or crying. I tried to imagine him being afraid. Then I realized he wasn't speaking of personal experience but professional observation: he had seen people lose control. His profession—like Tom's—concerned people who lost control.

'Are you here to arrest me?' I said.

'For what?' He turned the cup in his hands. 'You think the accident is your fault?'

'But it must be, somehow. I was the driver.'

'Fault would mean you drove into them on purpose. Do you think you are such a person—capable of such an act?'

Tom believed everyone is capable of everything, fundamentally. To him, violence is circumstantial. The nicest man, given the right set of circumstances, may become the most brutal genocidaire. Everyone? I'd pushed Tom, even you, even me? How do you think these atrocities happen, he'd countered, if not for people like you, people like me?

'If I can't remember,' I clarified. 'Then I don't know. I can't tell you with any certainty.'

'Perhaps you were driving carelessly.'

I looked at him. Was this a gentle form of interrogation? Was he asking me to incriminate myself? 'Was I?'

'Did you, for instance, overtake on the corner?'

Had I passed on a corner? I had. Yes! That was it. Suddenly,

I knew with absolute certainty. I felt a great wash of relief. 'Yes,' I said. 'The corner just below the village. That's what happened.'

Putting the tea aside, he kept his eyes on me. 'But that's not what happened. Let us be completely clear.'

'I'm sure. I can see it now. In my mind.' And then clarity clicked immediately to shame. Hot shame on my cheeks. 'Oh, God. I did. I'm so sorry. I'm so sorry.'

Spilling words, awkward, ineffective words, sorry, sorry, sorry, but only in fear and self-pity of what might now be done to me. No—not for the dead children, but for myself. I wanted to be sobbing, on my knees, begging forgiveness as the parents shouted: '*Die of cancer,* Mörder Hure, *die with cancer eating your face.*' But even in this notion I glimpsed a deeper selfishness, layers of selfishness like tissue. That if they beat me, if they stoned me, put me in the stocks and pelted me with excrement, only when my skin opened up: then might I feel. Their anger, their sorrow would make me real; like Frankenstein's monster, make me exist. I could not pull away from myself, this grasping, selfish woman who wanted to feel guilt not for what she had done, but so she could prove to herself that she existed.

My face was wet. I was crying. Strebel stood. For a moment he hesitated like a schoolboy, then he put a hand on my shoulder.

'No,' he said firmly. 'It wasn't your fault. You didn't overtake. All our evidence confirms it was an accident. That is what I'm here to tell you.'

'But I remember—'

'You don't remember. You did nothing wrong.' He looked at me again, tilting his head. 'There is just luck, terrible, cruel luck, and people like you, like the parents, like those poor children get caught in it.'

He took a white cotton handkerchief from his pocket, and I wondered what kind of man carries a white cotton handkerchief anymore? What kind of man hands it to a crying woman? I did not take it, so he began to dab at my face.

'Please,' I said. But of course he didn't understand what I meant. 'Please, please.'

Tom said I was ugly when I cried. I covered my face and turned away from Inspector Strebel, and then, at last, 'I'm not crying for them.'

He did not sigh with disgust. He did not leave. He stood as if nothing had changed, as if he had not heard.

'I'm not crying for them.'

'No,' he said very quietly. 'You are crying for yourself.'

I went to the sink and splashed cold water on my face. When I looked back at him he was putting his handkerchief away.

'Are you okay now?'

I nodded. A vague exhaustion washed over me.

'Come, then. Could you come with me to the incident scene?'

'Would that be helpful?'

'I always go to the scene a few days later. I want to know the place without all the cars and the confusion. That it's just a place and holds no special menace.'

I fumbled with the keys, dropped them. He picked them up, and again gave me that small smile. He pulled on his gloves, buttoned his coat. I had the feeling he was fighting the urge to reach over and button mine, too.

We cut through the village on the footpath. He said he preferred to walk, he spent too much time in the car or behind a desk. The morning was damp and gray: we couldn't see the lake or the mountains, and without them Arnau revealed its essential dullness.

Perhaps he felt this also, for he suddenly asked, 'Why are you here? Arnau? Alone?'

The question was so direct that I wondered again if, despite what he said, he was prying. Perhaps his whole visit was an elaborate means of revealing my motives. Even the handkerchief might have been a manipulation.

'My husband and I were going to build up the valley, our

dream house.' I was aware that he would notice my use of the past tense.

'Excuse me,' Strebel said quickly. 'I shouldn't have asked. It's not my business.'

'Isn't it?'

He looked down at me, dark eyes under unkempt eyebrows.

'Isn't everything your business in a case like this? Who I am, why I'm here, what I was doing driving past the bus stop on a day like that.' I heard myself spill this out. 'The dream house, it was a lie. He never even bought the land. But that's why I'm here. I believed him.'

Strebel said nothing. He let me move into the silence.

'We're getting a divorce,' I said, pushing my hands deep into my coat pockets.

'I know that. It's in your file. Swiss efficiency.'

'Does my file say he left me? For another woman. They have a baby.'

'No. We're not the KGB.'

Perhaps he meant to lighten the mood. But I felt a burning, like fury. 'Do you want to write it down? Maybe it's important. Maybe everyone should know. I thought we were enough, I thought we were happy, but he wanted that squeaky little woman instead.' And then I reminded myself. Three children were dead. Three children were dead and I hid my face.

Strebel put his hand on my shoulder, steady and unjudging. I felt like a stray dog to whom someone is suddenly, unaccountably kind. 'Squeaky?'

'I must seem despicable.'

Simply, softly, he replied: 'There is no way you should seem. This tragedy is yours also.'

By now we'd reached the main Arnau road. We turned left, downhill. I kept expecting to feel a turn of emotion. Even if the memory was gone, flown like a bird, surely the primal sensation must remain. A template.

But there was nothing.

I looked upon the road, the curve in the road, as I had for the past six months. And I realized I had always done this with unease. Even before Tom left—when I believed we were intact—I hadn't wanted to be in Arnau. There was nothing prescient about this feeling; rather, it had been the sense of dislocation, as if I'd accidentally disembarked at the wrong train stop. I'd loved Geneva and the bistros and the babel of languages and the weekends in Paris and Berlin. I'd followed Tom without complaint to Arnau. Happily. As I always had. Lagos. Addis Ababa. East Timor. Geneva.

Arnau.

I saw that I had clenched my fists. I relaxed my hands, put them in my pockets. 'Why did you want me to come here with you?'

Strebel noticed my hands, noticing, noticing everything. 'You think I'm trying to trick you. I'm sorry for that.'

'But surely you want me to remember.'

'Surely? No, not at all. Memory is so...' his long fingers wriggled in the air. 'So unreliable.'

'But then you would know what happened.'

'I *do* know what happened. I think it's you who needs to know.'

'It must be there, the memory. How can it not be? How can I have done this... this terrible thing and not remember?'

Cars passed. I watched for a moment, the drivers' profiles shifting through the plain of my vision. Uphill, downhill. Intent they were, with shopping lists and marital grievances, lies to tell and food to cook. The banal world continued parallel to the world of tragic incidents. Relentlessly.

'Perhaps there is no memory to retrieve. During intense trauma the brain can focus on simply trying to survive.' He wanted to calm me, but he heard me—I heard myself—gasp and then swallow.

Briefly, he touched my wrist. 'Memory is narrative. It is not truth. It is the worst witness. Police hate witnesses. We groan inside. People swear they remember a man in a red coat, when we know it was a blue one. Or they remember a man with a hat because their father wore hats.'

'Sergeant Caspary told me "Almost instantly."' I looked straight ahead now, at the hard, dark mountains in the distance. 'In the hospital, when she came to talk to me, she said two of the children had died "almost instantly." What does that mean?'

'They were deceased by the time the paramedics arrived.'

'But alive for those minutes? What—five minutes, three minutes between the crash and the arrival of the ambulances?'

He was quiet for a moment, then: 'It won't help. This sort of talk.' He walked on, toward the bus stand. I followed and we sat down. There was a heavy industrial smell, and I realized it was new plastic, because of course the shelter was new. The cement under my feet was clean and fresh with only a few splats of gum.

'Please look.' He gestured to a series of neon orange hieroglyphics painted on the asphalt and pavement. 'The truth is physics. The car, the road, the surface of the road, the trajectory, the weather, the victims' weight. Gravity is merciless but completely objective. You braked. You braked hard. See the marks there?' He gestured and I saw the skid marks, the definite skid marks, and around them the orange arrows, numbers, squiggles. 'You did what you could,' he said. 'This wasn't your fault.'

Suddenly, fitfully, he pulled off his gloves. 'I really don't like these. I have a perfectly good pair of wool ones. But my wife—' I could tell he was embarrassed, he'd revealed something too private.

'I used to buy gloves for Tom,' I said. 'I thought he liked them. But perhaps he felt the same way.'

Turning his face to me, his dark eyes met mine. But he quickly looked away.

'Tell me their names,' I said.

He waited, as if deliberating. 'Mattias Scheffer. Markus Emptmann. Sophie Koppler.'

'Sophie. She lived for a little while.'

Strebel nodded. 'Yes. A few hours.' He adjusted his coat collar. 'We should get back before the rain.'

I thought back to Mrs Gassner tying her shoes. It had been about to rain that morning, too.

Magulu, May 10

Martin's fuel pump arrived yesterday with the Thursday bus from Mwanza, and he is now installing it. There's a crowd around the car and, periodically, he slithers out and shouts at them to go away. He shouts in what I assume is Ukrainian, probably the filthiest slurs, and sometimes he shouts in English, calling them niggers and kaffirs and cunts. But the crowd doesn't care. They laugh at him. He's a sideshow clown. The second he slides back under the car, they move in again, resilient, insistent as a tide. Someone steals a wrench, and it almost makes me smile to see his fury.

'There are always more of them,' I am tempted to tell him.

When he is finished, he sits at the bar and starts drinking. As I pass by he calls out 'Princess!' and offers to buy me a drink. I ignore him. He follows me into the hallway. I turn.

'What do you want?'

'You're very beautiful.'

'I'm not going to sleep with you.'

He laughs, then talks in a low, soft voice: 'Sleep? No. *Fuck.* I'd like to fuck you. And then maybe hurt you. You'd like that.'

I keep walking. He catches my arm, his fingers digging in. 'I know.'

'Know what?' I turn to face him. Looking into his eyes I feel like I'm watching a snuff film.

'I know exactly who you are,' he says.

He jerks my arm behind my back. I hear the sound of his zipper. He presses against me so I can feel his erection and rubs himself slowly against me. 'I know,' he whispers. 'I know everything, princess.' When I try to move, he pulls my arm higher. He'll break it if he wants to. Very quickly he comes with a sigh, and lets me go, zips up. He walks casually back toward the bar.

And I stand with my pounding heart, this constriction in my chest and this absolute fear. My breath comes in quick little bursts. *I know exactly who you are.* I know who you are. I know everything.

But how can he?

As my breath slows I decide he knows me the way a rapist likes to think he knows women, that my resistance merely masks my lust. Even as I need to run to the bathroom and vomit in the sink and take off my shirt, I consider the pettiness of Martin. For all his brutality, he holds onto a lie that he must at all costs turn into a truth: that I desire him, secretly, that other women do.

Or maybe I've got it wrong. Maybe Martin knows he repels me. And this excites him.

Or maybe he just doesn't care. The way the villagers taunted him, laughed at him—the way he'd turn around and kill them if he was paid to, even the women, even the children. *No matter how they die, burning, screaming, guts falling out, whatever. There's always more of them.*

But they would kill him, too, without hesitation, hang him from a meat hook, hack him to pieces with a machete. They are bound together, this merchant of violence and his victims, as if they need each other; as if, like a snake eating its tail, there's no distinction. Tom would say to me that violence becomes an identity, how people see themselves in the world, and to ask them to stop being violent is asking them to erase themselves.

Martin Martins leaves that afternoon. The sound of his car rubs the smooth, familiar air. I can just see him through the window of my room. A dozen barefoot children chase him, shouting, laughing. And when he speeds up, pulling away from their vortex, they start to throw pebbles. Then stones. He is leaving, he is leaving without them, he is leaving them behind, and they are furious.

Magulu, May 12

Dorothea invites me for dinner. When I get to her house, Kessy is sitting on the sofa watching TV at top volume. He's not in uniform, just jeans and a T-shirt. He's quite at home. He shakes my hand—the three-part shake I've come to know here, but it's a cursory greeting; he's riveted by the football. Dorothea comes in and speaks curtly in Swahili. At first he ignores her, and so she turns off the TV. He looks at her, shakes his head with disdain, gets up and walks out. She immediately plumps the cushions where he's been sitting.

'This is just a private club to him,' she says, mimicking him: '"*Lete beer, lete nyama choma, lete chai, ongeza sauti.*"'

She gives me a Coke. 'These Swahili men, they think they can just tell you what to do. Get this, do that. White men do not treat their women in this way. You see for yourself in the cities. Women are all looking for a white man, even the old ones, the drunk ones, the poor ones. They are all better than one Swahili man.'

'There are white men like Martin,' I tell her. I think of his sticky cum on the back of my shirt. I think of the bruises on my arm.

Dorothea makes a sour face as she sits down. 'Yes. He is *mbovu*. You know what Gladness told Kessy?' She looks at me over her Coke. Tonight, she wears the red pageboy wig and a purple dress. She slips her kitten heels off as she curls her legs underneath her. I'm surprised by the soles of her feet, which are flat and callused, as if she is accustomed to going barefoot. She raises an eyebrow, 'Samwelli found the old fuel pump from Martin's car.'

She makes sure I am listening, then she leans forward. 'It was not broken.'

'Does Samwelli know about cars?'

'He cannot even fix a flat tire on a bicycle.' She makes her derisive little snort, then taps my leg. 'But he gave the pump to Kessy.'

'And Kessy knows about fuel pumps?'

She nods. 'There was nothing wrong with it.'

'But,' I say. 'But why would Martin do that? Come up with such a story?'

'Kessy says he is looking for someone. Kessy says he's looking for you.' She touches me again, her hand now staying on my knee. 'No one knows why you are here. And then another *mzungu* comes—this *mtu mbovu*. And then the box, with those things. Too many coincidences.'

'It's for someone in the village, you said so yourself.'

'Yes, I tell this to Kessy. You are a good person, I tell him. Such a man as Martin Martins cannot have business with a good person. But, friend,' she hesitates—and I can see she needs to speak but does not want to offend. 'Friend, why are you here?'

I stare up at the plastic flowers in their vase on top of the vast cabinets. Below, in a special place of honor, she keeps the photograph of her sons. I look back at her, the small, intense, intelligent face. Of course she wonders. She and Kessy have been speculating.

And yet what might I tell her? Why am I taking so long to answer, as if I have a stutter, and cannot find purchase in the word I need to begin.

Kindermörderin.

She's looking at me, scrutinizing my face, and whatever it is she sees there leads her to say gently—forgivingly: 'There is a mine north of here. Run by South Africans. Maybe this Martin is working for the South Africans.'

I say nothing, so she carries on, gathering confidence. She has enough conviction for the both of us. 'Titanium. Yes, of course. That is why he is here. Yes, I know it. He is nothing to do with you.'

I should tell her he's a mercenary. But then she will ask, Why was a mercenary here in Magulu? Was he here for you, friend?

Was he?

She walks into the kitchen and comes back with serving bowls of beans and rice and rich, thick goat stew.

Arnau, March 19

The coffee cup was in the sink. The chair was slightly askew. I stood and listened, though I was quite sure he had gone.

The flat was very quiet. Even the Gassners' TV was mute. The silence felt like a withdrawal, a withholding, that might at any moment surge back with a scream.

He had been here again. *He*, I concluded, because the coffee was black, and I didn't know any women who drank their coffee black. Once, I had expressed a pet theory about this to Tom: that men, single men, often forgot to buy milk or sugar, so they grew accustomed to making do without. Tom took his coffee with full cream milk, making the exception when we lived in Addis, where the coffee was served black and sweet and strong. He had laughed a little at my idea, asking how I'd done my research—how many single men I knew. Not many, of course.

So I had no basis, no basis at all, for the notion that the person coming into my flat was a man. It was an impression. The scent of him hung upon the air. Or I could determine the disturbance of molecules by some atavistic radar.

But what did he want? To just sit here with his coffee? I could find no other trace of him. He hadn't rummaged through my drawers the way a stalker might. Hadn't taken anything the way a thief might. Deliberately, he had left the cup for me to find.

I put my bag of shopping down. I washed the cup and placed it on the sideboard. I pushed the chair flush against the table. I felt a creeping coldness. The small hairs at the nape of my neck rose like tiny antennae. He was not in the room, he was not in the flat, but the cup was his message: he could come anytime he wanted. When I was not there. When I was there.

It was pointless to ask Mrs Gassner, though she must know who it was. He could not have entered without her complicity. She perched like a praying mantis behind the peephole of her door. Perhaps she had even given him a key.

Outside, along the street, there was a taxi stand. I took one to Thun. The driver, whose darker skin and heavy accent suggested recent immigration from the Middle East, kept glancing at me in the rearview mirror. When we'd reached the lake road, he snapped his fingers, 'Yes, madam, it is you, the American lady. The accident. Those children. Three of them. I know, yes, my sister, she is marry to the cousin of the woman who work for Mr Emptmann.'

I said nothing.

'They say you were driving like crazy woman. You were drunken woman.'

I kept my eyes on the lake, on the gathering momentum of Thun.

'If you kill my children I kill you that is sure thing.'

I entered the police station tentatively, but no one seemed to recognize me. No one turned away or murmured their disgust. No one spat or threatened me. A young police officer behind the Plexiglas window spoke in a quick interrogative burst. *'Kann ich Ihnen behilflich sein?'*

'Strebel,' I said with my terrible pronunciation. *'Kann ich mit Kommissar Strebel sprechen?'*

'Let me see,' he replied in English. 'Your name?'

'Pilgrim Jones. No—Lankester.'

'Which is it?'

'Jones. But the file may be under Lankester.'

'Wait.'

I waited.

Strebel appeared, pushing open a security door with a hesitant smile. 'Miss Jones?'

'I wasn't sure—the name,' I fumbled.

'My name?'

'My name.'

'You don't know your name?' He raised a wayward eyebrow.

'I mean, who I might be to you. Jones or Lankester.'

'Well, which do you prefer?'

'Jones.'

'So I got it right.'

'It's odd to hear. After so many years.'

'But it's a nice name. Complex in the beginning, then simple, so people have to think a little bit, but they don't forget and they don't mangle the spelling.'

Again he gave me that half smile. It didn't promote levity or humor or the complicity of friendship. It was carefully appropriate and meant to reassure: in all this madness, I'm not swayed, not partial, not your friend, but not your enemy. In its strict neutrality, Strebel's smile was deeply sincere.

He shifted his weight and tilted his head. 'How can I help, Miss Jones?'

I knew, then, I could not tell him about the cup and the chair. That even if he believed me—which was unlikely—I would seem ridiculous. And I wanted this singular man to like me.

With Tom, I'd never considered how people felt about me, because they liked Tom, they loved Tom. They leaned in to hear what Tom had to say. But Strebel did not know Tom. He spoke to me, not around me, as if I was a portal to Tom. With Strebel I wasn't Tom's wife.

'Has there...' I began, uncertainly. 'Has there been anything new?'

He frowned. 'New?'

'I mean, evidence. Or—' I put my hand over my mouth. Was I lying? By asking the question I had not intended to ask, by showing concern that was merely improvisation, was I being dishonest? This clever man would ferret out dishonesty.

'Evidence?' Strebel noticed the gesture. 'No, no new evidence. Only what we have. As I said.' He peered at me, then fussed with the papers on his desk. 'Let's go, shall we? Lunch? I'm a little hungry.'

'Is that appropriate?'

The smile—only this time, something warmer. 'Miss Jones,' he said. 'You're not a suspect.'

The café was around the corner, nondescript with an unhappy rubber plant in the window. The waiter knew Strebel and hailed him with menus and a gesture to the table by the plant.

'The soup is always good here,' Strebel said to me. 'Everything else, very mediocre.' I saw him pat his breast pocket, then turn to me. 'Can you tell me what it says, the day's specials. I've forgotten my glasses.'

'Consommé,' I began. 'That comes with a side salad.'

'So you read German?'

'Strictly menus.'

'No to the consommé.'

'*Blumenkohl?* Cauliflower?'

'Yes, cauliflower.'

'And chicken with vegetables.'

'What about you?' he said.

'The cauliflower.'

'It's excellent here, they add a bit of Appenzeller.'

While we waited for the soup, he said, 'How is it for you? Sometimes people can be cruel.'

I did not meet his eyes. A cup. A chair. I hope cancer eats your face.

'It's fine,' I said.

'Even so,' Strebel said. 'People want to blame. They want there to be bad so they can believe in good. So they can be good.'

'Isn't there bad? Isn't there good?'

'Only degrees. But that's my experience. I'm not a philosopher or a priest.'

He seemed to me a little of both.

The food came. It was the first meal I had eaten with another person since Tom left.

'You're right,' I said of the soup.

'I think Swiss cooking is like Scottish cooking. We praise blandness.'

'Except for cheese.'

'Well, cheese is not food. It's sacrament.'

I almost smiled. He noted this struggle. He put his spoon down. 'Why did you come today?'

The question cornered me, and he spoke in the gentlest voice, so I had to lean forward to hear. 'What I'm asking, really, is do you have anyone to talk to?'

I looked away.

'Miss Jones—'

'Pilgrim, it should be Pilgrim.'

'Well, I'm Paul, then.'

'Paul.'

'You're very isolated,' he said. 'I'm worried for you.'

'For me?'

'That you should have someone to talk to.'

'Tom suggested his girlfriend's shrink.'

Strebel laughed out loud. 'Really! What a sensitive guy!' He chuckled on, and then stopped abruptly. 'I'm sorry. I know that even if you could find it funny, there's no room in you for laughter now. But, really, I hope you find it funny one day.'

He reached out to touch my arm. 'You can talk to me, okay?

Look, try. Ask me something. You'll see, I'll answer as Paul not Inspector Strebel.'

'How do they—' I stopped myself. Again, I felt the conundrum of honesty. Did I really want to know, or was I just asking what I thought he expected me to ask? I was so tangled in words, in what I should think versus what I did.

'How do they get through the day?' he finished for me.

'Yes. How do they get through the day?'

He took a moment to realign his side plate and butter knife in front of him. 'They brush their teeth,' he said. 'They do the laundry.'

I thought of the cup: the ritual of making coffee, the kettle, the cafetière, the measuring of grinds. The rigid sequence.

'And they breathe their loss. Bitter air. And it takes a long time. But life is persistent. For you, too.'

'And you?'

'Me?' he raised his eyebrows. 'This is my work.'

'But when you're not a policeman, when you're Paul.'

'Yes, I see. Because I'm always a policeman, an investigator, aren't I? It's a state of being.'

'A suit of armor?'

He tilted his head to consider me. 'No,' he said. 'Because you can take that off.'

We sat for an odd moment in silence, as if too much had been revealed and we didn't know how to return to the mundane. The waiter came with the bill. Strebel paid. 'We should get back before the rain.'

'You said that last time.'

'Ah. Next time we must make sure it's sunny.'

In the street, he hailed a taxi and told the driver my address. As the door closed, as the car pulled away, he glanced through the glass and then raised his fingers as if to doff an invisible hat.

Magulu, May 15

I sit on the bed in the room that was Martin Martins.' I look in the empty waste-paper basket, the empty drawer, the empty cupboard. I feel ridiculous. Did I think I would find a clue? To what? Anyway, Gladness has cleaned everything with her usual thoroughness. The room reeks of bleach; though, underneath, the smell of cigarettes lingers. I think back to every instance I saw Martin. What he was doing, what he was reading. Wasn't it an old *Spiegel*? He drank beer, he slept in his room, he slept with a prostitute, he watched the TV in the restaurant, he smoked Roosters. This is the behavior of a man waiting for a spare part for his broken car.

So why do I have this cold pit in my stomach? Martin's lie about the fuel pump. His *I know you*.

Too many coincidences, Kessy said.

But who decides how many is too many? Who can see conspiracy in the random? I forgot to pay a phone bill. *MAHNUNG!* Mrs Gassner could not tie her laces. Tom brought me to Arnau because he'd met Elise by the lake. In proximity—the imposed proximity of chronology—these events clustered and swarmed, connected.

But taken separately—

Perhaps Martin lied about the fuel pump for some reason

quite beyond me or Kessy or Dorothea. Perhaps he was waiting, or hiding. Perhaps Kessy is wrong and the fuel pump was broken.

Why am I so ready to believe Martin Martins intended me harm? He called me princess. He saw my coldness, my vanity: the hard, little pea of my heart. He saw what I keep from others, and so I imbue him with special power. I give credence to his story of being a mercenary.

Or have I fashioned a projection of unexamined guilt? What better tableau than a professional killer on which to display my moral dilemma—my inability to feel anything for three small, dead children. Martin Martins absorbs all light like an imploding star.

I have taken lives, like a petty god. I have importance because of that. I am no longer Tom's wife, no longer his ex-wife. I am a looming giant in the lives of the children's parents, Godzilla, stamping and tramping, crushing and smashing. I am *Kindermörderin*. I am Martin.

I note the shambling rustle of pink bougainvillea outside the window and the filament of a spider's web. Beyond the bougainvillea lies the kitchen courtyard. I can see Gladness hanging up sheets on the line. Around her scatter ubiquitous chickens, and an emaciated kitten toys with a piece of colored wool. Gladness bends and plucks white pillowcases from the green laundry tub. I recall how she watched me when Martin told me his story. Suddenly I realize that she's the one who slept with him, and she was worried I might fuck him for free. In the same matter-of-fact way she does everything here, she sleeps with the customers. It's all money. Apart from Dorothea, with her commands and her talk of STDs, no women come near the place. But there are plenty of men.

I go to my room, retrieve the box from the back of the cupboard. I estimate its weight at six pounds. Hate does not diminish, I'm learning. It can shift atoms, congeal into matter. It takes shape in the material world.

Magulu—Butiama, May 16

I do not say goodbye. This is force of habit: all the leavings in my life with Tom, associations with associates abandoned every two years. There were no parties, no one said goodbye. People left Dili or Lagos and the only evidence of their leaving, of their ever having been there at all, was the new people in their house. Tom taught me; leave quietly, don't slam the door.

As I pay the bill at the Goodnight, Gladness doesn't ask where I'm going or why. Her job is to usher in and usher out. I give her a good tip. '*Safari njema*,' she says. Travel safely.

The bus leaves at noon from under a huge fig tree near the market. It rattles as it idles, exhaust fumes stinking. The crowd here is focused, active; there's incentive to leave Magulu. People shove bags and even children through the windows. Touts sell tickets. The driver sweats as he manoeuvres boxes and sacks into the luggage compartment. Boys sell hard-boiled eggs. Others carry large boards on their shoulders—window height—bearing plastic combs, mirrors, packs of cards, key rings, dolls. They resemble peacocks, moving their displays stiffly up and down the length of the bus.

A young man in a tie tries to co-opt my seat by the window. I bought my ticket from the bus office—a table under the fig tree manned by the agent, a Rambo-esque vision in a red bandana and mirrored shades. I paid extra for the window seat.

As the young man won't move—he has settled in, folding his arms, crossing his legs, determined as a suffragette—I summon the tout. He shouts at the young man and smacks him on the head. When I have reclaimed my seat the tout comes back and stares meaningfully. I pretend I don't understand that he wants a thank-you tip—which is a mistake, because he places a very fat old woman next to me.

She glances down curiously at the box on my lap.

'*Vitabu,*' I lie. Books. She looks away. And moves so that part of her buttock takes up part of my seat.

We reach Butiama at dusk.

Only a decade ago Lake Victoria lapped at the edge of the town. The dusty shacks and crumbling buildings might have then seemed almost picturesque. But the lake level has dropped, and a wide hem of mud and trash now separates the town from the silvery-blue water. The dark mud smells, the day's sun has heated the garbage rotting within it, and I find myself almost gagging on the thick, fetid air. The woman next to me shrivels her nose, shakes her head.

Outside, a medieval scrum surrounds the bus, as if people want to lynch the passengers rather than greet them. We can't disembark because so many beggars, thieves, taxi drivers, touts for other destinations, screaming relatives are blocking the door. I realize my best option is to slip behind the old woman, drafting her bulk like a cyclist.

I have not thought what to do now, where to go. The ticket touts shout out destinations: Arusha, Mwanza, Dodoma, Kisumu, Mbeya. Pick one, I think. But not Mwanza, where they burn witches, where they kill albinos. In the frenzy, I am separated from the old woman, and I feel as if I have just lost a friend. Almost immediately, the crowd notices my solitude and I am surrounded by shouting faces. I feel hands grabbing at my suitcase, grabbing at the box under my arm. 'Sistah!' '*Mzungu*!' 'Arusha!' 'This way! This way!' 'Sistah!'

Frantically I scan the faces for one that might be open, sincere. I see only the same hungry expression of the men in Magulu when they nearly attacked Kessy.

'This way! This way!' a boy in a white shirt is saying. 'This way, this way, this way.' He takes firm grasp of the handle of my suitcase. I look down at him, his dark, indecipherable eyes. The white shirt is huge, a man's shirt engulfing him, making him thinner, smaller: vulnerable. So I soften immeasurably toward him, and he senses this in an instant. He pulls me, shoving aside his competitors as if they are not larger and heavier and meaner. He pulls me confidently, a fish on the line. 'This way! This way!'

We are free of the crowd, but still he doesn't let me go. 'This way.' We cross a road. A man tries to sell me a bottle of water. The boy shouts at him. We enter a narrow alley, turn into another alley, another, another. I think about the girl Kessy found deep inside a maze. I think about her toes, smashed with a hammer, a kind of meticulous cruelty. Kessy saved her, and he was punished, rendered helpless in exile. I remember him saying to me on the road north of Magulu, 'Who is going to stop them? Me? With my club? My flashlight? My laws?' The terrible cruelty extends to Kessy: for a man to find himself capable of good, and then be stripped of the means ever to do good again. I think of Dorothea holding the hand of a dying girl, holding the photograph of her lost sons. These emotional assaults seem so carefully crafted—bespoke—that I can almost believe in God.

The boy turns back to look at me. His expression is serious, but sure. 'This way.'

Alley folds into alley, an origami of shadows. 'Where are we?' I finally say.

'This way.'

And we burst out into a courtyard illuminated by evening sun. There is a water pump, a fig tree, a Land Cruiser. For a moment

I panic, for I'm certain it belongs to Martin Martins. But a large, black Tanzanian sits behind the wheel. The boy seems to know him. They speak in rapid Swahili. The boy turns to me, assertively: 'This man will take you.'

He has his newspaper half-folded in his hands, the sports pages. He smiles. 'Only three hundred dollars.' Then he taps the side of the door with the newspaper. 'Missionary car. It is in excellent condition.'

'But where are you going?'

'Very comfortable. God has personally blessed this car.'

The boy looks at me and nods. 'You go with him.'

'Where?' I demand.

'You go with him. He will take you.'

Perhaps they think I'm someone else—some other white woman.

'Who is the car for?'

'You,' the boy says, smiling. 'It is for you.'

'But who am I?' I say and, almost—almost—I laugh. Because I wouldn't be completely surprised if the boy and the driver said, 'Of course we know! You are Tom's ex-wife! Yes, Mr Tom. He is a very good man!' So I try again, 'The car—has it been ordered?'

'Ordered?' Boy and driver look to me.

'Ordered,' I repeat, hopelessly now. 'A name, an organization. Someone who paid for the car.'

'Order? No, no, madam, there is no order.'

'You pay for the car,' the boy taps the hood in reassurance. 'Only three hundred dollars. It is in excellent condition.'

The driver extends his hand to me, 'My name is Davis. Welcome.'

'But I didn't order a car. I didn't arrange for a car.'

'Yes,' Davis says, giving me his own version of the boy's bright and certain smile. 'But it is an excellent car.'

I consider my trajectory, my arrival at this point: I view myself from high on a Google map. A white woman in a backstreet of a Tanzanian town stands by a white Land Cruiser. A series of dots illustrates my journey, back through Magulu, through Kilimanjaro Airport, north across Kenya, across the Sahara and the Mediterranean, the boot of Italy, the Alps, Arnau. I have to think quite hard about the distance I've traveled, that the journey is a physical reality; because it feels as if I've just stepped through a portal. I have to look closely at the figure on the Google map and say, yes, that's me, definitely me, that far out, that far away. I could very easily believe I was someone else, that Arnau had never happened.

When I finally understood that I must not stay in Arnau, I took a taxi to Zurich airport. I did not know where I was going. I thought vaguely of Addis Ababa. I thought of calling Strebel. I thought—very briefly—of my parents. At the airport, I began to walk, absorbed by the other travelers, their sense of purpose buoying me, instilling in me the confidence of direction. Calm, assuring voices came over the PA system in different languages. I imagined that if I listened closely I would hear my instructions: 'Passenger Jones, Passenger Pilgrim Jones. Please go to counter E13.' Traveling with Tom, there had always been a car and driver, business-class tickets, everything preordained.

For several minutes I had stood in front of the departures board. Dubai, Shanghai, Sydney, Boston, Mumbai, Istanbul. Anywhere. Cairo, Tel Aviv, Kilimanjaro. Tom's alimony was extremely generous. I had so much choice.

And if I had chosen Cairo? Or Sydney? What unconscious criteria led me to Kilimanjaro? A memory of snatched conversation, a picture in a magazine? No. I was propelled away, not toward. I thought of my father's favorite saying, 'The journey is all, the end is nothing.' I was sure he'd never considered the intense vertigo of a totally blank future. I had no image in my head, no expectation. Only where I would go and not hear *Kindermörderin, Kindermörderin.*

I walked to the KLM desk and bought a ticket for Kilimanjaro. It wasn't a decision, it wasn't a choice.

All my life had been a segue.

Meeting Tom. Being left by Tom. Even the accident. Even Magulu.

And even in this moment when I step toward Davis—who stands at attention, his smile intact; even at this moment—in the fading light of a courtyard in western Tanzania—I'm not making a choice.

I'm yielding.

Davis takes my suitcase and I do not resist. He puts it in the back of the Land Cruiser. He reaches for the box but I shake my head. No, I must hold this. He opens the passenger door. I get in. There's a glow-in-the-dark crucifix rosary draped on the rearview mirror. Davis starts the car. We drive off.

Who is Davis? Am I to be taken to some forlorn place? Murdered? The truth is I don't care. I have nothing to live for—a bland expression that I now understand. That I welcome. Because life, like a wire, requires tension on both ends. You care to live and someone else cares that you live. What's the point of holding the slack end?

We drive out of town, Davis saying nothing, focusing intently on the road and the objects veering into it: suicidal donkeys, overloaded cyclists, battered pick-ups groaning under the weight of a million green bananas. Children, always more children.

'Where are we going, Davis?' I ask.

'Tanga,' he says.

I have no idea where Tanga is. Or why we're going, or how far.

And only now do I recall Dorothea: 'The *uchawi* will direct you.' But I put the idea to one side, onto the shelf with my parents' kachinas and saints, their Buddhas and bundles of sage: the tchotchkes of belief.

Night narrows around us. The road burrows through it like a tunnel.

Arnau, March 20

The front door buzzed.

I did not answer immediately. Who could it be? Now, after dark. A boy I vaguely recognized running off, laughing and shouting curses? Another plastic bag filled with dog shit? I was weary, but had no right to be so.

'Hello?' I said through the intercom.

'Strebel,' he said. 'Paul.'

He came up the stairs, hesitated at the door, his hair at odd angles, his tie askew. He gave the impression of a man in a hurry, with something important to say.

'Come in.'

He did, and looked around, looked at me. 'I'm sorry to intrude.'

'It's fine, please.' My calm tone belied the fear that a new witness had come forward. Someone to say: That American woman aimed her car straight at those children, she drove straight, straight on.

Strebel and I surveyed each other.

'Do you have anything to drink?' he asked, as if to allay my fear. 'Not tea; a drink drink.'

'Wine?'

'Thank you, yes. Please. A large glass.'

'I have red. Bordeaux.'

He nodded. 'I should explain.'

I grabbed a bottle, handed him the corkscrew. Neither of us spoke again until the wine was poured. He took a sip. 'You can ask me to leave.'

'Why?'

'If you don't want me here.'

'The wine,' I said, because I did want him here. 'It's not very good.'

'Oh, the wine.' He looked at it in his hand. With the other he tried to smooth his hair, but he only flattened it on top, leaving the sides askew.

'Tom always bought the wine. He knew all about it. I just choose by the labels.' I rotated the bottle with its pretty blue label so Strebel could see.

'I think there's a lot of fuss. Like coffee. We should just get on with it.' He took a purposeful sip and gave a hesitant smile. 'I was at my granddaughter's birthday.'

We sat and he slid the glass back and forth over the tabletop. He took another sip. 'I've been a detective for twenty-six years. I should be able to deal with things like this. We're trained to be objective.'

'Objective? About the sight of three little bodies in the road?'

He rubbed his eyes, as if to remove the image. 'I really shouldn't be here.'

'But you are.'

He regarded me in a way that felt acutely masculine. I knew he was thinking that I was attractive—he was allowing himself that thought. He said, 'The wine, it really is not very good.'

'It's awful.'

Strebel lowered his eyes and then he stood.

'Is that why you're leaving? Because of the wine?'

'I'm leaving because it's absolutely not what I want to do.'

We moved toward the door. I began to open it. But then

I stopped. Strebel was close to me, and I turned so that my shoulder brushed against his chest. I'm not sure if I did this on purpose. But when it was done I was overcome by the need for him to touch me. He stayed absolutely still.

I cannot now remember the way our bodies turned to speak, whose hand first touched whose face, but there was a kiss. He was afraid to offend, afraid to assume too much. I took his hand and led him to the bedroom. For a moment he hesitated. 'I'm too old,' he said. Then he kissed me again.

He was not Tom. Perhaps that was what mattered most.

'I want to tell you something,' he said much later. I stretched my body against the length of him, the warmth of him. He would go soon, after he had said what he needed to say, and we wouldn't sleep together again. This much I knew.

'I want to tell you what happened.'

'Why? Why would you do that?'

'Because of how we were talking the other day. The distress you feel at not remembering. But the parents expect you to remember. They need you to explain. It's like my granddaughter's coloring books, where you color in each part, carefully between the lines, so simple, and then you have a whole. Then you have the picture.'

'But who would want that picture? Of the children, like that.'

Turning toward me, he propped himself onto one elbow. 'The parents want to make sense of it. My wife—'

He stopped.

'Let's not pretend you don't have one.'

He kissed me, perhaps grateful for the reassurance, and then he went on: 'My wife has dreams. They make sense to her, but I think only in the retelling. She chooses what to leave in and what to leave out. I think there is no meaning, dreams are images, the brain processing. But she needs meaning. So she imposes it. And in my way, as a policeman, I also impose order. Motive, justice. It's natural. Otherwise we're just atoms rushing around.'

'But the inquest.'

'If the inquest is based on your current statement, it will satisfy no one but the file clerks. There will be a recitation of technical facts and a conclusion of "no fault."'

'Are you suggesting I make it up?'

'No, no.' He touched my cheek with his fingertips. He wanted to reassure me. 'I'll tell you.'

'Isn't that illegal?'

'Completely.'

I thought of the man who came into the flat, who sat in the kitchen drinking my coffee. Would it help him? Was that what he sought by entering my space? An explanation? I may become real to him—colored in. The way, sometimes, I'd pressed my face into Tom's shirts when he had been away. The smell of the starch had confirmed him. I nodded.

'Good.' Strebel kissed me lightly on the forehead. 'So. We start with when you woke up. What did you have for breakfast? The twelfth of March. Begin there.'

'Toast. Tea.'

'What kind of toast? What kind of tea? If things are specific, they seem more real.'

'The local granary bread. With butter. Irish Breakfast tea.'

'I used to like Earl Grey. But my doctor said, "Absolutely no caffeine."'

'I think Earl Grey tastes like soap.'

Instead of laughing, he spread his hand over my hair, moved his face close to mine and murmured, 'Pilgrim.' We held on, and in those brief seconds so much was possible. But then we let go.

'I got dressed after breakfast. Navy blue. Tom liked me to wear navy blue. I wore a navy blue turtleneck and a navy blue wool skirt.'

'Navy blue is a color for old women and the police.'

'It's discreet, tasteful.'

'You're thirty-two. Why do you want to be discreet?'

'Is that part of the story? My capitulation to navy blue?'

A soft laugh. 'No. I'm sorry. You wore navy blue. You brushed your teeth.'

'I brushed my teeth and put on a small amount of makeup. Discreet, tasteful makeup.'

He gave me a small, acknowledging smile.

'Then I left the flat.'

'At what time?'

'Eight-fifteen. My language class in Tunn starts at nine.'

'You got into your car?'

'No. Mrs Gassner was in the hallway. She couldn't tie her shoelaces because of the arthritis in her hands. She asked me to help. And I remembered the phone bill. It was weeks overdue. She warned me, '"They cut you off no mercy."'

'And they have.'

'And so has she.'

'No mercy?'

'She calls me "*Kindermörderin*."'

'Ignore her. She'll stop when she finds someone else to persecute.'

'But I am a child killer. A killer of children.'

'No,' Strebel said. 'You cannot even say you caused the death of children. It is not correct. It is emotion, not fact.'

'Legal fact.'

He lay back. 'If you need to cry and blame yourself, then you should. You should find a way to sink into that, but not drown. Don't deny all the complex feelings. But, right now, I need you to be here with me, helping me. We don't, you know, have so much time.'

'You have to go home.'

'As you say, we won't pretend.'

'Of course. I helped Mrs Gassner with her laces, and I ran up to get the phone bill. Then I got in my car. I saw her drive off.'

'And that's it?'

'I sat for a while, thinking about Tom. Being angry about Tom. Minutes. And if I hadn't—'

Touching my lips with his finger, he said, 'Listen. When my daughter was very small, three or four, we were in the bathroom brushing our teeth, and there was a power cut. Everything went completely black. It was only for a moment, a few seconds. But she cried hysterically. When the lights came back on, she said, "I thought I was dead." She couldn't understand it was nothing to do with her. Maybe lightning. Maybe a tree falling on a power line. That's what I'm trying to tell you. You didn't make the darkness. You did not kill those children.'

'Tell me, then, who did?'

'Let's keep going. You started the car.'

'I started the car, I was thinking of Tom.'

'Then you drove through the village,' he said. 'You thought it might rain. You thought about the gray clouds and how you wanted it to be spring.' He was watching me as he spoke. 'You came around the corner, the one below the village. The traffic was light. You weren't speeding. And then suddenly a dog ran in front of you, right in front of you.'

'A dog?' I said almost in wonder. 'What kind of dog?'

'Black, maybe dark brown. Dark and quite large. You don't know much about dog breeds?'

'I had a mutt growing up.'

'Then it was just a dog. And you braked to avoid it.'

'A large dog. A black dog, possibly a dark brown dog. That's why it happened?'

'Yes.'

'And then I saw the children.'

'Did you?' He could not keep the inquisition from his voice.

I closed my eyes. 'No. I can't even feel them.'

'Pilgrim.' His face was close, a lover again.

'It was the dog's fault?'

'No. Yes. There is no fault. You got out of bed. Everyone got out of bed that morning.'

'What should I do now?'

'Come in and make another statement. Just this, what we talked about. I'll tell Sergeant Caspary to expect you.'

He lifted his hand gently from my face, his departure beginning.

Tanga, May 21

REMEMBER!
YOU ARE ONLY THE CUSTOMER!

The sign is displayed atop the counter, the script the kind of red block letters used to warn of fire or falling rocks. The counter contains Tanga's best selection of notepads, all three of them dusty, stale and lonely as week-old pastries.

I regard again the admonition, and glance at the young man perched on the stool. I assume he works here, but he shows no interest in me. He has not even looked over. He stares at nothing—or something I cannot see, a bewitching vision. The shop, so bright at the entrance, closes into darkness behind him. It's impossible to know how deep or large it is, what might be back there. The man sits between the shadow and light. Half his face is exposed, every pore, every fault; the other half invisible.

'This one.' I tap the glass, pointing to a notepad with a faded green cover.

He gets down from the stool—an abrupt movement as if spurred by an electric shock—and, taking a set of tiny keys from a hook above the counter, unlocks and slides the cabinet open.

I'm fascinated by the idea that such security is necessary. He pulls out a red spiral notebook, furthest away from my choice.

'Not that one, this one,' I tap again, more vigorously.

With a sigh he replaces the spiral notebook and selects the green cardboard one. 'This is an inferior item. It is made in Tanzania. The paper is very poor. You will not be satisfied.'

'Thank you for your advice. But it is the one I want.'

After paying him, I walk out into the halogen blast of midday and to the post office. I write to Mrs Gassner, enclosing a check for the phone. The stamp shows a giraffe standing in front of Kilimanjaro, and I imagine Mrs Gassner squinting at it, concluding I'm on holiday.

The post office overlooks the arc of Tanga's bay. Giant mango and fig trees line the headland above the sea, which is the deep blue of hand-tinted postcards; no shallows here, no shades of aqua or turquoise, only depth all the way out to the Indian Ocean. An island sprouts in the middle of the bay, an upthrust of coral rag topped with a crew-cut of green. It is hardly bigger than the three ships anchored beyond it.

Nothing is new here, I observe, so unlike the accidental present of Magulu. Even Tanga's modern buildings are decades old, cement monoliths stained with mildew and moss, cracking open like tombs. The old colonial buildings live haphazardly among them, their wooden balconies drooping, their thick, white-washed walls crumbling into the narrow, shadowed alleys. I am careful not to trip on chunks of broken plaster.

Mr Davis and I arrived here a few days ago, shortly before dusk. We had traveled in silence, for it turned out he spoke no English beyond his introduction. When he stopped in front of the Seaview Hotel, he said, 'This is a good hotel for you.' I paid him three hundred dollars and he drove away.

My room is on the fourth floor, on the corner. A small balcony overlooks the market square, and when I stand at the very edge I can just see the bay. When the heat abates in late afternoon, people appear with baskets as if answering a secret summons. Sounds drift up, the bright trill of bicycle bells, schoolboys running—the slapping of their cheap plastic shoes. The air vibrates with the short, sharp whistling of swifts as they turn and wheel against the dimming sky.

The market closes at dusk, the square empties again and is dark within the hour. Under the one working streetlight, taxis wait. The drivers get out and sit together on the hood of one of the cars, smoking and laughing, listening to football on the radio. I have only once seen a customer. They all drive white Toyota Corollas, though this provides no uniformity: each vehicle is in a different state of decay.

Later still, when even the taxis have gone home, beggars gather under the light. Some of them carry plastic bags containing leftovers from the restaurants around the market—rice and *ugali*, I think, perhaps pieces of fruit—and this they share amongst themselves. I recognize a few of the beggars from the market: the man with elephantiasis afflicting one leg, the man with no fingers or nose, the blind boy. The man with elephantiasis drives a hand-pedaled bike. When they have finished eating, the blind boy climbs onto the back of the bike, and they pedal off.

I sit and watch the dark, empty market. I'm not sure what's going to happen. Maybe nothing will. It could be that I have nowhere to go, so I am here. Anywhere and nowhere are the same place. But I keep thinking about the boy, about Davis. 'This way, this way.'

Arnau, March 21

After Strebel left, after midnight, I could not sleep. My heart looped between the warm feeling of him and the black dog he'd implanted in my mind. I still felt him against me and inside me, his long arms scooping my body to him: a formal lover, wholly aware that we must keep passion at bay. To relish would have been unseemly. We'd made love with great care.

I'd had few lovers in my life other than Tom, and only before Tom; boys my own age, fellow students, callow and unpracticed. I'd never been in love. And then, in October, in my second year at Brown, a man stopped me.

'I'm looking for the Joukowsky Forum.'

'You're nearly there.' I was hurrying to the other end of the campus, not wanting to be late for Dutch and Flemish Masters. 'Just up the block. On the right.'

'But I'm terrible with directions.' He had turned toward me and I noticed as if by instinct the soft, dark wool of his coat, the glossy silk of his tie. 'I think perhaps you'd better take me there.'

He'd smiled, the hint of mischief, or complicity—of the accomplices he wanted us to be. I turned—and the ease of that turning, the lightness of movement, belied the weight of the consequence. In that moment my singular life ended: my ambitions to be an art historian, my upcoming year in Florence. It wasn't a sacrifice. I was nineteen, I had faith in opportunity and time, in things working out. All I knew was that I was going to miss my class, and I didn't care.

We walked together and arrived at Joukowsky. There was a poster advertising a lecture about human rights in African prisons by someone called Thomas Lankester. 'It looks heavy-going,' I said.

'Very,' he said. 'But edifying.'

'Do I need edification?'

'I hope so.'

And we had laughed together, we had shared the little joke.

After the lecture, Tom took me to his hotel room. He was slow, careful, drawing out each sensation. In that heightened state I could see the threads in the white sheets, taste the after-shave on his neck. He stood over me, looking down. 'Beauty like yours,' he said. 'We should bottle it.'

Tom's life wasn't altered by our meeting. Or our marriage. I went with him, not in concession but because I was nineteen and he had chosen me. And he loved me. Surely—surely he had. Yet that love had ended, and I hadn't noticed.

The way I hadn't noticed a black dog.

The black dog had been crucial to the accident. If not the cause, then a deciding factor. It had caused me to swerve. Without the black dog, the children would not be dead. Without me, they would not be dead. The dog and I moving along our timelines. But the dog, like Tom, trotted on, away from the scene of carnage, regardless and unchanged.

I think that's why I went to the window, as if I might see the dog. It might be straying up the dark road in flagrant violation of Swiss leash laws, cocking its leg on the lamp post. But of course there was no dog in the road. No cars. Only the still sigh of 2 a.m. The night was clear. I glanced upward at the blinking stars, hemming the mountains.

Then, shifting my gaze, I saw him on the other side of the road.

He had a soft-edged shape, a middle-aged, balding man. I felt I should know him, that I did know him. From the village? Did he work at the hotel? Had I seen him in the supermarket? Was he a neighbor? Had he thrown a curse at me?

But I felt more than familiarity—rather, an intimacy. A connection that in the next second I had to dismiss because I did not know him, had never met him. There was only the *feeling*, and the way he turned from me and hurried off, as if he'd forgotten a pot on the stove.

I knew. He had got the key from Mrs Gassner. He had sat in my kitchen and drunk a cup of coffee. Waiting, watching, scenting. He had wanted some *sense* of me.

He had it now. He'd been standing there in the dark road for hours. He had seen Strebel leave. I had slept with the policeman overseeing his child's death. And while that small, ruined body was disintegrating, I had been kissed, I had been comforted, I had been pleasured.

Tanga, May 22

She is American. I know before she opens her mouth. She wears knee-length khaki shorts with pleats. They make me think of Melinda. But this woman has big, soft hips, and the pleats that were sharp and neat on Melinda's speed-walked frame are stretched to wheezing point. If Tom had been here I could almost have heard his eyebrows rise in disapproval. He did not like overweight people.

'Gloria Maynard,' she says, extending her hand. 'I'm here reinventing myself by saving the world.'

Gloria tells me she has already asked at reception. She knows I haven't given a check-out date, which has kind of piqued her curiosity. 'I've seen you walking around the past couple of days,' she says. 'Thought I'd say hi.'

I want to shout 'Go away!' but instead I extend my hand and say, 'Hello. Pilgrim Jones.' There's an odd moment when I don't know what to do next so I say, 'Come in.'

'Better idea.' Gloria waggles her car keys. 'Let's go to the club and get some gin and tonics.'

She sees me wavering—sees my empty room, my lack of immediate, certifiable excuse.

'I won't take no for an answer.'

She certainly won't.

She drives a white Toyota Corolla with one hand, smoking and gesticulating with the other. She flicks the gold fringe on the dashboard. 'Bought it from a taxi driver. Actually, he owed me money and in the end he had to give me his car. He had a little habit. Would you believe it, there's a big drug problem in this town. Walk along the front at night and you can buy anything you want. Crank, crack, smack, weed, meth. Because it's a port. Some of the stuff's on its way in, some on its way out. I reckon, this being Tanzania, the same stuff is coming in as is going out.'

This being Tanzania, I hear, and wonder how she knows— about the drug deals and buying a taxi from a drug addict and this being Tanzania. She looks so Midwestern. She is here to save the world. But why here? And why? And how? I now appreciate that my appearance in Magulu was not just odd but unsettling. Whatever questions I have about Gloria she will surely have about me.

The electric windows don't work. The passenger side is half-way up. 'Kind of a pain in the rainy season,' Gloria says. 'The rain gets in and the foam in the seat gets damp and it smells like a boy's bathroom.'

Outside, people flow past. I think how much better dressed they are here than in Magulu, but then I realize it is just after five and I am seeing people with jobs, people who can buy clothes and shoes. If I dared walk down the poorer streets, the tracks that drift off into bean fields and palm groves, I'd see the ubiquitous, tatty, patchwork poor. I hear Martin snicker: *There are always more of them.*

The sea, to my left, appears and disappears through thick stands of fig and mango trees and the shabby remnants of colonial houses. A red-brick hospital built by the Germans a century ago has long been humbled by ivy and the roosting swifts. In the foreground, the new hospital is already decaying, molding. Gloria has a strong opinion about the healthcare offered there and it's not a good one.

Several hotels follow with their overgrown lawns and dark windows. Once, during the pre-Independence sisal boom of the forties and fifties, things were different; visitors came and there were buffets and bands. Tanga was a thriving colonial town.

Gloria talks on, her little history lesson, and I nod, yes, yes, how interesting, but I'm imagining the colonial housewives— acolytes to their husbands' careers—trying so hard to keep busy with teas and luncheons, the sweat ruining their frocks; and, how, at the end of the day, when their husbands were passed out in bed and the servants had gone home, they could sit on the sofa, crumpled, stained, their hairdos limp. In the quiet unelectrified dark, they could undo the hooks of their sensible bras, take off their stockings, let the fat roll and the sweat drip and press the last cold drink to their cheeks, and think: *Thank God it's over.*

I recall how I'd take off my clothes after an evening with our Addis associates, our Lagos associates. I'd shed the little black dress like a skin and feel the very edge of unease, like a shift in barometric pressure. I pushed it away with such discipline: that inkling of my boredom. *Thank God it's over*, I would think, then tamp down that thought. Be careful what you think, thoughts become words, words become conversations and conversations become traps. Therefore: think less to say less. Then Tom would reach for me, Tom would touch me, and I was reassured that all I needed to be was Tom's lovely wife.

'This is it,' Gloria says, juddering to a stop in a sandy layby. I refocus now on the wrought-iron gateway encompassed by bougainvillea, through which I can see the bright blue of the bay. We walk down a long flight of steps, under a flame tree. The clubhouse is a surprise: a new building, well-made, with a large open veranda. Below us, there is a small beach, two pale brown children with a bucket and spade. About half a mile along, on the public beach, hundreds of Tangans thrash about in the water, their raucous laughter punching holes in the quiet of the Yacht Club.

As we sit at the bar, Gloria tells me why she's here—an orphanage for children with AIDS. I lean forward, attentive. 'I put my life savings into the project. I mean, what the hell was I saving it for if not life?'

But it has been difficult.

'The Tanzanians don't want to admit there's a problem. It embarrasses them. So rather than take my help, they refuse me permits—not all of them. Just a couple of the really crucial ones. It's a crock. But I also kinda accept that it's a test. If I stick around long enough and pay enough *chai* they'll trust me. I see their point. If I'm going to take care of sick and orphaned children, I'd better be walking the talk.'

Despite first impressions and near-chain-smoking, Gloria isn't a drinker. She sips her G&T carefully, eyes me purposefully. 'So, Tanga.'

There's no hint of a question mark in her voice, but very clearly she thinks it's my turn.

'Divorce,' I say. Rehearse. See how it sounds. See if it's big enough to hide in.

'Men,' she sniffs. Again the unquestioning question.

'Men,' I lob back.

'Mine was a first-class prick. Best day of my life when Milton left.'

Down the bar from us a group of men are drinking. They've had too much sun, their old skin blotched and peeling, bits of it actually missing. One of them catches my eye and winks. Sure enough, he calls out, 'Hey, Gloria, who's your friend?'

She doesn't even turn around, just gives him the finger. 'No one who wants to know you, Harry.' Then she leans in, stage-whispers, 'What every girl dreams of, right? An insolvent drunk with Kaposi's sarcoma.'

I laugh. It's an odd sound, and I think how I've held myself back these months, laughter forbidden. I feel something in that moment, maybe spiked by the gin, a possibility, as Strebel said, of life's persistence.

As if reading my mind, Gloria says, 'Hey, if you're thinking of sticking around, I got this cute guesthouse I'm caretaking. The owner had to go back to Holland. Dying mother. He's asked me to rent it or sell it, whichever comes first. It's right on the sea.' She glances at her watch. 'It's still light enough. Just up the road. I could show you now if you like.'

The tarmac—such as it is: a fickle strip of tar connecting potholes—segues into a narrow sandy lane. There are houses between me and the sea, hidden by high walls and security gates: a rare show of prosperity. But the walls are intermittent, punctuated by more abandoned mansions and grass lots with mud huts: those who have lost, those who never had.

We pass a boy grazing a cow on the verge. He's wearing a white shirt about ten sizes too big, and for a brief hallucinogenic moment I think it's the boy from Butiama. But we pass this boy so quickly and the idea that they are the same child is absurd. Gloria waves and he smiles and waves back.

Then she says to me: 'The key is not to have anything they can steal and sell. No computer, no TV. Then they won't bother you.'

'I just have a small bag.' I don't mention the box.

'Traveling light.' She says this casually, but she's still seeking a revelation. Why do I only have a small bag? Did I leave in a hurry? Did I leave in secret?

'My husband and I traveled a lot. I'm good at packing.' We shed our material lives, posting after posting, all those boxes, and we just left them behind, so by the time we arrived in Arnau, we had only the essentials.

'Ex-husband,' she corrects.

'It's recent. I'm still getting used to it.'

'Ah, poor doll.' She pats my thigh.

This, then, is who I can be for Gloria: the wounded divorcee.

Easing the Toyota around potholes, Gloria says, 'The electricity is totally unpredictable, so gadgetry of any kind is pointless. Hairdryer, TV, computer, and such. Though you don't have those, traveling light.' She stops at a low metal gate and beeps the horn. A security guard in blue uniform runs out to open it. He salutes.

'*Habari*, Jamhuri.'

'*Habari*, Mama Gloria!'

They chat for a moment. Her Swahili is good—fluent, I assume. And I think she's serious about her orphanage and her commitment. She tells Jamhuri I've come to look at the house. He glances in at me, smiles, the most brilliant wide smile, '*Karibu, Mama, karibu sana!*' Welcome.

We stand in the gloaming. The late evening light, soft and translucent, has made the world benign. The house is white and round and sheltered by red-blooming tulip trees. A hundred yards from the door, a low sandy cliff dips to the sea and a swarm of mangroves. White egrets flock to roost. The sun slips behind the mangroves, creating spangles and diamonds through the leaves. The air vibrates with the wild looping song of Bulbul birds.

'*Karibu*,' Gloria says, and hands me a set of keys.

Tanga, May 25

Gloria lives on the other side of the bay, but without a view of the sea. I've ridden over here on a bicycle I rented from Mickey. He owns a stable of bikes at the market.

'I'm no Martha Stewart,' Gloria gestures down the hallway. 'But it's got potential.' The house is a long cinderblock bungalow with seven rooms and three bathrooms set one after the other with military precision. 'I'm leaving it to the kids to decorate. I want their crap on the floor, their socks in the sofa, crayons on the walls. Noise, mess, you know, that'll make it home.'

The house waits ready for them. The rooms have beds, the bedding neatly folded on the mattresses. There are toys, stuffed animals and plastic cars, a bicycle with training wheels and pink tassels on the end of the handlebars.

'I've been promised the last permit.' She lights a new cigarette from the last. I study the orange-red packet with the logo of a racehorse. Why a racehorse? What connects horses to smoking? Or roosters? Gloria continues: 'A couple of days, they assure me I'll have it. I have ten kids already, and another sixteen needing space.'

She tells me she had a revelation. She takes a long drag, exhales through her nose—a talent which secretly intrigued me as a child, for I thought of dragons. 'I was in the dentist's office, back in Ashland, looking through an old *National Geographic* and there's a thing about children in Africa with AIDS. I was just about to start reading when the nurse came in and said Doctor Babbits was ready for me. I sat in the chair and Babbits gave me the gas. I have terrible trouble with my teeth. As I was sitting there with him drilling away and feeling a bit floaty, I saw those children. They were alone. They were hungry. They were scared and helpless. I started crying. It was unbearable. Babbits thought it was pain and gave me another hit. But it was the children.

'I went home—trailer home, trailer park. I kept thinking how I was this fat, useless, middle-aged woman with rotting teeth. Eating, watching TV, waiting tables in an economically fucked, bigoted little town in semi-rural Michigan. "More coffee, sir?" "Can I take your order, Ma'am?" Ten bucks, keep the change on a $9.47 bill. The sum of my life. "Will that be all?" What if it was all? Fifty-three lousy cents.'

Exhale. Fresh cigarette.

'I have got to quit these damn things before the kids come.'

The housekeeper brings in a tray of coffee and small, dry biscuits. Gloria looks at me enquiringly.

'White, no sugar,' I tell her.

'Figures,' she says, handing me a cup.

'Does it?' I recall my own deductions about black coffee drinkers.

'Ladylike, careful.' She takes hers white with three heaping sugars. 'So I sold my trailer, emptied my savings. You'd be surprised how much money you can save up when you've got nothing and no one to spend it on. I flew to Dar, didn't know anyone, anything. Sure, I was worried that I didn't have enough money, didn't know what I was doing. But that was just brain blah-blah. I had conviction: I had to do something about those poor kids, they were all that mattered. That was two years ago.'

I'm genuinely impressed. 'Just like that?'

Gloria snaps her fingers. 'I even changed my name. Used to

be Mary. Plain old Mary. Tired Mary. Mary of the sore feet. The other waitresses, we'd call ourselves Sisters of the Blisters. On the way to the airport I heard The Doors. And I thought, Gloria. Yes, I will be glorious. And you?'

These last two words jump out at me, unexpected as a barking dog. 'Me?'

She raises her brow inquisitively.

'I don't have a story, Gloria.' I can't hold her gaze, so I turn to regard the toys, clean and neatly sorted in boxes. 'Just the divorce.'

'Everyone has a story.'

'Tom was the interesting one.'

'Tom? The ex? Did he tell you you weren't interesting?'

'It wasn't like that.'

'Then what was it like?'

'Usually,' I say. 'Usually, people don't notice I don't talk. They're happy talking about themselves.'

'Now, that is certainly true. I love talking about myself.'

'He left me.' I know it's what she wants, the petty drama. 'For another woman.'

'Kids? Kids make a divorce real messy.'

We didn't want children. We wanted each other. Tom in the doorway, watching me put in the diaphragm. Pushing me against the sink, 'I need you all the time.'

'No. No children.' I start to tear up. It's like someone's sliced open an onion.

Gloria truly appreciates the tears. Her voice softens. 'You're still young. You've got plenty of time.'

'And you?' Ping! Lobbing back.

'Children?' She puffs out her cheeks. 'Son. James. But he's passed.' She reaches for the cigarettes. 'Yes, James passed quite a while ago now.'

'I'm sorry.'

'Maybe you wouldn't be if you'd known him. He turned out wrong.'

It seems so much to reveal, this wrong, dead son, but she wants me to know about him. Who he was and his being dead defines her, pins her like an insect on a lepidopterist's board. I study her face and search for him. Did he look like her? I wonder where he fits into the dentist's office, the need to save.

At any rate, Gloria moves on. 'Hey, I'm being pushy, too direct. That's the American in me. And, crap, am I going half crazy waiting for this permit. How about I show you around? We could do a little tour of Tanga's finest tourist attractions.' She adds this with a little smirk.

She won't take no for an answer.

Arnau, April 17

Two days after the inquest, I saw Mrs Berger. She was walking along the path from Arnau to the bridge. I was on the way to the bus and hurried to catch up with her.

'Mrs Berger?'

She stopped and turned. Her face was tightly drawn. Her forehead was deeply furrowed and the skin under her eyes smudged so dark a tone of blue I thought she had been beaten. She was a neat person, dressed so that everything matched her olive wool skirt. The neatness only exaggerated the disarray of her face. She looked at me blankly.

'Do you know who I am?'

'Of course.' She glanced behind me, to see if anyone was coming up the path.

'I...'

I began.

'I...'

'What?' she said.

'It's a relief,' I said at last. 'About the inquest.'

'A *relief*?' she said astounded. After looking into the hollows of her eyes for a moment, I looked down, as if on the ground among the wet leaves I might find what it was I should say. I'd chosen the wrong word. There was no relief. There was just another day.

She spoke instead. 'William is dead.'

'William?'

'My dog. He was poisoned.'

'By whom?'

She waved her gloved hand. 'One of them.'

'Are you sure?'

She began to cry, half turning away to hide herself. 'The vet. Yes. It was rat poison. Placed in a piece of meat. He died in agony.'

'I'm so sorry.'

'It's because I said I loved him like a child. You're not supposed to love a dog like a child. A child is a sacred thing, oh, the only beloved, not a dog, a stupid animal.'

'Have you talked to the police?'

'And should they care?'

'But it wasn't your fault.'

Now came a bitter eruption: 'Of course it was my fault. It was your fault. We together.'

'The inquest—'

'*The inquest?* What does the inquest have to do with anything?'

'Maybe William saw something—a cat, and you couldn't have—'

'And maybe you, maybe you accidentally stepped on the accelerator instead of the brake.' She spoke in a rush, as if she had to get it out, had to lose control for just a moment. 'Maybe not even accidentally. Maybe you are crazy, your husband left you and you drove at those children. Maybe you are wicked and spiteful. People say this, and maybe it's true.'

'People say—' but I couldn't finish. I stepped back, but she stepped forward, her face close to mine. 'You keep to yourself. Don't think I will talk to you. Don't think we will commiserate. You will leave and everyone here will forget about you. But this is my home. For the rest of my life I am not who I was before, I have the story. Always behind me they whisper, "She was the one, those three children, it was her."'

Tanga, May 26

I unhook my shopping basket from the handlebars and leave my bike with Mickey at the market. I take the *daladala* to Raskazone. Its route ends a couple of hundred yards before the Yacht Club. I'll have to walk the last mile to the cottage. The tout urges me into the back. He says I'll be one of the last off. Never having told him where I'm staying, I wonder how he knows. I assume I'm marked: a single, white woman, a circus freak or celebrity; everyone knows I'm renting the white cottage at the end of the peninsula road. Hopefully, everyone knows: no computer, no TV. Just a small suitcase and a box.

The *daladala* defies physics. Clearly, the center should not hold: the doors, floor and side panels should fall off. The wheels should pop like buttons, roll into the sea. But somehow it proceeds down the street, the tout hanging out the sliding door, Arabic music blaring. We are crammed inside: a total of eighteen adults.

Outside the Bomba Hospital women are ululating. Someone they love has died, a not uncommon event at the Bomba according to Gloria. Three people want to get on the bus, but only two get off. One of the aspiring passengers is a woman holding a baby against her chest with one hand and a young boy in the other. She argues with the tout, and he lets her on, directing her to the six-inch space next to me. She looks at me, then shifts her eyes to the boy, a question.

I nod and the boy climbs onto my lap.

He does not fidget, sitting solemn-eyed. He wears a school uniform, a blue shirt with striped tie and khaki shorts. I study the back of his neck, the deep groove of his nape and the perfect shape of his head. His skin is polished and smooth. He smells faintly of soap, a local brand like Lux.

The *daladala* jolts along the road, hitting a pothole so he is thrown back against my chest, his head on my shoulder. His mother chides him in sharp Swahili. 'It's okay, it's okay,' I say. Because I want him there, I want him to lean his head against me, I want my body to hold his, to protect him from the road.

The tout bangs the side of the *daladala*. We've reached the end of the route. The boy turns and looks at me with large, dark eyes, 'Thank you, madam.' I smile, 'You're welcome.' I want to kiss him, I want to hold him. Absurdly, I want to make everything right for him, everything, forever; I'll pay for his schooling, his college, his shoes, his books, he'll become a doctor.

He and his mother get off ahead of me. Tightening the sling that holds the baby, she takes his hand roughly, pulling on his arm. Don't, I want to say. He hurries to meet her step, and they walk away up one of the sandy roads that spoke outward. He doesn't look back.

When, I ask myself, was the last time I held a child? I have no idea. But in that moment I realize I will never hold my own child. I cannot allow that life when I've taken it.

Kindermörderin.

Something tears in me, something structural. I give way, my legs buckle. I'm kneeling on the sand.

'Mama,' a voice says. A warm hand on my arm. 'This way, this way.'

I'm walking. There are arms around me, holding me up. Voices. The word *mzungu*.

I see a pair of feet in sandals scuffing the sand. I realize they are mine.

Down steps, a long flight of stone steps. Familiar, but I'm not sure.

A little girl in a red dress swoops down, as if on a swing. I see bouquets of flowers on her dress. Her mouth in a little 'O' as if in song.

Now I'm sitting.

A man says, 'It's the heat.'

There's a cold glass of water in my hand.

Wa— wa—

The thirst I felt in hospital, waking up. Months ago, years ago, in another person's life.

'Come on, love, drink up, you'll be fine.'

He's smiling. His teeth are terrible, he's missing half of them. 'Slowly now,' he says. 'You're Gloria's new friend.'

The water is sharp, too cold against my teeth, so I press the glass to my cheek.

'Thank you.'

He puts his hand on my forehead. 'Burning up. Are you taking anything for malaria?'

I shake my head.

'That's a bit daft, then. It's bad here, especially this time of year.'

'It's not malaria,' I say. It's a boy, a small boy on my lap, the weight of him and smell of him. Not a story, not words: but a child of marrow and blood. How does a child cease to be?

'Let's get you something to eat. And keep drinking that water.' He shouts out to the barman, instructions in Swahili. I look past him, out at the sea. I know where I am now.

'Harry,' he says. 'That's my name.'

'Hello, Harry.'

He hands me a plate of greasy chapatti. Where has this come from? 'Best food in the world,' he says. 'That and a Coke.' And like a magician he pulls a Coke from the air. And a beer for himself.

The chair I'm in is comfortable, and the fan turns slowly overhead. I take a bite of the chapatti and a sip of the Coke: it is the best food in the world. He's sitting opposite me, leaning forward, his elbows braced on his knees.

Bit by bit the world puts itself back together, like a Lego house. The sea, the clubhouse, the gathering dusk, the somnolent town on the edge of a continent. And Harry, grinning.

'Better now?'

'Yes, much.'

'I once had a spell like that in Bujumbura. Heatstroke. Out for days. This very nice Indian fellow kept visiting me. He brought the latest *TIME* and a basket of fruit, took excellent care of me. And then he jumped out the window, I saw him go right off the balcony. A few days later, when I was feeling better, I asked the nurse about him, what a tragedy, I said, such a nice chap. What Indian? she wanted to know. No one's jumped out the window.'

It turns out that Harry has lived all over Africa. In 1973, for instance, he drove a bulldozer all the way from Khartoum to Kampala. 'I was contracted to make a road but there was a war. I made the road anyway. There's always a bloody war.' He smuggled khat into Somalia when the government decided to make it illegal in the 1980s. 'The ban only lasted six months, but it was good money while it lasted.' He flew over the Congo, low on fuel, searching for a missionary's airstrip, the details of which he'd written on a bar napkin. 'It was like looking down on broccoli. Goddamned broccoli as far as you could see. Four hours, five hours, six hours. I'm watching the fuel gauge going down, down, down.'

He's a drunk now, he laughs. Fixed almost permanently to the bar stool. No one else sits on his stool, and if a stray yachtee or tourist tries to, the old boys warn them off. 'I should be holding it down right now,' Harry says, looking over his shoulder with mock concern at the empty stool and the two other old boys on theirs. 'They'll be worried about me.' But he settles in the chair, tells me he almost died eight times. 'Three plane crashes, a puff adder bite, a car crash, cerebral malaria twice. Oh, and some woman stabbed me.'

'Some woman?' I say.

'Wife.'

'How many wives have you had?'

'My own? Or other men's?' He gives me a wolfish grin. 'Eight. Eight wives. Of my own. Two more than Henry the Eighth and I didn't kill even one.'

I imagine the young incarnation of Harry—the other face he once had. The blackberry-dark eyes and straight nose, even if he wasn't handsome, he'd have been a buccaneer.

He's studying me right back. 'What an arsehole,' he says.

'Who?'

'The arsehole who left you.'

I sip the Coke. 'How do you know he left me?'

'Gloria mentioned you were divorced,' he winks. 'With a certain relish.'

'Why do you assume he's an arsehole?'

'The way you are.'

'And how am I?'

'Scooped out.'

I'm very careful not to look at him but out at the evening, the swifts in the sky, the dark mass of the sea.

Harry, however, continues to look at me.

'I never left a woman,' he says, and this return to jauntiness is for me, I sense, to bring me back. Whatever his physical disrepair, Harry is a sensitive man.

'Eight wives and you didn't leave one of them?' I say, jaunty too.

'Oh, I made it impossible for them to stay.'

'How?'

'Drinking, whoring, wandering.'

'Why did you keep getting married?'

'I loved the words. The promise, the hope. That I could be a husband.'

'And what is a husband?'

Harry takes his beer. 'We're going to drink properly, then?'

'What do you mean?'

'Drink, talk about love.'

'Is that the proper way?'

'What else do you talk about when you drink? Politics?' He offers me his hand.

Insects swarm under the security lights outside the club. We get in his old Land Cruiser with one very weak headlight. There are rust holes in the floor. 'Watch your foot.'

He drives into town, the main road above the port, parks on the street, and leads me into Le Club Casa Chica.

It is very dark and loud in here, so I feel muffled and semi-blind, and I think this is the purpose of a nightclub, to hobble senses: to obscure, to mute, to subdue, render hostage the self that discerns.

People know Harry, wave their arms, call out his name. I can't hear, but I see their lips move. Harry old friend; Harry, me matie. I notice the women in here are exceptionally sylphlike, narrow-hipped and long-limbed. Harry slides into a booth, taps the space beside him and I think this is for me. But a slinky, bony girl materializes in seconds, melting over him. I sit opposite. A waitress with shining red lips brings drinks with paper umbrellas.

'Sugar,' Harry puts his arm around the girl. 'This is my friend, Pilgrim.'

I extend a hand, and as Sugar takes it I notice her exquisite, impractical manicure and the hugeness of her hands. Sugar is, of course, a man. They are all men. Harry winks, holds up his drink.

'I assume the arsehole wears suits.'

'What?' I say as if I can't hear him, but I can, I'm just not sure I want this to go any further. He leans in, repeats, 'The ex wears suits.'

'Very nice suits.'

'He's a lawyer.'

I'm taken aback. 'How did you know?'

He laughs, 'I have many years of experience with a wide variety of arseholes. The suit narrows the field to professional arseholes. I think to myself: an arsehole who wears a suit; so not a pilot or a doctor, both really very chronic arseholes. The suits are nice, you said. A successful arsehole. An arsehole who dumps his beautiful wife in a crummy way; therefore an arrogant, self-righteous, selfish arsehole. A born arsehole, not a circumstantial arsehole. Because, let's face it, we can all be arseholes if we get stuck at Customs, if another man is fucking our wife. An investment banker? Real estate tycoon? No, not quite right. Something he represented, something you were looking for. You liked his goodness, what he stood for. Conclusion: had to be a lawyer. Probably a defence lawyer, death penalty cases something like that.'

Sugar makes a sad, sympathetic face, though her makeup looks like a Kabuki mask. 'Men. Why we always choose the ones who are shits?'

'But he's someone else's arsehole now,' Harry says, leaning across the table. 'You see that, don't you, pet?' Then he shifts back, lets Sugar take his hand in her large, decorative paw and lead him to the dance floor. I order another cocktail, sweet and overbearing like comfort food, and watch them, Sugar oozing and gyrating and Harry surprisingly able to follow the beat.

Harry's got it a little bit wrong: I didn't fall in love with Tom because of his goodness. I never examined him, never drew the chart of Tom. Shoulder of goodness, hock of deceit, the fine brain. I saw the brilliant whole, without considering the parts, the atoms, that made Tom, Tom.

Under the spinning disco ball, I realize his otherness was absolute. On that summer day on the edge of Lac Léman, I see myself letting go of his hand. And Elise stepping up to him. He looked at me across the distance, asking me to come back. He didn't want to talk to her. But I turned and kept walking, and maybe what he was seeing was not Elise staying, but me walking away.

Geneva, April 18

The Rue Saint-Léger was a street of children. Families burst out of high wooden doors, prams, dogs, nannies, children whirling like pinwheels. I waited at a discreet distance, pretending to do the *International Herald Tribune* crossword. I looked as if I belonged.

Elise came out of No. 41, the baby in a harness across her chest. Her hair was tied up carelessly, her face bare. She wore sloppy jeans and a man's sweater—one of Tom's, a gift I'd given him years ago. She crossed the street, into the park.

The trees were lovely, the buds just emerging: an entire summer compressed like silk scarves in a magician's pocket. It was a warm day, though the sun was dulled by the muslin of high clouds. Elise walked toward the pond, and from the bag over her shoulder, pulled out a loaf of bread to feed the ducks. Perhaps she might fling the baby into the water, perhaps she was a lunatic. But she simply fed the ducks and kissed her baby's head.

'Pilgrim?'

I turned.

'What are you doing here?'

He was standing on the path, having come into the park

behind me. He was carrying a box from a bakery, containing, I supposed, sandwiches for him and Elise.

I looked away, my face scalded.

He took my arm. 'Come, come with me.' He glanced toward Elise, but she hadn't seen us. Once outside the park, he led me into a café. In his impeccable French he ordered two coffees.

For a long time I kept my gaze down. When I did look up I saw Tom, my husband, and it was everything I could do not to reach across the table and touch him.

'Why,' he said, quite gently. 'That's what you want to know.'

The waiter brought the coffees and shared a joke with Tom. Oh, everyone loved Tom.

'Mrs Gassner told me you didn't buy the land.'

He pressed his lips together. Something I'd never seen before: Tom at a loss for words. Finally, he managed only, 'Elise.' Whatever he intended to say next, he abandoned.

I began to laugh. It seemed better than the alternative, the great hard sobs lodged in my throat and the ugly tears that would stain my face and redden my nose. I giggled. Tom stared.

'Are you all right?'

'Tom. Tom, Tom, Tom.' I tapped my fingers on the table, a little drum, the background music of my life. Tom-tomtom-tom.

I stopped, and we sat in silence.

At last, he said, 'I don't know how it happened, I can't even remember how.'

'Really? You can't remember cheating on your wife? Did you do it all the time, is that why. I just didn't know?'

'No.' He shook his head vigorously. 'It was after work, and we went out for a drink. I wasn't even drunk.'

'But you found her attractive, you couldn't resist her.'

Again, he pursed his lips. 'I won't do it, Pilgrim. I'm not going to betray her.'

'But you betrayed me.'

'There's a difference. I didn't intend to betray you.'

'This is about intention? Oh, Tom, such a lawyer. It's about what you *did*.'

He wasn't looking at me, he was playing with a little sugar packet.

'You left one Sunday evening,' I said. 'And you didn't come back.'

When he turned his gaze to me, I saw his eyes were red and damp. I did what I'd seen him do to hostile witnesses on the stand, soldiers who'd put children in churches and burned them to the ground: I waited. Because it's a human need: to justify.

'I can't explain Elise.'

'Then explain me.'

He deliberated, he wanted to get it right. 'The world is so broken. And I would come home and all I wanted was for you to be there, clean and smelling so wonderful, and I could wash myself in you.'

'We could have had a child.'

Strangely, he regarded me. I had confused him. 'But you never said so. You never said.'

'I didn't think. I mean, I did. I thought we had time.'

'We didn't.'

'*Quelque chose encore?*' The waiter was standing there with his white apron and benign smile.

'No,' said Tom. '*Merci, mais non.*'

No, there will be nothing more.

We walked outside, and I wondered what we should do—a quick, chaste embrace? *Des bisous?* Three or two?

'I heard the inquest is over.'

'Yes.'

'How are you?'

'It's all right, Tom.'

He took my face in his hand and kissed me, the hungry Tom kisses, this act of open mouths and tongues, two humans inside each other. When it was over, I lightly touched his shoulder with my hand and walked away. He was watching me go, I knew. But I didn't turn around. I took the train back to Thun and the bus up to Arnau.

My stomach tightened like a fist as I walked from the bus stop, up through the *malkerai*, toward the flat. I saw the downstairs curtains twitching. Mrs Gassner's face appeared.

Tanga, May 28

'Can't you see what he's trying to get you to pay for?'

I've just mentioned Jamhuri, who has told me about his child. She's very sick. Gloria is driving me to the Amboni Caves north of town. She takes the road past the Hindu crematorium—a pretty, white colonial-style building surrounded by frangipani trees. It's right next to the town's fuel depot, and I wonder if this is a cause for concern.

'The child has epilepsy,' she says. 'He wanted me to take her to a witch doctor. I won't pay for that crap. So now he's asking you.'

'A witch doctor?' I attempt a look of minor incredulity.

'You can't sling a cat in Tanga without hitting one,' Gloria says. 'But of course Jamhuri only wants the big gun. A certain Mr Sese.'

'What does a witch doctor do?'

'Oh, it's not so much about the witch doctor, doll. It's about the believer.'

I frown as if I don't understand. But I'm thinking about Dorothea. *There is a place where many strange things happen. There are ghosts and spirits.* I see her clearly in my mind, her grief and her terror of the box: *'Take it away from here, take it far away from here.'*

Gloria interprets my expression as disbelief, and rises to the challenge. 'Last month, I took Jamhuri's little girl to a specialist in Dar. He prescribed phenobarbital and reckoned she'd probably grow out of it in her teens. But you know how these people are—well, you don't, do you? Jamhuri was expecting she'd get an injection or an operation and be completely healed, just like that. I don't think he even tried the pills. That's why he wants to go to Mr Sese. He thinks she's possessed by *shetani*. He wants you to pay for his daughter to see Mr Sese.'

'*Shetani?*'

'Ghosts. Spirits. They're everywhere. Apparently.'

'And Mr Sese is—'

'The pre-eminent witch doctor.' She leans toward me in a stage whisper. 'He advises the president.'

Gloria brakes at an intersection, takes this opportunity to turn and regard me with her curious owl stare. She's trying very hard to locate the rat she senses scurrying through my words.

A loud honking erupts behind her. 'Where the hell do you think you're going in such a hurry?' she yells out the window, but shifts into first and pulls forward. 'Don't get me wrong. These guys like Sese are very powerful. When I first got here, I had a girl who came to cook and clean. She was a little thing. After a couple of months, I noticed she was turning gray. No kidding, her skin was turning gray. Like wet cement. I finally got her to talk to me. She said she was dying. I didn't doubt that to look at her. I took her to the doctor. Full panel of blood work. A small fortune. No AIDS, no cancer, no TB, everything fine. The doctor told me she was indeed dying—from a powerful curse. I said, "You can't be serious, you're a doctor." He said, "Of the body, not the spirit."

'He told me there are certain curses so powerful that the person who casts them must also die. The only way you can kill your enemy is to kill yourself. For instance, there's this cooking pot curse. You sneak into your enemy's kitchen and steal his cooking pot. You shout a curse into it, wishing their death.

Then you smash the pot and bury the shards in the bush. If your enemy manages to find all the pieces and put the pot back together, then he will be saved. If not, well, *kufa kabisa*—he's dead. But—' she sticks a stubby finger in the air to make her point. 'But, you die too. That's the deal you make with the *shetani*. A twofer.'

'Twofer?'

'Sure. Two fer the price of one. And, you know, that little gray girl, I found her one morning in her room, curled up like a dead moth you'd find in the window. I suppose she'd died in her sleep, there was nothing to be done, she'd got it into her head that she was going to die, she'd willed herself to die. And so she died. I don't know why she thought she deserved it. But that's a powerful thing: to do with a thought what most of us can only do with a gun.'

I glance at Gloria's profile. She is all soft. A small, putty nose, skin loose and soft as dough, her great soft body pillowing in her soft, drapey clothes. I notice for the first time that her pale blonde hair is actually dyed. Her roots reveal a mousey gray. Did Mary dye her hair—or does this belong to Gloria alone?

After a moment I ask her, 'What do you believe, Gloria?'

She hoots a laugh. 'Moolah, doll. I believe in Almighty Moolah.'

We pass the old Amboni Sisal estate, just bush now perforated by the occasional row of sisal. How precisely the sisal was planted, the immaculately measured rows. What were the colonial farmers thinking? That they could take this unscrupulous bush and make it neat as a formal garden? This *Africa* where people smash cooking pots and die of curses.

At some point, Gloria makes a left turn onto an unmarked dirt track. Only when we've driven several hundred yards do I see a small sign announcing: *Department of Antiquities—Amboni Caves*. Gloria makes several more turns—none of which are signposted—past a school, through the middle of a small village and a flock of chickens, cutting a hard right in what looks like someone's front yard, and then down a steep, rocky hill. The bottom of the car crunches over rocks and jars against rills of erosion. Gloria doesn't seem concerned. The car rattles and squeals.

We enter a thick screen of fig trees and cross a dry riverbed. The shadows are deep and cool and grateful, and soon we arrive at the caves. An old man in a Muslim *kofia* gets up from his chair under the trees. He stands very erect, like a soldier.

Gloria turns off the car. 'Watch how he doesn't give us a receipt. Not that I blame him, given what he must get paid.'

She greets the old man with great politeness, which he returns. They speak at some length in complicated Swahili.

He takes the money and disappears into a small, dark hut. He emerges carrying a flashlight and no receipts. 'Swahili or English?' he asks, looking at Gloria.

'Oh, I'm not going in. I've been before.'

'But you've paid, madam,' the guide says in perfect English.

'I'm waiting for a call. You go on.' She opens her handbag and scrambles for her phone ringing inside. 'The Ministry of Health. Let's see how much they want.' Then she sneers, '*Uchawi*, my ass.'

The guide leads me up a set of steps carved from the rock. 'This is limestone,' he says. 'Long ago, it was beneath the sea. And the sea created these caves. But now the sea is very far away. Yes, the world changes.'

The entrance has been domesticated. Beneath the tall archway of stone and the canopy of wild vines, the sandy floor has been swept and plastic patio furniture placed on a natural terrace. There are potted plants and, on the table, half a clamshell for an ashtray.

From here I can see Gloria. She is standing with her back to us, gesticulating, as if she's angry or perhaps just adamant.

'Let us begin the tour, madam,' the guide insists. And so we enter the caves.

He talks about the bats, which cluster like dark grapes on the cave roof above. When he shines his flashlight they twitter and fidget. I don't have to worry about them, he assures me, they never attack. The danger is not from the bats but from the cave itself.

A couple and their dog were exploring the cave, he says, sweeping the flashlight to the right, illuminating a small chamber. 'The dog fell down this hole.' The ground without warning, a socket; impossible to see unless you were looking for it; impossible to know its depth. 'The husband and wife decided to climb in to try to get the dog because they could hear it barking.' He pauses for effect and to make a small sigh. 'They were swallowed by the cave. Never seen again. Completely gone.'

We walk on. I think about the story, how it doesn't make sense. If the couple were never seen again, how does anyone know they went looking for their dog down this particular hole? But I have no doubt that people have gone missing here, in this maze of dead ends and sightless corridors, unseen holes. There is no natural light. We are within the earth, like rabbits. The guide says the tunnel system goes so deep and is so extensive that cave experts have not been able to chart it. However, some believe it goes all the way to Mount Kilimanjaro—five hundred miles west.

He shows me another low and unexceptional cave where three Mau Mau fighters hid during the war for independence in Kenya. And here, around the corner, the rock has formed a chair. He is not satisfied until I sit in the chair and say, 'Why, yes, it is exactly like a chair!'

We climb up a ramp of earth, squeeze between a crack. 'Are you afraid of the dark?' he asks. 'I am going to make it very dark.' He turns off the flashlight.

This is not darkness but a kind of obliteration.

I think about Strebel's daughter telling him she thought she was dead.

The guide turns on the flashlight.

'No,' I say. 'Just a few more minutes.'

He turns it off, makes a dry little cough.

My body blends with the darkness. The barrier of skin dissolves. I diffuse into the air, into the exhalation of my breath. I am the tiniest particles, un-being.

He sighs, turns the light back on. 'Now I show you the image of Jesus.' When I hesitate—for I feel the loss of that moment—he registers his annoyance, 'You must come, please. The tour is for a limited time.' We walk down another tunnel and he illuminates a smudge of mildew that vaguely resembles a face.

'Yes, it looks exactly like the face of Jesus.' My voice surprises me, as if it is coming back to me, an echo, from very far away. 'Exactly like the face of Jesus.'

I have no idea that we have turned toward the mouth of the cave, only that I can feel my pupils begin to shrink. Daylight filters in, low down along the ground. We surface slowly into light.

Just before the entrance, I notice a small side chamber crammed with plates of fruit, sticks of incense, bottles labeled as rose water.

'What is this?'

The guide hurries on, waving his hand impatiently, 'Just local people. Pagans.'

'But what is it for?'

'I am a Muslim! This is for primitive people.'

'Can I look?'

He sighs. He is a repertoire of sighs. This one expresses long-suffering acquiescence.

'Why do they make the offerings?'

'For good health, for money. Some women ask for help to get a child. For many different things.'

I kneel down. 'Has this been here for a long time?'

'Yes. Many, many years. As a boy I remember it.'

In my place, exactly here, the desperate have knelt with their hopes and desires. Women have begged to conceive. Mothers have prayed for their children to be well again. Men have asked for opportunity, for rain, for a new fishing boat, for good luck at sea.

How foolish to believe life could change with the lighting of incense, the purchase of rose water, the offering of eggs. And yet, when you have reached the end of yourself, what else is there? When the tangible world has failed you, why not indulge in the possibility that a corner of the universe might stir, send a shiver of atoms through space, that you might be delivered after all.

The guide shifts his weight. Any moment now he will sigh. I am about to obey, to stand.

But something among the bottles catches my eye: a small jar containing a piece of flowered cloth. I reach in and take the jar.

'No, no!' The guide steps forward, alarmed. 'You must not touch the offerings!'

I'm not really listening. I take out the cloth. It is red cotton flannel with yellow and white flowers.

I look up at the guide, showing him the jar, 'Do you know who put this here?'

'Madam, please, I do not know. How can I know? Local people coming here do not report to me. They are free, this is their place. You must not touch these things.'

'But if a white man came here you would know. Everyone would know.'

'These are not your things. They are not for you to touch or meddle. You must be respectful.'

I replace the jar, stand and wipe the sand from my knees. I try to sound sensible. 'Is it a curse?' I want to see the truth in his eyes, I want to have some instinct. But he is hidden, he is vanishing back down a path into the bush.

'I know that cloth. I recognize it. I want to know who put it here.'

'The cave, madam, it has had an effect.'

'I have money. I can pay you. More than he did.'

He moves nervously, definitively toward the entrance, 'Your friend is waiting for you, madam.'

Back at the car, Gloria seems preoccupied and barely greets me. She turns the ignition. With a little cough—rather like the old guide's—the engine starts.

'Why did you bring me here?'

'What?' She's looking straight ahead.

'Here. Why are we here, Gloria?'

She grips the steering wheel and takes a deep breath, so her whole body expands and subsides. 'Have you got a thousand bucks?'

Tanga, May 29

It was simple for me to go to the bank and withdraw it from my credit card with its virtually limitless limit. I hand the money to Gloria in an envelope. She takes it, weighing it for a moment in her hand, and then stuffs it somewhere down the front of her dress. 'Thank you, doll, really.'

'Thank Tom.'

We are sitting now in the Peace and Plenty, a café near the market where they serve mango smoothies and crisp samosas. Swallows roost in the high eaves of the ceiling.

'What's it like?'

'What?'

'Having money. You just buy whatever you want, go wherever you want.'

'I never thought about it.'

'You're kidding, right?'

'Tom paid for everything. Or it was an expense. Housing, taxis. A lot was on expense.'

She moves her jaw back and forth. 'No shit.'

'We weren't extravagant.'

'You don't know what you're talking about.' Her tone is suddenly savage. 'You go to the bank and get a thousand bucks and do not even fucking blink. Imagine, imagine that you could only get, maybe on a good day, forty. You'd stand there while the machine made its noises, like it's trying to decide whether to give you the cash or tell you, "Hey, loser, there are insufficient funds to cover this transaction."'

She places her hands flat on the table, creating a triangle with her body. She's suddenly like an animal which can make itself bigger to ward off attackers. 'Doll,' she hisses. 'Money changes everything. With money James would still be alive. And that's *everything*. My son was *everything*.'

'I'm sorry.'

'Now, isn't that the most *useless* fucking word. Oops. James would be alive if I'd had money. Sorry. And you're *sorry*?' She shuts her eyes for a moment and when she opens them there are tears. These she wipes away furiously, angry that Mary, soft Mary, is leaking out. 'My boy, my sweet boy's head exploded with a bullet. And there is not a single morning I wake up and my first thought isn't about him, and I'm not hoping that when I open my eyes I'll be in the past, where he is. Money gives you choices, doll. It gives you good schools and nice neighborhoods, and if those fail, it gives you lawyers. You don't even see that. You've lost nothing in your life but a dumbass husband and you think boohoo-boo-fucking-hoo, so sorry for yourself.'

She pauses here to sniff and exhale. 'Sorry is the ashes of your child in your hands blowing into the wind.'

All that comes from my mouth is one syllable: 'O.' But this is attached to a string of invisible Os that sound in my head like the women outside the Bomba Hospital ululating O-O-O-O. I am terrified of the gaping tomb that is Gloria. How deep, how wide, how bottomless the pit and what lives down there, what forms in the dark, in the mud of the soul. The sound, listen close, I can almost hear, between the sobbing and the weeping there is the mumbling, the muttering of spells.

'I have to go,' I say. And I almost run, knocking over a chair on the way out.

★

The lights sparkle on the dark sea like fallen stars. The fishermen are far out on the continent's edge in wooden boats with patched cloth sails. They light kerosene lamps to attract the fish on which they depend. But to the observer, the lights are decorative, ornate.

Waves break on the reef. I can hear the rushing of surf. I imagine the foam, pale and blue in the moonlight, the moon-dappled sea, the nets sinking quietly below. Do the fishermen ever fear the sea and its dark, unfurling possibility?

I pour another glass of wine, cheap South African stuff. Tom would be mortified. Tom will never know. There's a power cut, so I'm sitting in the dark. I want it to be quiet, but the expats in the big house down the street have a generator, and so we must suffer juggernaut noise for their uninterrupted light and TV.

On the table in front of me is the box. I run my hands over the fraying cardboard. I think about the person this once was: a young man, perhaps, a son, a brother, loved in the rambling, careless way of a too large family; protected as much as possible from the shame of his white skin, his ugliness, his need to stay out of the sun.

When he was a boy some children from school tied him to a fence so he would get sunburned. The pain was excruciating: his clothes felt like sandpaper. His skin peeled off in sheets, and they laughed and called him a lizard.

Years later, he got a job, washing dishes in a fish restaurant in Mwanza. He had friends, and maybe even a girl who didn't mind how he looked. She was dark-skinned, ebony, and wore a bright yellow shirt that seemed like a fabulous conspiracy—the darkness of her skin, the brightness of her shirt. He knew men hunted his kind. So he was vigilant. One of his brothers always came to the restaurant to walk him home after dark. He slept with the door locked. But they were waiting, one night: first they clubbed his brother, and then they took him, put him in the back of a car. Tied him up. He paid attention on the drive, he took in everything—the dark night and the intermittent lights, the smell of the car, of the men, of the night itself, damp from recent rains; the wide and forever darkness expanding across Africa; the sound of the car rattling on the road, the brakes squealing when it finally stopped. He did not protest or beg, he knew there was no point. He knelt down and looked straight ahead. He felt calm with certainty, but also he was tremendously sad. He saw through the dark, across the miles they'd driven to where his girl lay sleeping in her yellow shirt. He went to her, lay with her, put his arms around her warm body and she whispered his name.

And then the men cut his throat.

There must have been screaming. He would have screamed. A man dying to feed the hate of another. How does such a transaction come to pass? What kind of wrong extracts such a price? Who is the accountant?

I notice the neighbors' generator has stopped pounding. But the lights haven't come back on, so perhaps it ran out of diesel. I need to be outside, and push open the door. The air is humid and so heavy with salt it almost coats my skin. The tide has ebbed. The night is soft, lapping. I stand on the little headland above the mangroves and listen to the sucking of the sea, the popping of seaweed, and far beyond, just audible, the ocean against the reef. Everything is moist and sucking and briny, constantly rejuvenated by the return of the sea. I think about the incessant regularity of the tides, how they come and go, unlike the rain inland that fails or floods, or the northern seasons that falter or linger. The sea washes the shore every day, with whispering possessiveness, forever and ever.

Martin stands beside me. I didn't hear him arrive.

But then I'm only imagining him.

He lights up his imaginary cigarette. Ha ha ha.

'What do you want, Martin?'

'It's not easy being a mercenary.' His Rooster is the only light, a fierce ember. I imagine him extinguishing it on the back of my neck. 'Africa is full of problems people want solved. Do you know the last time I took a holiday?'

'No. When?'

'Ages. Fucking years. So don't go anywhere else. Don't piss me off. I've booked a week in Mauritius. A package deal, all inclusive, non-refundable, you see.'

'I see, yes.'

Somewhere Jamhuri snores softly. The fishermen's lights glitter on the reef, far out. And Martin steps away.

It's strange—isn't it—how I can take all the bits of the story and fit them one way, or another. I can make Martin appear and disappear. I can make him a mercenary in need of a holiday or a rapist or a man with a broken car. I can conjure a woman in a yellow shirt and the pale-skinned man who loved her.

I remember what Strebel said about narrative. But what he didn't make clear enough was how malleable the narrative might be, how slippery the stories. Physics might fix the course of a moving vehicle away from a dog. But what of the non-physical world?

There's a feeling I have now of crowding, shouting possibilities—that every version is true. And none. Put Martin here beside me. Leave him in Magulu, or at a titanium mine run by South Africans. Take away the tulip tree above me. Take away the mangroves and the sea. Put a different piece of cloth in a jar. In a cave. Or not in a cave.

I was mistaken. The fabric only looked like Sophie's dress. The red cotton flannel with white and yellow flowers.

I was right. It's the same, the exact same.

It can't be a coincidence.

It is a coincidence.

There's a cup in the sink, a hammer in the corner of a dark

room. The fuel pump was never broken. The pieces of the cooking pot were found. The girl's cervix dilated and the baby was born, happy, wailing. The couple and their lost dog were found, they are alive and well in a suburb of London.

All I had to do was turn around and go back to Tom and take his hand in mine and whisper, 'Let's have a child.' And we walked on beside the golden lake. Elise faded, a stranger, someone we wouldn't recall ever having met.

Tanga, May 30

Harry is at the Yacht Club bar. His face lights up. 'Hello, pet.' He orders me a beer. I drink it very quickly. He raises his eyebrows, but orders another. I think Harry would be perfectly happy if I became his drinking buddy. Possibly, I might, too, in a numb, muffled way. He wants to chat, wants to know what I've been up to. I tell him I went to the caves with Gloria.

'Gloria hates the caves. Why the hell did she take you there? It's a godawful place.'

'I have no idea,' I say. But I do. The idea creeps up my arm like a caterpillar. I take the beer, down nearly half of it. 'What don't you like about the caves?'

'Bad,' he says and takes a swig of his beer.

'Bad?'

He laughs now, but not really.

'Why are the caves bad, Harry?'

He shakes his head and pushes back from the bar, as if he might leave. But he can't, I know that. I lean in, whisper gently, 'Harry, I'm in trouble. Something happened at the caves that I don't understand. I saw something that maybe was left for me. A message. But I'm not sure. So I need you to tell me about the caves.'

'Why did she take you there.' It's not a question anymore.

'Tell me, Harry.'

He licks his lips, then moistens them more with beer. 'Jesus,' he says. And takes a long draft. There's a new feeling about him and I think it might be fear. 'I didn't see you coming.'

'Harry, you're not making any sense.'

'Sense? You want sense? Darling, don't stick around here.'

I put my hand on his, very deliberately, my soft, young hand over his gnarled mitt. Go on, I say with my hand. He puts his other hand over mine, and gives it a pat.

'I'm cursed,' he says.

'What kind of a curse?'

'I wasn't always like this, a sad old sod.'

I wait, and after half a beer, he obliges. 'A young couple went missing in the caves.'

'Yes,' I say. 'The guide told me.'

'People heard them for days. Longer. A week. They'd gone looking for their dog, that's what the theory was. But no one could find them. Too many echoes, too many tunnels.' He takes another sip, Dutch courage. 'The local police even brought a sniffer dog from Nairobi. But it couldn't smell anything because of the bat guano.'

I imagine them, the young couple, entering the caves with their little dog, the dog disappearing, their searching for him, possibly falling, possibly climbing into the hole. They lost their way, slowly, turn by turn, and did not quite appreciate the calamity: they thought they were found; they heard their friends calling for them; they thought they were going to be all right. And then terror when the voices faded.

'Did you know them?'

Harry shakes his head. 'Sisal people. Expats. Before my time.'

'Then what do they have to do with you?'

'Messengers. They were messengers.'

'They were bringing you a message?'

'She was. She came to me. She was pretty like you. Slim, dark hair. She was trying to help.'

'What was the message, Harry?'

The bar fills up and the noise gives Harry somewhere to hide. Sikhs in neat turbans and twined beards are laughing at the bar with plump Tanzanian men, with yachtees, with crusty old-timers like Harry. Three young Muslim men play darts while their wives in black abayas drink Cokes. Beyond us, the dark sea filters out, taking the fishermen with it.

I touch Harry's hand again, and he's about to go on, but—

'Hi, there.'

It's Gloria.

'Christ,' says Harry under his breath.

She says, 'Harry still telling you his glory-day stories?'

Finishing his beer, Harry takes a deep breath and finds himself again. 'Why aren't you home polishing your broomstick?'

'Oh, that's funny.' Gloria looks at me. 'We had a fling, Harry and I. It didn't end well.'

'Ended just fine for me,' Harry retorts.

'The thing is. The thing *was*,' says Gloria. 'He had all these stories. And then he just stopped calling. Acting like he hardly knew me. It took me a while to figure out he'd simply run out of stories. He's nothing more than his stories. A comic book.'

'I never enjoyed scorning a woman, Gloria. But you—it was a pleasure.'

Gloria appears to ignore this. 'Harry was quite the adventurer. Did he tell you about the goats?'

'Is this necessary?' There's an odd tremor in his voice, a return to the uncertain ground of the caves.

'Come on, Harry. She's not going to sleep with you.'

I don't want this, don't want Gloria's elliptical conversation, her bitterness peeking out like a blood-red petticoat. I start to get down from the bar stool, but Gloria puts her hand on my shoulder possessively: 'About twenty years ago now, Harry was screwing this woman whose husband owned a bean farm out near Tabora.'

Harry looks straight ahead.

'No,' I say because I don't want to hear this. I don't want to hear any more stories. I want to leave quickly, but I'm a little drunk and I can't get my bag off the back of the chair. The strap is all tangled.

'The woman's husband was away in Nairobi—Betty, wasn't that her name?' Gloria is merciless. 'So Harry decides to fly in and fuck her. It's late in the day and he's been drinking at a bar in Arusha, the Discovery Club, I think it was, but that doesn't stop hero Harry. Oh no. It's a bush strip at dusk, and when he lands he hits a herd of goats.'

Harry says, quietly, 'Do you want me to finish the story?'

Gloria hesitates, and for a moment I see Mary revealed, a woman brutalized by life. Gloria could stop this right now, could wave a hand and laugh, move the conversation on to something benign. But she doesn't. She looks to Harry.

'They weren't goats,' he says.

There's a nasty pause.

'They were children. Playing football. The propeller killed some of them and mutilated others.'

I have my sandals on now.

'And their parents put a curse on me. That's what I was trying to tell you. They cursed me.'

'I have to go.' I walk out of the bar. I hear Gloria's hard laugh. Harry calls her an old hag. I hear him demand, 'Why'd you take her to the caves? That bloody awful place.'

'Oh, you and your stupid curses, you filthy old drunk.'

Up the steep steps, I'm on the road now, walking south along the headland. The road is sporadically lit by the houses. The streetlights have no bulbs, and I wonder who would want their gaudy brightness exposing the sweet wrappers, cigarette packets, cow dung. Let us find relief in obscurity and this still quiet strip of potholes, hemming a continent, defining the end of something and the beginning of something else. For just a moment, rest, then continue the stolid walk of the unforgiven. Drink and drink, for in the bottle there is absolution.

Is that what I must do, then? Drink?

Or seek some other form of self-annihilation?

The shadow of some other curse.

You and your stupid curses.

Why did she take you to that godawful cave?

When did the couple realize they were going to die? Was there something beyond fear, to be entombed in the sleepy, absorbing dark? They reeled back through that morning, looking for the moment when their trajectory fixed in time. A specific set of circumstances aligned, locked in place.

Perhaps they reached the end of the driveway and turned back because they'd forgotten the phone bill. Seeing the dog, panting and excited, they decided he could come after all. Perhaps they forgot the leash. Perhaps it broke.

At this end of the road, the houses don't have lights; there is only the occasional glow of a kerosene lantern. I pass the *dukha* where a woman sells eggs and soap. And other commodities. I have seen her walk with men toward the abandoned mansion behind her stall. She makes no effort of allure—she wears curlers and flip-flops. Her big, loose breasts sway recklessly beneath a dirty T-shirt. She scuffs her feet on the sandy earth as she takes her customer to an old bed in the back with no sheets. I imagine her scratching her nose as he works toward his conclusion.

She is in her shop, almost a silhouette in the *chiaroscuro* light. Her chin is in her hand, the whites of her eyes very bright, her skin very black. The shop contains her and frames her like a Vermeer, with that densely suggestive narrative. She sees me but slides her eyes away, uninterested.

Now the bitumen surrenders to the sand track. In the darkness I step carefully, trying to gauge the depth of the potholes. Jamhuri has put on the outside light. I call his name as I open the gate and there's silence. I call again, louder, and finally he answers in a rush, 'Mama! *Karibu*!' and hurries around the corner to give me a salute. I can see the wrinkles on his cheek from where he's been asleep. He escorts me to the door, and I step inside. I'm thirsty from my walk, so I go to the sink.

There, on the sideboard, is the box, the flaps frayed, the messy knots of sisal string. Did I put it there? I feel certain I didn't. But in the next moment, the next breath, I can't be sure. Did I forget?

Or is the universe arranging itself? Moving objects, shuffling them, dealing them like cards, ha ha ha: a cup, a child, a dog. If it can move a car toward a bus stop, it can surely move a cardboard box.

Something flickers at the edge of my vision, like a face at the window in a horror film. I turn, look out. But there's no one. Of course. Only Jamhuri, shuffling in the dry leaves of the tulip tree.

And in the breathless silence I put out my hand to touch the box. But it moves through the cardboard—as if through a hologram. I pull my hand back and hold it with the other. Again, I reach out. This time I feel the rough paper, the shape of the box: corners, angles, planes.

I go to the door. Step out.

'Jamhuri,' I say. 'Jamhuri.'

Arnau, April 19

The cup, the black grounds therein. I almost welcomed the little routine: how I would wash the cup tenderly, and put it back in its place for next time. This was our slow waltz, a kind of courtship.

But today: he hadn't drunk the coffee. The cup was on the table, still full, the dark brew still lukewarm. The chair was askew. Not how he normally left it, neatly returned against the table.

I went from room to room, trying to figure out if he'd been there, too. And what he'd done. I wasn't ready for change. I was dwelling in time like a nest.

Everything was just as I'd left it. As I lifted the cup from the table my sleeve caught on the chair and I spilt the coffee all over my skirt. I was a good housewife, and under the sink I kept a bottle of seltzer for such mishaps. I crouched down, pulled open the cupboard door. The seltzer stood among the extra dish soap, laundry detergent and white vinegar. But as I took it in my hand I noticed something else: a large roll of duct tape. The heavy silver kind.

I hadn't bought it. I was sure Tom wouldn't have bought it. And even if he had—for some unimaginable reason, because what on earth would Tom do with duct tape?—I felt sure I would have known it was there.

Perhaps Mr Gassner?

I could hear both Gassners downstairs. The French doors were open to the first real spring day. Sounds drifted up, a stray Gassner cough, the clatter of cutlery being put away, the inevitable TV.

Perhaps Mr Gassner, what? Came up here and put a new roll of duct tape under the sink?

The plastic wrapping was intact. I held it for a while, wondering what I should do and what it could mean.

I just put it back.

Tanga, May 31

Jamhuri leaves me at the edge of the track.

'Just go, Mama. Someone will meet you, someone will take you to him.' He is already backing away. He doesn't want anything to do with this. He has no idea what's in the box, but he knows it's something important, something that brings a white woman to a lonely stretch of coastline with evening drawing close.

To Mr Sese.

The path leads into a grove of tall, thin palms. Goats nibble on patches of rough grass that manage to grow on the pale sandy earth. Beyond the palms, the path disappears into thick bush. I try to reassure Jamhuri again, but he turns on me with frightened eyes and hurries down the track. It is several miles back to the main road.

I take off my shoes. The path invites bare feet with soft, yielding sand and the gentle sway of its route. I can just hear the sea. The leaves of the palms clatter in the barest breeze. Something of Jamhuri's fear has stayed with me like a trace of his sweat on my skin.

As I near the tangle of bush, a boy appears. He wears a white shirt, enormous on him, so that he seems a scarecrow. I sense I've seen him before, but there are so many ragged children. The boy looks at me with intense, unashamed curiosity. I am a blue elephant in a pink tutu. I am a circus grotesque wearing bells.

'This way, this way.' I know it can't be the same boy from Butiama, only another boy saying the exact same thing. I see the shirt is torn at the back, almost entirely, revealing the sinewy black body beneath. 'This way, this way.'

The path threads the scrub, making sudden, inexplicable turns. After several minutes we burst onto a dry, white inland wash. Bicycle tracks crisscross the sand, originating from the low shed of a salt works on the other side. I imagine men with bare hands gathering the salt residue from the high tides, rendering it slowly in the steaming vat. I imagine the merciless salt on their rough hands.

Halfway across the wash, there is an island of ragged trees. As we approach, I see ribbons tied to branches, strands of tinsel, bits of colored cloth. I glance around: we are alone. Except, of course, for the man in the trees.

The boy looks at me again. Stares. Perhaps he's never had the chance to examine a white person. Our skin is like the underbelly of fish. 'This way,' he says, gesturing to the island grove. I reach in my pocket, find some coins and hand them to him. He smiles and runs off across the sand, the gap in his shirt flapping open. I step into the trees.

There is litter on the ground—the torn wrappers of incense sticks, empty bottles of rose water, shredded newspaper, dead matches, the caps of Sprite. The scrubby trees shed their leaves eagerly, and I smell the decaying leaves as well as the smell of the old man, which is—surprisingly—Old Spice. Mr Sese wears a Mao-style polyester suit, town shoes and thick glasses. He steps forward, shows me to a chair. 'Madam, welcome.'

He is not some mad-eyed Rastafarian in rags and beads. He looks like a librarian. 'Would you like some tea?' The flickering light glints off his glasses so that for a moment I cannot see his eyes, which are thick and pale with glaucoma. I can hear Dorothea: So, he has no medicine for that.

Mr Sese offers me a cup in one hand, holding a large red thermos in the other.

'It's just tea?'

He laughs, 'Yes, just tea.' He pours. 'I cannot give you medicine without knowing your complaint.' He sees I don't quite understand. 'Just as with your medicine, with mine there is a different treatment for a different ailment. Would you like me to test the tea?'

I take a sip to make his point. Then I hand him the box. 'This is why I'm here.'

He opens the cardboard flaps, glimpses inside, and shuts the box with scrupulous objectivity. 'And how did you come to be in possession of this?'

I tell him the story: Magulu, Kessy, Dorothea. 'She's a doctor, a proper doctor, but still it frightened her.'

'Madam, I'm an improper doctor and it frightens me.' He peers over his glasses. 'Your friend, she appreciated the powerful nature of this spell.'

He puts the box down on the sandy earth. He considers his words. 'This magic finds the person for whom it is intended.'

'But I have it.'

'Yes.'

I shake my head. 'I only took it because they didn't want it. Dorothea and Kessy. They were afraid.'

'It was not for them.' He is matter-of-fact.

'Then who was it for? It came on the bus.'

Did it? I think back. Was it a Thursday? Kessy said some children found it on the roundabout. And then Martin, and then Martin—

Slowly Mr Sese shakes his gray head. 'Madam, the nature of such magic is very sly. It uses people. And it has come to you by whatever means. It has come to you.'

'It wasn't intended for me,' I say, deciding to stand, to leave.

'Then why have you kept it?'

'Because of Dorothea. She asked me to help.'

'You could have just thrown it away. As you don't believe. Yet, you brought it all the way to Tanga. To me.'

The boy, I think, the boy in the white shirt. *The* uchawi *will direct you.*

This way, this way.

'How can I throw it out?' I look at Mr Sese. 'It was a person. Isn't there a ceremony? Can't you take care of it? That's why I'm here, isn't it?'

He puts his hands up as if to slow me down. Then he closes his eyes and mumbles under his breath. I'm relieved that he looks ridiculous.

Finally, he opens his eyes. 'They are okay, the dead. Don't worry about them.'

I take my wallet out of my bag. I'm pulling out two crisp, bank-fresh bills. 'Is twenty thousand enough?'

'But the living. The living are always the problem.'

As he doesn't take the money, I put it on his chair. I start away, and he says, 'He is coming for you.'

'What?' I look back at him. He is a charlatan, chanting gibberish and cleverly deducing that a woman with a box of body parts might be disturbed and frightened. She is easily persuaded that someone might be after her.

Is this Gloria's work? Martin's?

His voice is low, a librarian's whisper. 'He has already come.'

'Who? Who are you talking about? How much did they pay you?'

'I will try to help. Yes, I will do what I can.' He reaches out for me, and for a moment catches my hands, holds them in his. They are extraordinarily warm.

But I pull away, hurry back across the salt pan. The wind has dropped, so the dusk is still and deep, and the light almost lavender on the white sand. I retrace my footprints and find the path that takes me to the track. I want to be in the white cottage, the door closed: home, this new idea. The act of returning home is redemptive: through the gates, across the threshold and we may begin again, we may be the better, wiser person than when we left; forgiven and forgiving.

On the main road, I wait for a taxi. Surely, there are taxis on this stretch. But none arrive. I begin to walk into the quickening dark night.

People watch me as I pass. But I can't see them. They exist beyond the hem of light cast by buses and cars. I know they are selling dried fish and mangoes on wooden tables. They are laughing, dissenting over politics and the behavior of relatives. They are casting spells and buying curses. They are placing offerings in caves, among the roots of baobab trees, imploring, requesting, hoping for an alteration in the scheme.

The taxi slows, dogs my heels from a dozen yards before I realize it's there, a white Toyota Corolla. I peer in at the driver, but the headlights of an oncoming car blind me, stun my vision. I can't see anything but the negative of the light.

'Raskazone,' I tell the driver. 'Past the Yacht Club.'

I get in the back. The taxi moves forward. There's the smell of cigarettes.

'How is old Mr Sese?' Gloria asks chattily. 'Has he been helpful?'

She is revealed now, hands resting casually on the steering wheel. For a moment I say nothing. I clench my fists so that my nails dig into my palms. I feel uncertain: that odd wavering sensation. The coming in and out. O-o-o-o-o-o.

'How did you know I was here?' I hear myself say this, as if from a great distance.

Gloria takes a drag. 'How did I know you were here? Magic!' She makes a spooky ghost noise then laughs. 'Jamhuri works for me, doll. I pay his salary.'

We drive. The road dips and turns vaguely inland. We pass small villages, collections of huts, lit only by kerosene lamps. The lamps blink like fireflies. There are faces—pieces of people—and then only road in the headlights. For long stretches there's nothing but sisal. Once neat rows gone to bush. The before and the after is relentless.

Moving, we are moving over the roughshod road and under the trees, under the restless rustling trees. Through the dark town. Past the hospital, past the Yacht Club.

'I shouldn't have told you about Harry like that,' Gloria says at last. 'He's harmless these days. Defanged, declawed, sitting at the bar. It's the self-pity I can't stand.'

Gloria's smoke loops up like a genie. She carries on, she has what she wants to say, why she's come to find me: 'Life is full of sorrow and shittiness. But it's what you make of it.'

Now we are on the narrow sand track. A bearing has gone in the Corolla's wheel, rattling like a stone in a tin can.

'That's what I'm getting at, doll. What have you made of it? What have you *done*? Have you done anything good? Anything beautiful? Have you created anything? Music? Art? Have you made anything better? Even in a small way? A small light in this dark world? Have you even been *happy*?'

She throws the lit nub of the cigarette out the window. 'You should ask yourself what the hell you think you're here for.'

I feel an odd narrowing, as if in my bones. A sense, I suppose, of intense definition. I am present.

'Your small, selfish little life.' Her voice leaks in a hiss of vehemence. 'Your guilt, your poor little broken heart. So fucking pointless.'

We arrive. There's no sign of Jamhuri, but the gate is open. Gloria drives in, stops the car. I know it's impossible, but there seems a momentary pause, a gap of total silence, between the dying of the engine and the rushing of the outer sea, the high tide surging in the mangroves. There's a wrinkle in time. And then the earth lurches forward.

'Get out.'

I obey.

She leans out the window. 'It's what you make of it anyway, doll.'

The car starts up again, and as she pulls away, the broken bearing pings. Gloria switches on the radio to the tinny sound of Swahili gospel. *We love God, God will help us, God-God-God, ping ping ping.*

A spark flies up from the muffler as it hits a rock. Only one tail light works, burning the dark like her cigarette, until it is extinguished by the bend in the track.

I turn toward the house.

The door is open.

Arnau, April 21

I opened the cupboard under the sink, a reflex, really. What I'd begun to do whenever I came back.

This time the duct tape wasn't there.

I checked again, behind the detergent and spare bottle of dish soap. I stood and looked around, I felt it was what I should do. The kitchen. The living room. The small bathroom. Each revealed itself utterly normal. Dormant. The sofa wasn't floating in the air. The toothbrush didn't chatter.

But the bedroom door was shut.

The closed door formed a dull void. Only a sliver of light glistened from the narrow gap between the door and floor.

I waited in front of the door. I placed my hands against it, palms flat against the grain.

'Hello?'

No one answered.

'Hello,' I said again.

I listened for a shuffle, a footfall. I watched the gap to see the crossing of a shadow. But there was no one.

I put my hand upon the handle, the round knob cool and smooth, an ergonomic fit. I turned it.

The room was exactly as I had left it, the curtains open, the bed made.

I thought perhaps that I'd closed the door by mistake, although I've never liked closed doors. Always the implication of what's behind them.

Perhaps the wind had closed it, a draft from another room.

And then I noticed the arrangement on the bed.

A plastic bag, the supermarket kind. Carefully folded.

The roll of silver duct tape.

A small swatch of fabric. About four inches in length. Red cotton flannel with white and yellow flowers. Individually, the objects were unremarkable.

But as a trilogy.

It didn't take me very long. My winter clothes I put in a trash bag in the basement. If Mrs Gassner found them before the trash collectors, she would sell them, for they were of excellent quality. I had so little else. All those years with Tom, the packing and unpacking, there was so little else.

And I left.

Left you.

Carefully, without slamming the door.

Tanga, May 31, 8:13 p.m.

And now you stand at the entrance to this other house, on this other continent, and it's as if no time has passed at all. As if we just stepped through the door at Arnau and onto Tanga's sandy earth. You—my silent dancer—you are pale, almost translucent in this half-moon, sea-fractured light. Your hair is thin, you wear your raincoat and I think you must find it too warm. You are overweight in the way of middle-aged men. I recall how I saw you that night in Arnau. After my lover left. And I wonder if that is when you decided to kill me.

I believe I know the smell of you, some part of my brain recalls it, the distinct yet subtle odor of your hate as you sat drinking my coffee in that pathetic flat. Where I stayed put like a well-trained dog.

You watch me walk toward you, under the tulip tree, across the threshold of sand. You think how much thinner I look, almost gaunt. The sharper angle of my cheekbones, the outline of my chin and jaw. You can imagine the skull beneath my skin.

'*Sagen Sie nichts,*' you say, you plead. 'Don't, don't speak.'

This is the first time I have heard your voice. We don't appreciate how a voice gives dimension. Perhaps this is why you don't want me to speak: you want to control your interpretation of me, keep me paper thin. You are entitled to whatever you need.

I think about a friend of my father's and how he had his cancerous larynx removed. He spoke holding an electronic device to his throat. This gave him the ubiquitous, halting voice of a computer. For a long time he kept the old greeting on his answering machine just so that he could listen to his own voice. I don't know why I think about him now with such sadness: how he hunched over the answering machine, finally, one day, pressing delete.

You hold a blue plastic bag and a roll of duct tape. Is it the same roll you left in Arnau? The bag is from the market in town, a *malbolo*. You are crying, your bland, wide face completely wet with tears. I might as well have flayed you alive and ripped out your guts. I have destroyed you.

I step into the house and shut the door behind us.

'She was the good in the world.'

Even if you had not forbidden me to speak, how might I reply? No correction can be made. We talk, we speak, so many millions of syllables spilling from our mouths in a lifetime. And it's just narration.

Sorry, the most useless fucking word.

But what we do—

Gloria said.

What we make of sorrow and shittiness.

I offer you my life. What you need.

I step toward you.

Kneel down.

You put the bag over my head.

You wind the duct tape around my neck. I hold out my wrists and these you bind. I hear the sucking of my breath against the plastic and the sound of your feet. I see the outline of you fade into darkness. I feel myself begin to panic, the bag clinging to my head like a skin. Lie down, I tell myself, in this embracing dark.

Un-become. Un-be.

Rain, air.

Arnau, March 12

Out of the corner of my eye, to the left, I see a dog leaping, bounding, tail in the air, and a woman yells his name. An English name: *'William!'* I glance in her direction and the dog is suddenly rushing at my car and I jerk the steering wheel to the right. I slam on the brakes. I feel the weight of the car shift with the swerve and hear the squeal of the tires and I look ahead and see three children and they are looking at me, riveted, faces bright with concern for the safety of the dog. A girl and two boys.

I want to stop the car, I'm certain I do. I'm supposed to. I've been a lovely hostess and I've spoken carefully and I've worn navy blue, I know if I turn the wheel again now there is still time, the merest fraction of a second, for instance Elise stepping up to stand beside Tom on the summer day by the lake and me walking ahead, the boats on the bright water, the fluttering of birds. All that is required is that I turn back to him. All that is required is that I allow the neurological signal from my brain to travel to my hands so that they may turn, turn the steering wheel hard to the left. But there is only Tom leaning in to hear Elise, her hands upon the air, and so I drive on, I keep going, I drive on, straight on.

I drive straight on.

And I see the fluttering dress as the little girl flies into my vision, a demented angel falling from the sky with her mouth rounded into an 'O' of surprise, and she hits the windshield and the glass shatters, tinkling, tinkling like bells, sparkling like snow, and the child in the red, flowered dress lifts back up into space; the wires connecting her to heaven retrieve her and she disappears from me and I feel oh a great gurning loss that she has been taken. I saw her face and she did not know that she was dying, did not know I was killing her.

STREBEL

It was raining. It always rained when these things happened, though Strebel knew this was just his impression, that the memories were collecting, cramming together into one rainy day. The benefit of rain was fewer rubberneckers, fewer bystanders, and therefore fewer people to come forward later with completely useless information.

Strebel got back in his car and sat for a moment, the rain battering, obscuring. It had just started an hour ago. If the rain had begun earlier, the accident would not have happened. The woman with the dog would have stayed at home. The rain would have washed away the slick, invisible residue of oil that accumulates on tarmac and the car would have driven—skidded—differently.

He could go on. He knew the parents would. Those itchy little ifs, like earwigs, burrowing into their brains. He didn't want to be here, didn't want to be involved—essentially this was a traffic incident. But his boss knew very well what it could turn into, given the driver wasn't Swiss. Given the victims were photogenic children. At least the driver was American, not a Muslim or an illegal immigrant. He was confident he could control the outcome.

The children had been on their way to the Fun Park, they'd been thinking about sweets and rides that tossed them in the air, they'd been happy, excited. Strebel rubbed his face and turned on the engine. He drove to the hospital in Bern. There had been talk of airlifting one of the children—the little girl—to Zurich. But not any more. The traffic was appalling, due to the rain, and he considered putting on the siren. But there was no rush now, no rush at all.

In the parking lot he looked out at the hospital, a rectangular block, as if the building was trying to hide in blandness. It might not be noticed, might not remind people that there was always a bed with their name on it. He thought about what he needed to say. The words always sounded wrong. It was impossible to convey the sorrow he genuinely felt, a sorrow that never abated. A sorrow that made no difference at all. He looked through his notes at the name. The name had to be right. He had to know ahead of time if there was an odd pronunciation or inflection. Sometimes he had to practice with foreign names so that he didn't stumble. Sophie. Not Sophia. Sophie Leila Koppler. Was that Ley-la or Lie-la? Was it Middle Eastern? He'd have to ask Caspary.

Strebel got out into the rain and let it pummel him. It was better if he looked wet and bedraggled; his sympathy would appear more authentic. Next of kin didn't need some wide-eyed optimist.

Inside the hospital, the wet soles of his shoes squeaked on the white floor and a drip from his hair ran down the back of his neck. He knew the way to the trauma unit and wished he didn't. In the lobby, he saw Caspary who pointed to a middle-aged man in a dark blue raincoat, standing by a potted plant.

'He only just got here,' she said. 'He doesn't know.'

'Is there anyone else?' Strebel asked. 'The mother?'

Caspary shook her head. 'She died of cancer last year.'

Child and mother, both in one year. *Well done, God*, Strebel thought and turned to watch a nurse hand Sophie Koppler's father coffee in a styrofoam cup. He didn't drink the coffee, but stood with the cup in his hand. When he finally noticed it, he seemed baffled. Who had given him the coffee? And what was he doing here?

I come into people's lives at the worst possible time, Strebel thought. He started toward Mr Koppler, then turned back to Caspary. 'Ley-la or Lie-la?'

'Lie-la.'

Mr Koppler didn't notice him approach, even though Strebel was walking directly at him. Strebel gently touched his elbow. 'Please sit down, Mr Koppler.'

Mr Koppler complied, almost spilling the coffee; Strebel took it from him, placed it on the floor.

'I'm Detective Chief Inspector Paul Strebel,' he said. 'I'm so sorry to tell you that your daughter Sophie has passed away.'

'Sophie?' Mr Koppler looked at him, bewildered.

'There was a car accident.'

'But she wasn't in a car.'

'She was hit by a car. On the side of the road. At the bus stop below Arnau.'

'Sophie?'

'Yes. Sophie Leila. Your daughter. She's been killed.'

'But she wasn't in a car. We walked.'

'Mr Koppler, I'm so sorry, but we need you to identify her body.'

'She was taking the bus.'

Strebel sat quietly. People in these circumstances attacked him. A woman whose young son had been battered to death by her boyfriend hit Strebel so hard that her ring split his cheek and he needed half a dozen stitches. Or people collapsed; their internal scaffolding gave way and they fell to the ground like detonated buildings. Or, like Mr Koppler, they seemed not to hear, not to comprehend.

'She wasn't in a car.'

'She was waiting at the bus stand with Mattias Scheffer and Markus Emptmann. A driver coming downhill lost control of her car and hit the bus stand,' Strebel explained in a soft voice. 'All three children were killed.'

Mr Koppler nodded vaguely, and after a moment he stood and they walked slowly down another corridor to the chapel, where Sophie lay, cleaned of blood and glass, under a white sheet. But you could never imagine she was asleep. This was always when the pretending stopped, all possibility of error eliminated.

'But how,' her father said, looking through the glass. 'She wasn't in a car.'

★ ★ ★

Ingrid was clearing away the dishes. She said, 'The downstairs toilet is broken again. The plumber promises to come tomorrow, but you know how they are.'

Strebel glanced over at his wife and felt a sudden rush of hatred, like a blast of wind. He wanted to run over and slam her hand into the rubbish disposal and hear her scream, and pull up the mangled appendage, bloody and battered, then say, 'Look, look at this, blood and bone and gristle. It's all we are, all that's ever left.'

In horror he got up and retreated to the living room, then turned on the TV. People were laughing, he had no idea what about. His whole body felt odd, as though his blood was fizzing. His breath wouldn't quite come, but knotted in his throat. Was he having a heart attack? He checked himself for symptoms but there was no numbness or pain in his left arm, no tightness in his chest—nothing specific, just this internal *heat* and profound anxiety at the rage he'd just felt against his wife. He sat on the sofa and tried to make sense of the TV. The actors were running around, chasing someone—something? each other?—laughing. A poor imitation of laughter.

'Paul?' He heard his name. Initially he thought one of the actors on TV must be named Paul. 'Paul?'

'Paul! Is something the matter?'

He looked up at Ingrid. The rage was gone, but its absence only clarified his profound ambivalence. And in this he felt a further confusion. How could feeling nothing be so intense?

★ ★ ★

Leaning over, he turned off her light. For many years her bedside lamp had been a source of irritation. Ingrid liked to read in bed, while he preferred to close his eyes straight away. But she would always fall asleep, the light on, the book open on her lap, her lower lip slack as a moron's. He was never asleep—could not fall asleep until he knew she was. He was a natural insomniac and bedtime was rife with ritual. The fresh glass of water by the bed, the hot shower, the special pillow, the ridiculous lavender sachet under his mattress: the superstitions of the sleepless.

But he liked to pretend to be asleep—a kind of lie to her; he liked the separation, the isolation, and how he could turn thoughts over in his head without interruption; without: 'Dear, it's Beatrice's birthday next week. The twentieth. You haven't forgotten? I spoke with Caroline and I suggested we buy a new bicycle.' He knew he was required to participate—his wife, his child, his grandchild. He did his best.

Ingrid shifted position in her sleep, entering her own fiefdom, dreaming voluptuously. No doubt she would need to refer to one of her books on interpretations. Her dreams were never just dreams but omens, premonitions, signs. She did not tell him about them any more. She knew better. But she kept a 'dream journal' on her bedside table. On waking she would scribble at wild speed and he often wanted to suggest she take up shorthand. The pen scratched the paper, scratch, scritch, her face intent and closed to him.

Now she was dreaming of her father coming out of a hole in the bed or a red fish that turned into a woman or a flock of white birds trapped in the kitchen. He did not dream, and he'd once made the mistake of telling her this. 'Everyone dreams, Paul. You just don't care enough about what your subconscious has to say.'

He turned on his side, slipping delicately out of bed. His rule. If he had not fallen asleep within an hour, he must get up. He felt not the least bit tired, although he knew the tiredness stored itself away, like bales of hay. Tomorrow they would tumble, bury him with exhaustion.

In the kitchen, he heated milk in a small pan. In the dark, quiet world outside, people were committing unspeakable crimes. Unspeakable, but not unthinkable. He sat down, drank the milk. Was Beatrice old enough for a bicycle? Hadn't she just started walking?

★ ★ ★

Ernst Koppler had put nothing of Sophie's away. Three dolls sat on the dining table, carefully aligned along a Dora the Explorer plastic placemat. Strebel knew vaguely about Dora because of Beatrice. Dora was supposed to be a better role model for little girls than the numerous princesses—Snow White, Cinderella; Dora was independent and proactive. Her ambitions didn't involve marriage to a handsome prince.

A number of stuffed animals were stationed or abandoned about the room: a penguin on the floor near the sink, a camel on the sofa; something—a cat? a monkey?—with large plastic eyes and pink fur crouched on top of the TV. On the coffee table were two rubber snakes, a green crayon, a yellow sock, a book about a baby elephant, a plastic spoon, a purple ribbon, a mini handbag decorated with pink and gold sequins, a princess crown, a yellow bath duck, a ladybird key ring, a plastic Swiss cow.

Sometimes it took parents years to put their dead child's

possessions away. By then, Strebel had observed, it was too late: the ability to move on had been forfeited. Objects wielded great power. Left out, they became museum pieces, totemic. Artifacts. Packed away, they became memories—the past. Strebel understood the psychology of grief—not that it was complicated. Detectives were required to take sensitization courses. They had to look at houses as potential crime scenes. Mothers who beat their children to death cried just as hard as those whose children had drowned accidentally in the river. Toys, therefore, could become clues, evidence.

But not here. In this house the toys, the casual mess, suggested the expectation of return. We'll clean up later. *Later* hung upon the air with the almost visible density of dust. There was a smell of dried apples. Strebel realized this was coming from Mr Koppler. He had not bathed recently, his clothes were the ones he'd worn at the hospital two days ago. He looked like a tramp.

Mr Koppler sat in an armchair. Strebel took the couch. But as he sat something squeaked. He rescued a doll from under his left buttock, and held it, not sure where to put it. Mr Koppler looked at the doll, and Strebel knew he was seeing Sophie talking to it, seeing the little girl babble. Are you hungry, little baby? There, there, Mummy'll give you a bottle.

The doll held them captive for long moments, before Strebel finally broke the spell. Very carefully, he put it on the coffee table.

'Mr Koppler, I know this is very difficult for you. I need to go over your movements that morning.'

Mr Koppler shifted his gaze, passing over Strebel to the pink cat-monkey on top of the TV and out the window. He was a man leagues down, on the bottom of the ocean. He could not move against the pressure of the water, could not see because light did not reach such depth.

'She didn't want to go. But I work. My own business. A stationers in Interlaken.'

'Go? Go to the Fun Park?'

'Yes. They planned it. They asked me. They're trying to be kind. After Hamida died.' Mr Koppler's expressionless face rotated back toward Strebel. 'They never spoke to me before, those women. Not to Hamida when she was alive. She was one of those immigrants.'

Strebel let a brief silence absorb this memory. Then he continued: 'The trip was to the Fun Park. With Simone Emptmann and her children, and Vidia Scheffer's son, Mattias. Correct?'

'Yes,' said Koppler. 'They were all going to take the bus because Vidia's car wasn't big enough.' Mr Koppler rubbed his hands very slowly against the top of his thighs. 'The baby. Simone's little girl. Her car seat was the issue, I believe.'

Outside, the sound of a car. The silence slipping backward. Strebel waited. How many times had he done this? Waited for a parent to recount the last hour of a child's life. The hour when anything else could have happened.

Mr Koppler began again: 'We left the house at about eight-fifteen. We crossed the Arnau Bridge. She wanted to stop a moment and watch the water in the ravine. She believes fairies live down there. Hamida told her that. We reached the recycling center, the parking lot, at about eight-thirty. Sophie told me again that she didn't want to go. We talked about it. She—she started to cry. I said I had to go to the shop and she must understand she couldn't come with me. She'd be bored. She'd… she'd get in the way. I said that. That's what I said. "You'll get in the way." So she agreed. She wanted to help me. That's how it's been between us after Hamida, we help each other. I left her and walked back across the bridge. I got in my car and reached the shop at nine-fifteen. In time to open at nine-thirty. It was busy. There was a conference in town and I had a lot of customers. The phone rang several times but I let it go to the voicemail. That's why. That's why when the hospital called…' He let the sentence drop.

There was nothing else. Mr Koppler rubbed his thighs again,

sat back in his chair and shut his eyes. Strebel put away his note-book. He glanced again about the room and saw the pink cat-monkey that longed for Sophie's touch, longed to nestle in her arm when she fell asleep, her soft breath smelling of bubble-gum-flavored toothpaste.

'She could have come to work with me,' Mr Koppler said, his eyes open again, tight and small behind thick glasses. 'She would have been no trouble.'

Statement by Mrs Alicia Berger; interviewing officer:
  Sergeant Teresa Caspary
14 March 2015 14:32

I left my home about twenty past eight to walk William.
[Sgt Caspary asks Mrs Berger to clarify who is William.]

He's a Rhodesian Ridgeback. They are very large dogs, and some people therefore find them intimidating, but they have excellent dispositions and are easy to train. Being a widow for more than five years now, I have taken William to be my best friend.

I walk with William every morning, weather permitting, at almost the same time and on the same route. He does enjoy his walks, so the weather must be really bad to deter us. And that morning the rain was holding off. It was just a little on the chilly side.

William and I never alter our route. I believe a dog has a natural territory, and by taking the same route I am allowing William to designate and maintain—to patrol— his territory. I must add here that he is always on a leash. I have a humane collar, a harness that goes over his chest and shoulders rather than around his neck. William is beautifully trained and very obedient. I never have to even tug a little on the leash to remind him of his manners. Which is why I find his behavior perplexing.

[Sgt Caspary asks Mrs Berger to describe the route she walks with William.]

Well, we descend from our house on Hillside Crescent to the pedestrian walkway connecting the crescent to Field Road. We follow Field Road south to the footpath leading down to the village green. We then take the footpath as far as the recycling center. It's very pretty there, overlooking the river ravine, among the trees. We then cut through the recycling center, cross the road at the pedestrian crossing, and go straight home along the Arnau Road.

Shortly after crossing the Arnau Road—

[Sgt Caspary asks Mrs Berger to define 'shortly.']

Two minutes. One minute? Say two minutes after crossing the Arnau Road, William suddenly lunged away from me. He's never done it before, so I wasn't expecting it. I don't know why he did it, as if he saw a cat or something, but even then he's seen cats before and never behaved in such a manner. I was so surprised that he yanked the leash right out of my hand and I saw him run across the street, right in front of a car. There was a terrible crash and I closed my eyes. I think I might even have fainted for a moment as I thought the driver must have hit William because when I opened my eyes I was sitting on the pavement.

I didn't see what happened. I didn't see the American woman's car. I just kept my eyes tight shut. I couldn't bear to see what was happening to my William.

The noise seemed to just go on and on, though I suppose it was only seconds. I was certain that William was dead and I couldn't bear it, just couldn't bear it. When I finally opened my eyes, I saw that the vehicle had hit the bus stand, but my concern was for William. I saw blood on the ground and I just started screaming. I'm so sorry about the children, but William is like a child to me, and I thought the blood was his. I was just reacting to what I saw at the time, not thinking. I just didn't have the courage to go over. And then I saw Mrs Emptmann running. I know Mrs Emptmann only really by sight from the market and generally seeing her around the village. I can't explain it but when she started screaming I knew it wasn't William. I knew it had to be worse. It was the way she was screaming with her mouth open so it looked like a red hole that went down to Hell and she was making the sound of Hell. I'm sorry, I don't know how else to describe it. And then I saw William. He was on the grass by the recycling center, sniffing the ground, right as rain, not a scratch on him.

'As if he saw a cat or something.' Strebel reread that line and closed the file. It was exactly as he'd wanted. A dog chasing a cat. The 'as if' and 'or something' would be lost and the story would become: Mrs Berger's dog saw a cat. He knew an accident must have a cause. The dog, therefore.

The number had been disconnected due to non-payment. What kind of person didn't pay the phone bill, Strebel wondered. Someone careless, irresponsible, vague? He drove to her address, a subdivided chalet on the high road above Arnau. It was an unexceptional place. What was she doing here? In this village where people raised children or retired with their knitting. Her file said she was in the middle of a divorce from a British human rights lawyer based in Geneva. Perhaps the divorce explained the phone bill: an argument over money, the unexpected stress of disarticulating a relationship. Was this relevant?

And why Arnau? Why this exile of faux stucco chalets and window boxes? Strebel could find no trace of a connection to this village or canton—anything that might have drawn her here. Americans were very nostalgic, he believed, they loved their ancestry; but Pilgrim Lankester-née-Jones had no roots here, not a trace of Swiss blood. She was misplaced.

When he rang her doorbell and there was no answer, he tried the concierge. A small woman with a wiry nest of gray hair came to the front door. She wore an apron and slippers. He introduced himself, showed her his ID. She peered at it, checked the photo against his face. She did not give her name in return, but he assumed it was Gassner, the name on the concierge's bell.

'Are you Mrs Gassner?'

A curt nod.

'I'm looking for Mrs Lankester, apartment two.'

'You have come to arrest her.'

'No,' Strebel corrected. 'Just to speak with her. Her phone isn't working.'

'I warned her! I said, "They cut you off no mercy." She didn't listen, did she? And now look! Americans. They think they know everything. They think the rules don't apply to them.'

'Mrs Gassner, do you know when Mrs Lankester will be back?'

'It's shocking, what she's done. Killing those children. I couldn't live with myself.'

Silently, Strebel begged to differ. People lived with a lot of awful things, some of them very comfortably. 'Please, Mrs Gassner,' he said. 'I'd just like to know when you think she'll be back.'

'She left an hour ago. Just carrying on as if nothing has happened.'

'Where?'

'I don't ask. Probably shopping. Spending her rich husband's money. Ex-husband. He divorced her, you know.'

Strebel let this pass with total indifference. 'Do you think I might wait for her?'

Mrs Gassner did an odd thing: she blushed. And then spoke very quickly, telling him that he absolutely could not, she wouldn't have it, a respectable building like this. He studied her—the sudden, clumsy discomfort—and noticed that she couldn't help but twice glance up the stairs. Was someone there?

'Are you sure Mrs Lankester isn't in?'

Unconsciously, Mrs Gassner glanced up the stairs again. Christ, she was transparent! Someone was up there, but not Pilgrim Lankester.

'No, no, no. I told you she has gone out. I saw her myself.'

Strebel imagined Mrs Gassner peering through the curtains. She knew exactly who came and went and when. And who was up there now. She'd probably let whoever it was in. Still, he conjured politeness: 'Please tell Mrs Lankester to contact me when she gets back. Here is my card.'

'You have to make her pay,' Mrs Gassner said with renewed enthusiasm. 'She must pay. An eye for an eye. It's your job to make her pay.'

'Please give her my message.' He made a point of peering inquisitively over her shoulder and up the stairs. 'Perhaps she can use your phone.'

When Strebel turned around to walk back to his car, she came out on his heels, 'Those children, broken and twisted, I can't bear to think about it, and she just carries on with her fancy life, oh, not so fancy now that the husband left, I can tell you, but he's still paying the bills.'

Strebel was in the car and Mrs Gassner was up against the window glass: 'She shouldn't even be in this country. She's divorced! He left her. For another woman. They have a child! And yet she's still here. On what visa? These people are all tramps, camping on our doorstep. Throw them out.'

Strebel started his car. 'Please give her the message.'

He drove off. Mrs Gassner's spittle had freckled the window. Before he turned into the main road, he glanced back in his rearview mirror at the chalet. Mrs Gassner stood in the doorway. But above her, he was certain he saw someone in the second floor apartment—just a fleeting glimpse. A man? The figure was gone, it was impossible to tell. Perhaps Mr Gassner was fixing a broken light.

But Strebel's feeling had a darker texture, which he hesitated to call instinct, and which never failed him. The feeling of what he might find on the other side of a door, in the trunk of a car, in the thick bracken of woods where a murder of crows had gathered.

* * *

It was after nine. Strebel rubbed his eyes, looked around his office. In his youth—before this was his office—the shelves had been stacked with paperwork. A detective might be overwhelmed by the amount of work, but at least he could see that it was there, being done. Now everything was computerized, the records kept in invisible folders in an invisible cabinet.

Strebel considered the virtual world. You could put things there, like files and photographs. And yet they didn't exist in the traditional interpretation of existing: i.e. something you could spill coffee on. He wanted—did he?—to be part of the modern police force, the bright young sparks who could tap-tap-tap and tell him the weight of water.

But at fifty-five, he remained awed by the landline telephone. How a voice could travel down a wire for thousands of miles. How? Physics didn't quite explain it. He could recall the first telephone in his village, a heavy, elegant rotary dial.

A few years ago, he and Ingrid had bought a microwave, the latest mod-con. They'd cooked a potato and stared at it like the Christ Child. Look at the little miracle! Hadn't they even laughed at themselves? But when was a few years ago? He felt a sick lurch when he realized he was thinking of the early eighties.

More than three decades ago. He was a *grandfather* now.

He tapped on the computer keyboard, opened the folder of the Arnau incident scene. He kept coming back to this case, as if it held some great mystery that he had to uncover. But it was the most mundane of accidents. Everyone involved was ordinary. Even the deaths of the children were ordinary—the ordinary result of an ordinary vehicle traveling at 60kph hitting an ordinary child's body weighing an ordinary 32kgs.

A little pink backpack. Two shoes, from the two different boys. The dark wine stains of blood. Glass everywhere. The ruptured edifice of the bus stand. The smashed car. The images were all data now, turned into rows and rows of digits by a computer genius in California. He wondered if Ernst Koppler had kissed Sophie goodbye before he said 'You'll be in the way.' If he had held her and pressed his lips to her soft cheek and felt his awkward body fill with love, that great lightsaber love for a child which he would never feel again.

'I keep losing things. My handbag, the house keys. My gloves,' Simone Emptmann had said to Strebel that morning, her voice coming to him now as if through a loudspeaker. 'I keep thinking he's staying with his grandparents and I can't remember when I'm supposed to pick him up.'

He was seeing her now in his mind. She'd sat very still in her kitchen. A pretty, uncomplicated woman who now looked as if she'd scalded her head in a pot of boiling water. Her eyes were red, cheeks flushed, the skin under her eyes was swollen and raw. A female relative—a sister? a cousin?—had come to take her little baby for a stroll so she could talk to Strebel without distraction.

'Earlier in the morning,' she'd said. 'That morning. When we were having breakfast. I looked at Markus. The sun was on his face and he was busy eating and didn't see me and I felt such sadness that my child was leaving me. But it's what they do; it's their purpose, to leave you. I don't think you're ever ready. Are you? Do you have children, Inspector? You know they'll grow up and have imperfect lives and people will hurt them and they'll be unsatisfied and selfish, and so I think maybe by leaving now he's only known happiness and love. That's what I tell myself. He's been spared disappointment.'

She'd folded her hands in her lap neatly, and he thought of little dead birds.

'I'm so sorry,' he'd said.

Now, he clicked the file of photographs shut and turned off the computer.

The office was dark and mostly quiet. Somewhere down the hall, the cleaner was pushing her trolley; one of the wheels squeaked. If something happened—a bomb, for instance—the squeaking would become important. Crucial. Interviewed by fellow police officers, the rubble still smoking behind him, he would strive to recall the squeaking in detail. The pitch, the direction. As he had never heard the squeak before, could this suggest a different cleaner—an interloper, the terrorist—had pushed a cleaning trolley? In the absence of a bomb, the squeaking wheel had no meaning at all.

Detail established truth. The color of the dog. Without detail, truth was a metaphysically unstable idea: too general, too big; cause and effect going all the way back to first dates, to ancestors surviving winter storms, to dinosaurs, to organisms in a puddle.

But detail could also torment. He recalled Simone's terror, how it peeked out like a flash of red beneath the veneer of disbelief. 'You vaccinate them, you make them wear helmets on their bikes and seat belts in the car. You find ways to make vegetables tasty and not let them watch too much TV. You do everything right.'

You do everything right. And yet the minutiae of life—she'd forgotten her phone, she'd gone back for it and left the children in the bus stand. 'Wait here, I'll be right back,' she'd told them. The phone—so necessary, just in case—had lured her. She'd had her hand on the car door when she heard the noise. The car crashing, the universe splitting open.

At any moment the mundane might turn lethal.

Strebel began to gather his things but then he realized how much he did not want to go home. He was *in* something, as if traveling in another country, and did not want Ingrid's banal intrusion. The broken toilet or the latest idiocy from their son-in-law. He called her again.

'I'm staying at the office tonight.'

'But I made you dinner. Trout.'

'I'm sorry. Put it in the fridge and I'll have it tomorrow.'

'Come on, Paul.'

Come on? Come on, what? 'I'm sorry,' he repeated, hoping to sound sincere. No: not even hoping. His apologies to her were mere habit, like washing his hands before a meal. 'Goodnight,' he concluded. He didn't wait for her to say anymore, just hung up. And lay on the sofa.

He thought sleep would be impossible, the sofa was not comfortable, the lights were all on. But he did sleep, waking at dawn to the sound of rubbish lorries in the street below. He had no recollection of falling asleep. Time had jumped forward and the only evidence of how he'd spent the night was the red mark of the sofa's seam across his cheek.

'It is Detective Chief Inspector Paul Strebel,' he said through the intercom. 'I came a few days ago, I tried to phone—'

'Yes, I'm sorry, it's disconnected,' she said. 'Please come up.' An American voice, but softly accented. He hadn't had many dealings with Americans and he was aware of the stereotypes he tended toward, and also his initial suspicion of her character.

Pilgrim Lankester was pretty, even beautiful, standing in the doorway at the top of the stairs. 'The bill, I forgot to pay it.' Why? he immediately asked in his head. There would have been many increasingly agitated reminders.

As he moved into the room, he glanced around, taking in the oddly impersonal space. There were no photos or reminders on the fridge, no magazines or mail on the counter; no stack of notices from the phone company littering the tabletop. He thought of a businessman's hotel room. But the feeling he had wasn't of transience; rather of tentativeness—someone unable or unwilling to make an impression.

She offered him tea. He studied her as she boiled the kettle, retrieved the cups. Despite the bruises on her face, there was an undercurrent of elegance to her. Well-cut clothes and hair, cheekbones and deep-set eyes: Mrs Lankester was the kind of woman, intimidating in her perfection, whom he saw in Zurich or Geneva stepping out of boutiques or chic little bistros. He could smell her. Faintly almond. Not perfume, but a soap or cream.

Her manners and beauty masked her essential timidity. Most people wouldn't notice the way she bit her lip before speaking or hesitated mid-sentence. He guessed this behavior was habitual, not the result of trauma from the accident. He recalled she was only thirty-two, five years older than his own daughter. And while Pilgrim Lankester was vastly more sophisticated than Caroline, his daughter was confident, even bawdy. He suspected that Mrs Lankester had married young, and he would find Tom Lankester to be a strong character.

When her hand trembled on the teapot he said, 'Don't be afraid.'

'Of the tea?'

'No. Of me.'

She thought it was her fault. 'No,' he said, firmly, 'It wasn't your fault.'

Strebel would have been fine if she hadn't cried. Crying made her ugly, her eyes puffed and red, her cheeks blotchy. He felt sadness, loneliness coming off her in waves, and this triggered in him what he begged to be a paternal response, but what he knew was lust. 'Vulnerable women are beautiful,' a colleague had once remarked, and Strebel had disagreed. In fact, they'd almost had an argument, because Strebel took the line that there was something predatory in finding weak women sexual. He'd been around too many rapists.

But now he felt the urge to touch this young woman, to hold her and comfort her—and he could not pretend the urge was simply protective. He was appalled. And in equal measure, he was stunned by the small hollow at the base of her throat, by the upturn of flesh where her upper lip bowed. It was as if she'd suddenly come into focus; she was clear, so brilliantly, perfectly clear and distinct against the gray, oaty mass of his life. He felt a surge of happiness—of being *alive*.

Stupidly, he handed her his handkerchief, the clean, pressed one Ingrid gave him every day, though he asked her not to. He was fine with paper tissues.

He should leave. Immediately. He should concoct an emergency. But instead, he asked her to walk with him to the incident scene. Oh, certainly, part of him was saying this request was legitimate—she might remember after all, he might gain a new perspective; but the greater part simply wanted to be beside her. Wanted the smell of her, to observe her excruciating loveliness.

As they walked, Strebel wondered if he could ever leave Ingrid. He'd like to think it would be simple, a matter of a suitcase and a polite goodbye. But they were bound by filaments. Not just magazine subscriptions, not just the burden of bureaucracy—health insurance, life insurance, house insurance, bank accounts, wills, pensions; but connections of habit. There would be inconveniences, petty losses. He'd have to buy a washing machine and do his own laundry. She'd have to ask their useless son-in-law to fix the toilet. But at least Strebel would be able to wear his own gloves. He was annoyed by the endless, small acts of dishonesty.

'Do you want me to remember? Is that why we're here?' Mrs Lankester asked, and her voice reached him, though at first he couldn't understand. He'd been thinking so intensely in his native tongue, and had to make the switch to English.

He noticed she was clenching and unclenching her hands. She was terrified. 'You think I'm trying to trick you somehow. I'm sorry for that. But even if you could remember, I'm not sure I would want to hear. Memory is so messy.'

Ingrid would no doubt prescribe therapy of some sort. Psychotherapy, aromatherapy, candles and chanting, perhaps a cleanse or colonic. Strebel imagined the scurrying shamans who prayed on grief and uncertainty, plucking visions from the air and placing them like ripe fruit at the feet of their acolytes. Paying acolytes. How could you trust anyone you paid for a service? A prostitute gave you what you wanted. A therapist gave you what you wanted. What a mistake to believe in the sanctity of memory or dreams. A man might as well believe the romantic murmurings of a call girl.

He stared at the new bus stand. Should he be awed at his countrymen's ability to reinstall a bus stand within days of its destruction? Or should he fear the haste to paper over tragedy? Then he glanced at Mrs Lankester, sitting next to him, her dark hair and neat form. In a pique, he tore off his gloves, then wondered if this was because he wanted to touch her.

She said something about her husband not liking the gloves she bought him, and Strebel remembered he'd admitted this to her only moments ago. Why had he felt it appropriate to leak some matter of his personal life?

'Tell me their names,' she said. The names of the children.

Names? He could name them all, every single one. Even the first child, the little baby who'd gone through the windshield. The rainy night. Rain, but of course. Thirty years ago, his first week on the job. He'd thought it was a doll. 'Restrain her,' his captain had said, and it had taken him a minute to realize the order concerned a woman. Restrain the woman who was running and screaming like a wounded animal in the rain toward the broken doll that had been her child.

Strebel looked over again at Mrs Lankester. He could not help himself. Her eyes met his. She was lost, and he would find her.

Distract me, he pleaded silently. From all this.

All this *dying*.

Midmorning and Ingrid was already on line four, wanting to know, 'Shall I pick you up on the way or do you want to come in your own car?'

'Just a minute,' he said, as if professionally distracted. 'Just a second.' What was she talking about? He looked about the office, knowing he wouldn't find the answer. There was no Post-it stuck to his computer. Ingrid sighed in his ear.

'It's Beatrice's birthday party.'

'Yes, I know. I know. Yes, I'll see you there. I'm in a meeting right now.' He hung up. He realized he had no idea when he was supposed to be there.

He called Caroline, hoping she wouldn't mention it to Ingrid. 'Oh, Papa,' she said, just like her mother. 'Five o'clock.'

She had tied colored balloons to the gatepost. As he neared the house, even through the closed door, Strebel could hear the sound of children screeching like monkeys. Inside, he almost clamped his hands over his ears: the high, intent girly 'eeeee' threaded through a harder boy 'wwrrrrrrr,' providing bass.

A boy wearing a wolf mask ran past him, growling. The wolf chased a group of girls, the cupcake pink of their dresses, their constant incautious movement, whirling, kicking, spinning, and the boys amongst them, growling back at the wolf, daring him to come closer. Strebel glimpsed Beatrice, her mouth open with sound, her tongue stained with red juice. She was screaming, and he began to move toward her, to save her or comfort her—the screaming, the red mouth, she was wounded, *a beetle on its back*— and then he realized in the next beat of his heart that she was screaming with excitement.

'Papa,' Caroline said, ambushing him from the side, her arm around his waist. 'The bike is a brilliant idea. You and Mum are so clever.'

'Good,' he nodded and kissed her just above the ear. Her hair seemed blonder than he remembered. Did she dye it? What was wrong with her natural color? She'd been a sweet child, he could never remember any fuss. He'd read her stories and carried her on his shoulders on the way to picnics. She'd broken her arm at school and he'd run like a madman through the emergency room to find her. Now she dyed her hair. Now she was married to a sporadically employed truck driver—a total dunderhead. She'd wanted to be a nurse but she'd failed the exams.

Suddenly he's six, suddenly he's thirty. Simone Emptmann's voice was in his head again. 'We were running late, we're always running late. I lose my temper because we're late for school and the train, for everything, and he's lost his shoes or needs a pee. We were late that morning. I shouted at him. "Don't you understand, Mattias? We're late!" It's so important to be on time. Because time runs out, you miss the train. Suddenly, you're standing on the platform, a minute late and the train is gone. Suddenly, he's six, not a baby, and you get afraid because you know you'll look again and he'll be thirty. You never think—never, never, never— that he just won't be there. At all.'

The noise of the children was like a hive of bees in his head. He smiled anyway at Ingrid who took this as an invitation to come and stand beside him. 'Do you remember Caroline's sixth?'

'Absolutely,' Strebel said.

'That dreadful clown who couldn't do magic tricks. He couldn't even make balloon animals,' she said. 'You almost had a fight with him about his fee. And then it turned out he was filling in for his brother who'd just died of leukemia.'

He had no recollection of the troubled clown. 'You made a chocolate cake,' he offered hopefully.

She looked at him. 'I doubt it. Caroline's allergic to chocolate.'

Of course. The rashes, the vomiting, the specialist in Bern, and how they'd tried carob as an alternative but it always tasted like clay.

'Cake time!' Caroline shouted and the children swarmed into the kitchen, hooting, screaming, growling, surrounding a straw-berry pink cake with the focus of cannibals. Caroline reached over and lit the candles. Everyone sang. Strebel heard his own voice droning. Beatrice leaned in and blew. She wore a jeweled clip in her hair that was coming loose from too much play. He noticed for the first time that she was a plain child and she would be a plain woman. He felt sorry for her, for the day she'd under-stand her lack of beauty; a wild surge of pain seemed to flush from his chest up his neck to his face and he suddenly found it difficult to breathe.

'I have to go,' he whispered to Ingrid. He ignored the way she grabbed at his shirt with her fingertips. It was as if he'd snagged it on a branch. He almost ran out into the cold and gathering dark. He got in his car. He drove mindlessly, up valleys and on dark, narrow roads. He hit the lake road, and drove south almost all the way to Interlaken. He thought of continuing on, all the way around. But then he pulled into the parking lot of a Café du Thé overlooking the lake, turned around, and drove the several miles back. Here he took the turn-off uphill, to Arnau. He was there in twenty minutes. He hit the intercom.

'It is Paul Strebel.'

The next time he saw Pilgrim was at the inquest. She wore dark gray and he wished she hadn't because it suited her. He should have told her to wear the most unflattering things she could find, but even then, she couldn't undo her beauty. It was a kind of mask, all that people saw. In the same moment, he was startled to remember that he'd slept with her. He'd slept with someone so beautiful, and he had found her beautiful the whole time.

The parents did not look at her, but Strebel knew they were attentive. They wanted to see her stripped and raw: at the very least *altered*. Disfigured. Two rows behind her sat Alicia Berger, and there was no mistaking her dejection.

The inquest began. Simone Emptmann composed herself, but Strebel saw the bitten nubs of her fingernails. Her husband, Michael, wore a white rose in his lapel. His eyes were red buttons, and he sat without touching his wife. Strebel judged their marriage would last another six months. Blame lay between them, a tar pit into which the past and future slipped. Every recrimination, every disagreement, every hope slid fluttering and squawking into the slurry. *Why did you forget the phone? You're always on that thing.*

Vidia and Bobby Scheffer wore black and held hands. Mattias had been their only child, and Vidia was perhaps now past childbearing. Strebel knew they had erected a wooden bench in the field in front of their apartment where Mattias had liked to play. A half-dozen family members surrounded them.

Ernst Koppler was quite alone. He did not take off his coat, and this was smeared and dirty. He had shaved, but not well; there were little nicks of blood all over his cheeks and chin and dried shaving cream on his ear lobes. His thin hair was greasy, carelessly combed. Strebel knew, Mr Koppler knew: no one would love him and he would love no one ever again.

The presiding judge spoke reverently of the great tragedy. He reviewed the evidence. The forensics and eyewitness statements all tallied, all aligned. Vidia Scheffer wept softly. It was exactly as Strebel expected it to be and had worked for it to be: humane and compassionate, detailed and thorough, a finding of no-fault. But it was a whisper in response to the screams locked within the parents.

Later, Pilgrim was waiting outside his office. 'Come in,' he said. After they sat down, he smiled delicately. 'How are you?'

She nodded that she was okay.

'What will you do now?'

'Go. Away.'

'Where?' And for a wild moment, he wondered if he could go with her. Cairo or Sydney or San Francisco.

'I have no idea.'

'America? Home?' he offered, and she made a little motion with her hand, a kind of question mark.

'I thought maybe London,' she said. 'But I don't know how…' and her voice trailed off.

She gathered her handbag and started to stand, and then startled him by sitting again and saying, 'Would it be possible to see the photographs. From the accident.'

'No. And even if I could permit—'

She looked at him directly: 'Paul, please.'

He felt her then, when she had been warm against him, her back curving under his hands, the dizzying scent of her. He felt hot with embarrassment and lust. He longed for her, for hours, days of her. Instead, he got up and left the room. He paused in the corridor. How could it be that he would never kiss her again?

Ten minutes later he came back with a plastic evidence bag. He shut the door behind him. 'This is completely irregular,' he said, and felt immediately churlish. He wanted her, he could not have her.

For a long moment she held the bag. 'Can I open it?'

'Yes,' he said and watched her long, delicate fingers press open the seams of the bag. She'd touched him with those fingers, she'd caressed him.

She took out a red dress with white and yellow flowers on it. 'This was Sophie's?'

Strebel nodded.

'Will it be returned to her father?'

'Now that the inquest is over, yes.'

'Will it help him?'

'I doubt it.'

Pilgrim put the dress back in the bag. He took the bag. And then he reached out for her, surprising himself. His hand on her shoulder, along her collarbone. She didn't look at him but he felt her, the warmth of her through the gray sweater.

There was a crack in the possibility of things. An opening.

But he said, 'Take care of yourself.'

★　★　★

A few weeks later he checked up on her. She'd gone. Of course. The system told him she'd left for Tanzania, a flight out of Zurich. He wondered, why Tanzania? And then he leaned back in his chair and covered his face with his hands. Not because he was crying. He felt he might find her somehow. In the dark curtain of his hands some residue of her might remain.

May's green organza draped the fields and the air hummed with bees. Boats were out on the lake.

Sergeant Caspary knocked on his door, 'I thought you would want to know, sir. The neighbors reported a bad smell and uncollected mail in the letter box at Ernst Koppler's residence.'

She drove with him to Arnau. The smell, it turned out, was just rubbish. But Mr Koppler was missing.

'The neighbors?'

'The woman next door—Elizabeth Schmidt—she phoned it in; she says she can't remember when she last saw him. Maybe not for a week?'

Strebel and Caspary walked next door.

'I feel so bad,' Mrs Schmidt said, welcoming them in. 'I should have been looking out for him. Bringing him meals, I don't know. And now—'

'And now?' Strebel pressed.

'He must be dead,' she whispered. 'What could he have to live for?'

Caspary sat her down.

'Am I in trouble?' she said.

'No,' Strebel assured her. 'But anything you might recall about Mr Koppler—even if it seems unimportant, might help us find him.'

'Someone told me she'd been a teacher back in her country. His wife. Hamida. She died, too. Last year. You know that of course.'

Strebel nodded.

'One of those "Stans." Kurdistan. Uzbekistan. There are so many. I wondered if I should talk to her about it. What she'd taught. Being a teacher myself. But standards are so different there. And there just wasn't the opportunity, you know, we weren't drinking tea together over the fence. Even when she had cancer, we didn't know until she started wearing a scarf. And even that—we thought she was Muslim. So it wasn't really until she died.'

'And that was difficult for Mr Koppler.'

She nodded. 'It wasn't so much that he was alone with Sophie, but Hamida's family kicked up a fuss. They had moved away to be with other family in Germany. Stuttgart, I think. They wanted to take Sophie with them. That was the only argument I ever heard. The grandmother—Hamida's mother—came one day. But Mr Koppler wouldn't let Sophie go, and the law was on his side. And anyway she didn't want to go. She loved her father.'

'How was Mr Koppler after Sophie's death?' Caspary asked.

'He didn't go to the shop, I know because I went to get some school supplies and it was all closed up. But he did go out on foot, sometimes at odd hours. I don't know where.'

'What day was that, when you went by the shop?'

'Last Tuesday.'

'Twenty-first of May?'

'I had lunch with my sister.'

'When was the last time you definitely saw him, Mr Koppler?'

'I just can't be certain. Please understand. He'd been such a regular person. Even after Hamida. Well, he had Sophie, and children need routine. But since the accident. How could anyone be the same?' She gazed out the window for a moment. 'He was standing in the road. Only a few days ago. Three days ago. Looking around him. He was there for quite a long time. I thought to go out to him. But you know. What can you do?'

Outside, Caspary offered, 'Suicide seems likely, sir.'

If only he'd taken her to the office, Strebel was thinking. She'd have been no trouble, no trouble at all.

'We're also looking for the car,' Caspary said.

They walked next door to Koppler's. Inside it looked exactly as it had when he'd been there—the quiet, patient mess of toys and books. In the garage, flies were eagerly breeding in half a steak. He knew enough about flies: the steak, the rubbish had been there for weeks. The house was filthy.

'And we found this,' a patrol officer said, holding up an empty box of rat poison.

'Is there any evidence of rats?' Caspary wanted to know.

'Not that we can see.'

Was that how he'd killed himself, then?

Strebel wandered through the house. Beyond the bathroom, Mr Koppler had a small office where he'd done his accounts. He'd been a meticulous man, but chaos smothered earlier order: unpaid bills, junk mail, sympathy cards.

Yet, placed to the side, a letter: the lower left corner of the envelope carefully aligned with the corner of the desk. Strebel picked it up. Inside he found a small note paper-clipped to another envelope. This second envelope, folded in thirds to fit the first, was addressed to Mrs Gassner. The stamp had been circled in pen: a bright, pretty picture of a giraffe. The postal imprint was smeared but he could make out the letters T-A-N-G-A. Or was the 'G' a 'Z' and he was reading part of the whole? 'Tanzania.'

He opened it.

May 21
Dear Mrs Gassner,
    As you know I left the phone bill unpaid. Please find enclosed

my check for fifty-six francs to cover the outstanding charge plus
the reconnection fee for your next tenant. I apologize for this
inconvenience.
  Yours,
  Pilgrim Jones.

The name, the actuality of her, was like a punch in the gut.
He shut his eyes, the better to see the glow of her skin, the
curve of her breast. He lifted the paper to his nose, imagining
the almond smell. He heard Caspary coming up the hall, and
shoved it in his pocket.

'As strong as it gets.' She held up a bottle of children's aspirin.

'I have to make a phone call,' he said, and went outside, far
enough away that he could not be heard. He turned his back to
the house, and pressed the phone to his ear. He stood like this
for a long time. He thought about the moment Mr Koppler said
goodbye to Sophie. Had he kissed her? Something eerily like
a prayer formed in Strebel's mind: please, please let him have
kissed her.

Caspary was coming out the door. He pretended to hang up.
He pretended to be himself. 'Nothing,' she said. 'I guess we wait
for the body. A hiker in the woods. Kids playing where they're
not supposed to.'

★ ★ ★

It took Mrs Gassner a matter of seconds to answer the door, as
if her *hausfrau* exterior belied the body of an Olympic sprinter.
'Inspector,' she said, looking at him with a spark of curiosity.
'Please come in.'

He demurred. 'This will only take a minute.' He brought out
Pilgrim's letter. 'We have just found this at Mr Ernst Koppler's
house. I wondered if you might know how it got there.'

'No.'

'There's no criminal intention here, Mrs Gassner, but I feel your help—your honesty—is important. Mr Koppler has gone missing.' He handed her the letter. She took it, regarded it with great mystery. 'It's addressed to you,' he said. 'How did it come to be in Mr Koppler's house?'

For a long minute she debated with herself. Could she concoct an adequate lie? Or might she apportion the truth? Strebel could almost hear her rifling through her options.

At last Mrs Gassner decided: 'I didn't know him, only in passing, at the market, the apothecary. I knew he married that Turkish woman.' Strebel thought to correct her but let it go. 'She trapped him into marriage. These immigrants are all the same and he was a fool. But the little girl, he didn't deserve that.'

Strebel was attentive, neutral, and she glanced up, almost imploring: 'I was doing the right thing, no matter what the law says.'

'Please, just tell me.'

She nodded. 'He came, a few days after the accident. At first I didn't recognize him. He was dirty, unwashed. He said he needed to go upstairs to Mrs Lankester's apartment. He didn't want to steal anything or make a mess, he just needed to see where she lived. Myself, I don't understand what it was about but I didn't see the harm.'

'So you gave him the key?'

'Several times.'

'And he was here that morning I came by?'

The very faintest movement of her head, just one nod. Strebel felt a surge of protective anger—almost jealousy. He wondered if Pilgrim had known of the violation, and had decided not to tell him. What had Mr Koppler done in there? What had he wanted?

'And the letter?'

'After the inquest—you know, it was a travesty to find no fault. Someone, even that Mrs Berger with the dog, should be held to account. This country is becoming too liberal. It started when they gave women the vote.'

Strebel remained impassive. 'And Miss Jones left without paying the phone bill?'

'Incredible! I found an envelope under the door with payment for the months remaining on the lease and her key. I went up. The place was empty. I found most of her things in the rubbish in the basement. Bags of clothes. Books, shoes, things like that. She didn't have much. It was a furnished apartment, you see.'

'And yet she forgot to pay the phone bill,' Strebel said, tapping Pilgrim's letter thoughtfully on his hand.

'That's the kind of person she was. Careless.'

'But she sent you the money.'

Mrs Gassner attempted to sidestep, 'I notice she has begun calling herself Jones. She must be on the lookout for a new man.'

'And then you gave this letter to Mr Koppler. Why?'

Now she was silent. And he felt she wasn't searching for a lie but for the truth—an explanation that made sense, that she could extract from the tangle of her justifications. 'I saw him,' she said. 'He looked terrible, he was suffering. We passed each other on the pavement by the cemetery. I suppose he was visiting his wife, his daughter. Can you imagine? Both in one year? He asked me if I knew where she was. I didn't see the harm.'

The harm, no one ever saw the harm.

'When was this?'

'A few days ago,' she said, and then, gesturing to the letter, 'Why were you at Mr Koppler's house? Has he... ? Is he... ?'

'What day?'

'Three days ago.'

'Monday?'

'Yes. Has he... has he—'

'Gone,' Strebel finished for her.

'Gone?'

'It appears so at this time.'

'He asked me where she was, that's all, that's all,' Mrs Gassner blurted. 'Africa. She's in Africa. On a photographic safari, I'm sure of it. Having fun.'

★ ★ ★

On his way back to the precinct Caspary phoned: she'd traced Mr Koppler's car to Zurich airport. Two days ago he took a Swissair flight to Dar es Salaam.

Strebel took a deep breath.

'Everything all right, sir?' the pilot asked, even though he was already pulling up the steps.

'Fine,' Strebel nodded. 'Yes, yes, not to worry.'

The pilot gave him a mock salute and shut the door. Strebel backed away from the plane and aimed for a lone tree on the edge of the runway. The propellers revved, bits of dried grass and dust blew up from the blast, and then the plane bumped off to the far end of the runway. Strebel watched it take off. The sound faded and was overtaken by the violent zzzeeeeee of cicadas.

He squinted. His pupils were pinpricks, terrorized by the sun. He was completely alone. Initially, this pleased him. He felt adventurous, a white man in the African bush. And the beauty of the flight from Dar es Salaam was still with him: the blue of the Indian Ocean, the fringe of turquoise suggesting shallows closer to shore, a ruffle of surf along the fringing reef, and the land eclipsed by wild green.

But the heat was absurd.

It hung on him like a great hairy animal, so that he could barely breathe, barely move. He was soaked with sweat—amazed at the speed with which this had happened. He'd been out of the Cessna's air-conditioned comfort for less than three minutes and he was sweating in places he had completely forgotten about.

The sweat collected behind his knees, behind his ears, at his throat. It trickled between his buttocks and into his groin, causing his thighs to rub. He was sure his eyebrows were sweating.

Blanched light, hot and white and unrelenting as a strobe, shot through the tree above him, creating not shade but a patchwork of lighter and darker. It fell messy and uneven on the dry soil at his feet. Where there were ants. A dozen or so, delicately meandering through the leaf litter, fully occupied with their ant tasks.

Christ, even his feet were sweating. He shifted his gaze from the ants to his feet in his sandals, the horny toenails and hair that leapt excited in little tufts from his toes. The feet of a middle-aged man were horrible.

Strebel switched his black leather bag to the other shoulder. A Christmas present from Ingrid. He would have preferred brown leather. He considered that she knew this very well, his penchant for brown leather, his clearly—adamantly!—stated dislike of black leather. She always bought him black leather: gloves, wallet, belt.

The wounds were never mortal.

Never too much to bear.

Peering down to the end of the runway where the short, cut grass yielded to long yellow grass and then to a copse of rough trees, he thought he could discern a white car in the shade. But his distance vision was increasingly bad. Anything past a hundred metres was a blur. He began to walk.

It was miles—ten, twenty, perhaps fifty; the longest airstrip in the world. Was this how it had been for Livingston? His thighs chafing? A stream of sweat down the side of his nose that dripped off his chin and onto his shirt collar? As Strebel neared the trees, he was certain the white blob was indeed a car; but closer still, he felt less assured by the Toyota Corolla, for it was mottled in equal measure by white paint and rust. One wheel was obviously a spare, several sizes too small. In a remote

Swiss village, sheep would have been living in this car. But here was the driver—he had the seat tilted all the way back and was fast asleep.

'Excuse me,' Strebel said, tapping lightly on the door. The driver made a low moan and opened his mouth. Then his eyes. He stared at the ceiling of the Toyota for a long moment, so long that Strebel's eyes were also drawn to the spot. But there was nothing there. In a series of movements—was it possible to be so slow and still considered moving?—the driver sat up, yawned, adjusted the seat, sniffed, scratched his neck, lifted his hands so they floated slowly, slowly down onto the steering wheel.

'Are you a taxi?' Strebel ventured.

'Taxi, yes,' the driver replied, scratching his crotch. 'You want hoteli?'

'Yes.'

'Twenty dollar.'

Strebel got in the back. It looked as if a wild animal had attacked the seat in a fit of pique. Nowhere did the seat retain its integrity, and Strebel was forced to straddle a crevasse in the foam that could swallow a child whole. But what were his options? He glanced out of the window into the white furnace, the grass wavering in the oily heat. What was he doing here? Tanga. *Tanga?*

The driver started the car and they crept away from the airstrip. Ingrid's arthritic grandmother could have outpaced them.

★ ★ ★

'This best hoteli.' It didn't look like much: a six-floor cement block with obtruding balconies. Strebel handed over the twenty dollars and got out. The driver came after him, talking excitedly. He was a large, bald man with hands the size of Christmas hams. He was shouting now, something in Swahili, and waving the money. Gauging the distance from the taxi to the hotel entrance at about ten feet, Strebel smiled a calm, traffic-stop smile; and, as if on smooth wheels, moved quickly to the door. Inside, he did not look back.

It took a moment for his pupils to dilate. The receptionist was a pretty, smiling girl. She wore a name tag identifying her as Alice. Her skin was perfect—smooth and clear so that it shone like polished wood. 'Good afternoon, sir,' she said in careful English. 'How may we help you today?'

'I'm hoping I have the right hotel. A friend of mine is staying here. She recommended it.'

'What is her name, sir?'

'Pilgrim Jones.'

Alice eschewed the large gray desktop—blind and silent. She flipped through a battered Guest Registry book. On the wall above hung a notice promising 'Wi-Fi in every r☺☺m!' Who had drawn the smiley faces? Alice?

She triumphantly closed the book. 'I remember her! A very pretty lady. She was here for only a few days. And then she went with Mama Gloria.'

'Mama Gloria?'

'She is very kind. She is trying to help the AIDS orphans.'

'I see. That's good of her. How could I contact Miss Jones?'

Alice thought a moment, then opened a door to a closet-sized office. Inside, a young man hunched over a table of accounts. They conferred.

'Miss Jones we don't know. But Mama Gloria. All the drivers know her. We all know her,' she waved a hand prettily, then pushed a registration form toward him. 'You are staying with us now? In-suite room is fifty US per night, breakfast included.'

'I'd like the same room as Pilgrim. If that's possible.'

Nodding, she selected a key and delivered it to him with a bright smile. However, this changed when she saw his money. She took one twenty and handed the other bills back. 'Oh, sorry, sir.'

'What?'

'These dollars. Pre-millennium we cannot accept.'

'Why not? They are legal tender. I got them from a bank in Switzerland.'

'Do you have others? We cannot take these.'

'I don't understand. Switzerland is the banking capital of the world.'

She smiled, a lovely smile that he realized was a wall. He could bash his head against it to zero effect.

Strebel rifled through his wallet and found notes that met her requirements. 'Please be comfortable,' she said.

In his room—Pilgrim's room—he removed his clothes. He peeled them, for they stuck like eggshell to the damp, pale egg of his body. He strode hopefully to the shower in the small bathroom—the 'in-suite.' There was a single tap. He turned it. The shower head sputtered, emitting a brief, violent jet the color of cola. Strebel wanted to shout and hit it, but there was nothing at hand except his bottle of shampoo.

Then the water came, cold and clear and steady. He stepped into it with deep gratitude that allowed him to comprehend the miracle of a tap. Why had he never considered how few people on the planet had experienced a shower?

★ ★ ★

He awoke later, abruptly, a copy of *Newsweek* stuck to his bare chest. He recalled only lying down, the overexcited squeak of the bed springs. Reading? An article about Sudan. Or was it Somalia? Terrible things, he couldn't comprehend—even as a policeman. The scale of atrocities frightened him because it implied original sin, rather than tightly contained circles of abuse. In Switzerland, specific excuses could be made: bad parents, mental illness. He had managed to fall asleep, mid-atrocity:

gangs of men with mirrored sunglasses and guns committed the most gruesome genocide to court international attention.

Ingrid had recently told him that horror was inconvenient, coming at you on the TV news before dinner. You resent it, she'd said, and you feel bad resenting it, and wonder what you should do to not feel bad. But the only solution is to undergo some kind of fundamental change in how you live your life, to become a doctor with Médecins Sans Frontières or a social worker for abused kids. At least stop buying goods made in Chinese sweatshops. It's so big, she'd continued, so impossible and awkward, and the easiest thing—therefore—is to feed the cat instead or make a note to buy more washing powder. And we always do the easiest thing, don't we?

She'd said this without looking at him, as if—he thought—she was talking to someone else. In fact, as if she was someone else talking to someone else, not Ingrid and Paul who talked of very little except, occasionally, the dunderhead son-in-law in a concerned, vaguely judgemental way. They never spoke to each other like this. She'd never ask him about his work. Long ago, they'd realized it was no subject for conversation.

After this odd outburst, she'd turned from him and quietly served up the sausages and *spätzle*.

Now he debated that she had meant something else when she'd said, 'And we always do the easiest thing, don't we?' The *don't we* seemed specific rather than general. Seemed to be woman-speak for: I know you have this big moral code that you live by out there, Mr Policeman, but you always do the easiest thing at home.

Recently, he'd noticed she had bunions. She'd had lovely feet when they'd first met. He'd seen that right away, her delicate, neat, high-arched feet in sandals. The elegance of her bare foot-prints in the Greek sand. Did bunions appear overnight, or grow slowly? And when? And why? What, exactly, were bunions?

He was overdue to contact her. He turned on his phone, but

it did not work. He turned on his computer, but could not find a connection. He dressed quickly and went downstairs to ask Alice.

'I am sorry, sir, the Wi-Fi, it is not working.'

'Yes, I know. But when do you think it will be working?'

She smiled shyly, nibbled the end of her pen. 'I think later. Yes, maybe later. Or tomorrow.' She directed him across the street to a small internet café, but the power was down. He waited as the clerk started a loud petrol generator. By then the server was down.

For a brief period both power and server colluded. 'Ingrid,' he wrote with lightning speed. 'All fine here in Reykjavik, though very, very busy at the conference. Don't expect to have much time to phone or write. Hope you are well. Love, Paul.'

The driver was leaning against the car, waving his arms and smiling as if Strebel was an old friend. Strebel felt trapped. He wanted to pretend he couldn't see the man, that his attention was diverted—a pressing phone call, for instance. But it was too late for that: the driver was now in front of him, giant hand out for shaking. Strebel shook back.

'Yes, yes,' the driver said warmly, then fished Strebel's twenty-dollar bill out of his wallet and pointed at the date. 'Banks not okay this!'

In a flourish of bonhomie, Strebel swapped the driver's bill for an acceptable version. The driver beamed, folded it carefully away.

'Where we go?' he said, still grinning. 'Where we go, doctor?'

'I'm not a doctor,' Strebel replied, wondering what about him had a medical air. 'Policeman.'

'Polici?' Now the driver wasn't so sure. He even took a step back.

Strebel shook his head. 'Not here. Back at home. Switzerland.'

'Switz? Eh?'

'Switzerland. Here,' he pointed to the ground, 'holiday.'

Was this the sort of holiday policemen took? To a foreign country to engage in some light, off-the-books investigating? He could just as well have gone to Sharm el-Sheikh with a couple of Sergeant Studer novels.

'German War Graves?' the driver asked. 'Amboni Caves? Tongoni Ruins?'

Strebel took this moment to dig around in his bag, but, in fact, he was trying to level with himself. The lies he'd told to come here, the absurd risk to his marriage, his career: these had been battering at his brain since he'd left Switzerland, like flies against a window. And they were getting louder; soon they would be like pigeons, a Hitchcockian rain of them, hitting with terrible, insistent thuds.

He had told his boss he was visiting a sick uncle in Bruges. He had told Ingrid he was in Iceland. He had withheld evidence, the envelope with the little giraffe stamp. Because? Because? Because he wanted it to belong to him, wanted it to be a message from his lover intended for him. A summons: Come, I need to be rescued!

Because of the scent of her.

'Pangani? Pangani good beach.' The driver looked expectant.

'Mama Gloria.'

'Ah, yes, Mama Gloria!' The driver clapped his giant hands and opened the back door with a flourish.

'No,' Strebel countered. 'Price first. And I'm sitting in the front.' He gestured to the ruined back seat. 'There could be someone lost in there. Are you missing any customers?'

The driver didn't understand, but peered inside, carefully examining the seat. When this show was over, he stood up and said to Strebel, 'Twenty.'

'Five.'

'Twenty-five.' The driver smiled.

'Five,' Strebel held up his right hand. 'Five dollars.'

They settled on ten.

'My name is Mr Tabu,' the driver said.

'Paul,' said Strebel.

As Mr Tabu drove along the shaded avenues, past shops and shacks, Strebel realized he was looking for her, a slim, graceful girl, on a bicycle or walking along the roadside. 'Pilgrim,' he would call from the taxi, and she would turn, smile, run to him.

Counter-intuitively, he hoped he didn't see her, because he was a grown-up, at least in part of his brain. He glanced at the vegetable plots out the windows, gradually replacing the little shops. He was indulging a fantasy. He could not really delude himself that he would find her and they would run off together and be happy. But the *yearning* felt good, like the transfusion of a young man's blood. He wanted to be foolish enough to believe in such a romance, just for a moment, to suspend his relentless sense of duty. To be, yes, an old fool, undone, besieged by lust.

The taxi bounded down a dirt road. A pack of mangy dogs barked and chased the Corolla's bald tires. The road led on through a field of dust-bedraggled corn and dead-ended in the open yard of a cement bungalow. Strebel, so lost in his thoughts, was confused as to where he was.

He got out and went to the door to find a large American woman standing with eyebrows raised as if she had been expecting him. She was overweight in the way Europeans expected Americans to be, from eating too much—fleshy, soft, undisciplined. She was also a smoker, he could tell from the smell of her. He introduced himself politely. 'I'm a friend of Pilgrim Jones.'

'Are you now?'

Strebel smiled benignly. 'I'm hoping to find her. My name is Paul Strebel. Are you Gloria?'

'No. I'm Bo Derek.'

He assumed that she'd invite him in and they would have a friendly, helpful chat. But her body blocked the door, her weight implied a bullying protection. She was definitely hiding something.

'I've come a long way,' he said. And gave her another smile.

'Well, you're out of luck, cowboy. You've just missed her.'

She was a hard-used woman, Strebel thought, like the wives of his father's generation, left up in the mountains to cope with the ravages of storms and childbirth.

'May I come in?'

Gloria tilted her head to survey him, then moved aside, 'Sure.'

Her home was makeshift, as if she'd scavenged the furniture from departing expats. Nothing matched, but it was comfortable enough. He noticed the boxes of toys, the shelf of children's books. Ah—the AIDS orphans. She offered him a seat but nothing else. He hoped for a glass of ice water. A very large glass. Preferably so large he could climb into it for a long soak.

'Look,' she said. 'I got twelve kids arriving any minute now. So let's cut to the chase. What's this about Pilgrim?'

'I'm trying to find her.'

'So you said. You've just missed her, so I said. Do you want to have the same conversation all over again? I'd rather not.' She fidgeted, tapped her fingers. She badly wanted a cigarette, Strebel was sure. But there were no packs or ashtrays in evidence. Had she just quit?

'Pilgrim left Switzerland just over a month ago,' he pushed on. 'I have reason to believe she may be in danger.'

'Here? Danger? From what? Falling mangoes?'

'A man associated with her has also disappeared.'

Gloria made a shocked expression. '"A man associated with her." What does that mean? Did they rob banks together?'

'She was involved in a car accident in which the man's daughter was killed. It's possible he blames her and wants to harm her.'

'That's terrible, just terrible, Detective—is it "Detective"?'

'Detective Chief Inspector.'

She gave him the look of a deeply impressed woman.

'How did you know I was a policeman?'

'Your shit-colored aura.'

Strebel wanted to laugh because he found this genuinely funny. The shit had stuck after all.

'Long way to come as a policeman,' she noted.

'I'm not here in that capacity. As I said, I'm a friend.' He gave her a neutral smile.

'I won't bother to argue that police can't have friends, although, personally, I think that it's impossible. So, yeah, I rented her a place out in Raskazone. The peninsula on the south end of the bay. Cutest little cottage.'

'When was this?'

'Coupla weeks ago, thereabouts.'

'When did you last see her?'

'At the club—the Yacht Club. Sounds very grand. But it's not. Just a nice, clean local place. Yachtees like it. Nice place to swim, cold drinks.'

'When?' he repeated.

She exhaled loudly and rolled her eyes. 'Two, three days ago. She was drinking with Harry Fonseca.'

Interesting, Strebel thought, that she'd given him a name. Harry Fonseca. He was careful not to let her know he'd picked up the hint. 'How do you know she's gone? Not just traveling and coming back.'

'How do I know she's not traveling and coming back? How do I know if she is? I don't know anything about her. I didn't say I know this or that.' She paused, looked Strebel over again, and went on, 'Maybe she met some young guy, some hot young buck and she's gone to Zanzibar with him.'

Strebel refused the bait.

'You went to the cottage. Why?'

'Pay the *askari*. Watchman. End of the month, salary due. I noticed she wasn't there.'

'Were you concerned?'

'Why should I have been? There wasn't a hex drawn on the wall in blood or anything. Just an empty house.'

Somewhere dogs barked and Gloria stood up. She moved to the window facing the road and looked out expectantly. 'I think that's them,' she said.

'Them?'

'My reasons for living.'

'Just one more question. Please, Gloria.'

She turned back to him, her eyes scanning his shit-colored aura. 'She's lovely, isn't she? The most beautiful woman I've ever seen. I'm not surprised you've come all this way for her.'

'No...' he started to say, to deny. But why bother? There was the sound of a heavy vehicle approaching, a diesel with a missing muffler. He ploughed on: 'Did you meet anyone called Ernst Koppler?'

But her attention was riveted elsewhere. He saw what she did: a decrepit bus full of children.

'I don't know why Pilgrim Jones came.' She kept her gaze out the window. 'I don't know why she left. Or where or how or who. In Tanga people come, they go. It's why the club doesn't run tabs. People go and sometimes they go without paying their bills. Pilgrim came, she went. Maybe she's coming back. I really hope she's okay. But that's it, as far as it goes for me. And I've never heard of the other fellow—Kaplin?'

'Koppler.'

'Koppler, right. No idea about him. We're done now.'

She was starting out the door. He watched her rushing, suddenly a nimble, glowing woman.

'Good luck,' Strebel said. But she wasn't listening, she was running to the bus, her arms outstretched. He watched for a moment from the doorway, the tentative figures stepping out of the bus. They were all so small, so thin. She crouched down and touched their faces one by one, just a brush of her finger. She was speaking to them in Swahili, the reassuring clucking of a hen, so she didn't notice Strebel bypass her, get back into the taxi and drive away.

Her performance had been almost perfect, he thought, but for 'Kaplin.' She hadn't misheard. She'd turned away from him as she lied.

Mr Tabu collected Strebel promptly at ten the next morning, and they drove to the Yacht Club. 'Do you know Harry?' he asked Mr Tabu on the way.

'Mr Harry, yes, yes. He like the club very much.' Mr Tabu laughed like a naughty child and then held his thumb to his mouth to suggest the tipping of a bottle.

The club's entrance was strewn with fallen bougainvillea blossoms, as if a wedding had just passed. Strebel trotted down the long flight of steps, confronting the sweep of the jade-colored bay. He'd almost forgotten about the sea. He had a Swiss ambivalence about it: the sea was an element of which he had no immediate or genetic experience, it frightened him; and yet he fancied the ocean's fluidity, how it took things somewhere else. Sailors or driftwood or an old plastic jug, lifted and taken to a cove a mile away or across a sea.

The bar was well kept, a bright, open design that welcomed rather than intimidated. It was empty but for a pair of old men and the Tanzanian bartender. Strebel debated how to approach: to slowly lubricate the conversation with alcohol, for clearly the men were drinkers; or to be simple and direct.

It probably wouldn't make a difference. Tanga was just another small town—a village if you were white, and in villages people didn't talk to an outsider. In those deep, dead-end mountain valleys of the Jungfrau where he'd started his career, the doors slammed in his face, mouths sealed shut. Eyes focused on a distant col. The dead child, the brutalized wife, the missing husband: no one would tell him a thing.

Strebel sat next to the men, introduced himself as Detective Chief Inspector Strebel from the Swiss Police, and put the two Swiss ID headshots on the bar. 'Do you know them?'

One of the old men said, 'What's this about?'

'They're missing.'

'Missing?' said the other.

'Pretty. She your wife?' Then looking at Koppler's picture, added, 'They run off together? He seems an unlikely choice.'

'You can never tell with a woman. Joanie went off with you.'

They had a laugh. Strebel offered to buy them a drink, but it was complicated: he had to become a day member and buy a book of chits. Now he understood what Gloria had said about 'tabs.'

'Just give us the cash,' said the one who'd had it off with Joanie. When Strebel handed over ten bucks, he checked the date, slipped the bill in his pocket, shouted, 'Mohemedi! *Naomba Tusker tatu!*'

Three beers came. Pink tickets bearing various denominations like Monopoly money were handed over.

'The girl was here. She took up with Harry. Though not— sadly for Harry—in the way Harry would like to have been, er, taken up,' Joanie's swain said. A long, throaty chuckle.

Strebel felt a surprise flinch of jealousy. How, exactly, had she taken up with Harry?

'And Harry, where could I find him?' Strebel sipped the beer. He saw the two men glance at each other and shrug in unison.

'Harry? Hard to say. He's usually here.'

'If he's not here, he could be anywhere.'

'He's like that. Breezy fellow.'

'The woman, Pilgrim,' Strebel said. 'I think she might be in some kind of trouble.'

'Oh, dear.'

'That's why I'd like to find Harry.' He wanted to make it clear, Harry wasn't competition. '"Anywhere." Do you think that's far?'

One scratched his beard, the other his hair; both looked doubtful. 'Breezy fellow,' they said. 'Hard to say.'

'When did you last see him?'

The old men exchanged glances as if to give Strebel the impression they were consulting each other, but in fact they were silently corroborating.

'Come to think of it, I only just realized he isn't here right now.'

'Wasn't he here for Quiz Night?'

'Come to think of it, I don't even know what day it is today!'

'Sorry we can't be of more help!'

Strebel drank the beer and asked about the weather. They told him the rains would be coming soon, the southern monsoons.

'I'll pay you,' he told Alice. 'I need someone to translate for me.'

She looked unconvinced, carefully examining her neat manicure. Strebel knew she was trying to decide what he wanted—sex? Or a Swahili translator? She suspected the former. All these old white men wanted sex. They were no different from the old black men, the young black men, the German backpackers, the shuffling but surprisingly horny and solvent beggars in the market, the Goan sailors from the harbor. Strebel supposed the constant challenge to her morality exhausted her. She must hear the whores talk in the hotel bar, and know that once they had been the same as her. Girls from villages with few options. Prostitution was a way to make money—more than you did in a hotel reception or shop.

Strebel noted the small silver cross around her neck and suspected that she wore it like garlic against the vampires of his gender. But like garlic, Christ's power was constrained by human greed. He thought of Pilgrim, a kind of whore, who had given up her freedom and spirit for a wealthy man. And Alice, considering the cost of her manicure and her hair extensions and, very probably, a dress she had seen. She could have these and all she had to do was take her clothes off for this old white man.

Ingrid had never made such compromises. A physiotherapist with a happy childhood and a good family, she'd come to Strebel free and clear, voluptuous, soft, hungry. They both made almost the same salary and they split the bills evenly. They had never fought about money; they had fought very little. Perhaps, early on, she'd resented the hours he worked, the interrupted dinners, the 3 a.m. phone calls.

Perhaps, once or twice, she'd even threatened to leave him. Did he remember? One Christmas when Caroline was little? She'd said he treated the house like a hotel and her like a maid. Something about his clothes on the floor, the unmade bed. From his point of view, what did it matter if the bed wasn't made? The bared sheets wouldn't melt in the sun or get dirty from the air. Leave it unmade, he'd said. Or maybe shouted. He took care of the cars—changed the oil, took the snow tires on and off. He kept up his side of things. Putting up bookshelves. Fixing the toilet.

'I want a translator,' he said to Alice, summoning up his most paternal manner. Even then she didn't quite believe him, but she nodded slowly. 'How much?'

'It's important to translate exactly what I say, exactly what is said to me. Okay?'

She nodded again.

'Someone may be hurt or in danger.'

'Yes,' she said, touching her crucifix.

'I'll pay you one hundred dollars.'

She looked down at her hands and again he felt her doubt. It was too much money. 'You are a Christian?'

For a moment he was confused—then he understood: his namesake apostle. And what she was hoping for: reassurance. He considered an answer that was the least lie—the least awkward words to pronounce. 'I believe in many of Jesus's teachings.'

Mr Tabu had put a couple of foam pillows in the back of the taxi, an attempt to hide or compensate for the state of the seat. Strebel and Alice dutifully sat on these as Mr Tabu drove them out to the Raskazone peninsula. The road followed the headland for several lazy miles past mansions gently dissolving in the salt air. The ragged road, the overgrown gardens, the cows and goats grazing on the verges: Strebel almost laughed to think how many violations of Swiss law he might tally in a single minute's drive. He wondered how it made him different from Alice and Mr Tabu, to live somewhere so neat and precise, so tidy and ordered.

For a moment, as they rounded the tip of the peninsula, a foul smell clogged the air, and he saw, to his left, a pipe extending into the sea spewing a brown smear of what could only be raw sewage. Less than half a mile away, back around in the bay, they had passed the public beach.

Now the road surrendered completely to sandy dirt, a narrow track. High security walls alternated with patches of scrub. A few hundred yards later, Mr Tabu stopped. 'This the house.'

Alice turned to Strebel, testing her importance, 'He says this is house.'

'Yes, thank you.' Strebel smiled appreciatively and got out. The wrought-iron gate was shut but not locked. 'Hello?' he called. He felt the emptiness, but said again, louder, 'Hello? Is anyone here?' No one answered. So he unlatched the gate and went in. The house in the yard was small and round with a roof of thatched palms. Several large trees with fat red blossoms shaded the front, and beyond them the shelf of land dropped to the dense green fleece of mangroves. Strebel imagined Pilgrim standing here as he did, and how the same sense of peace must have come to her. The wild twittering of yellow birds and the trees and the sea and green mangroves, the white house—the still, hot afternoon which held him softly in a cobweb of time, so that he felt if he went inside he would find a bed, and lie down and sleep until he wasn't tired anymore. He would lie down and she would come and lie next to him and they would sleep in the heat, just their hands touching, their fingers intertwined.

The house, however, was locked; he should have asked Gloria

for a key. He walked around, peering in—though there was nothing to see: a few pieces of old furniture, a basic kitchen, a pretty tiled bathroom, a bed secluded by a large mosquito net. He went back to the car and asked Alice if she could find a neighbor to talk to.

Together they walked down the lane to the big, new house and Alice knocked softly on the gate. A uniformed guard appeared and Alice spoke to him. She relayed to Strebel that the guard had only just started the job and anyway he couldn't give them names as it was against company policy.

Strebel was about to head back to the car when Alice touched his arm, 'What about him?' She pointed to a boy in an oversized white shirt tending two fat brown cows in the scrub.

Alice admired the cows, touching them in a familiar way. Strebel surmised she had been around cows her whole life: a village girl who'd had to learn to wear shoes. She spoke to the boy like a sister, and he admired her instinct for gentleness. Strebel noticed the white shirt. What was the shirt for, he wondered. Dirty, torn in the back. Was it one step above the poverty of having no shirt at all?

Yes, the boy told Alice, he remembered the *mzungu* lady. She came only with a small suitcase, nothing valuable. She didn't even have a car. She had a bicycle that looked like the kind you could rent at the market. Sometimes she even walked. He and Alice laughed.

'Why is that funny?' Strebel asked.

'Because white people never walk. We think you can't, that you are too weak. In my village, we even believed you didn't have legs.'

Briefly, he recalled a toy Caroline had had—a little plastic bus with plastic people who bobbed up and down when you rolled the bus along the floor. The people were just white heads on round pegs. They looked straight ahead, up-down-up-down.

'Did she have any visitors?' he asked, and Alice translated for the boy. He squinted in thought before speaking. 'The boy says Mama Gloria came sometimes. And there was a taxi with a white man inside. A few days ago only.'

Strebel took out the picture of Koppler. 'Was this him?'

The boy looked at the picture and Alice translated. 'He isn't sure,' she said, and added with no embarrassment: 'You all look the same.'

Holding back a laugh, Strebel asked the boy to think again— was the man fat? Thin? Did he have a lot of hair? Or no hair? Did he have glasses? Was he old or maybe young—younger? Maybe, Strebel tripped over the thought Gloria had implanted in his head, maybe a hot young buck to go to Zanzibar with.

The boy studied Koppler. It was hard to tell, he explained, because he didn't really see the man. The man never got out of the car. On the other hand, he would easily recognize the taxi driver; he was from the boy's tribe, Usimba.

Alice felt she must note that Usimba were not local people. They were from the middle of the country, near Tabora. And they were a very old tribe. She had read in school how they made paintings on the rocks that scientists said were many thousands of years old, maybe thirty thousand. Strebel nodded as if this interested him.

The boy agreed to speak with Mr Tabu and describe the other driver of the Usimba tribe. Mr Tabu nodded definitively, 'Yes, yes, I know him.'

Strebel reached for his wallet to pay the boy, but Alice discreetly stayed him. 'Do not turn him into a beggar. To speak is free, one person to another.'

Mr Tabu drove them to the bus station. A solitary bus trembled and shuddered under a canopy of mango trees.

As soon as Mr Tabu stopped the taxi, a swarm of ticket touts surrounded the car, offering Strebel passage—Morogoro, Dar, Pangani, Arusha, Mombasa. They leered at Alice, for they knew what she was: a pretty young black girl with a middle-aged white man. *Malaya*, Strebel heard, and he guessed at the meaning from the tone: whore.

He felt her fold herself in, as if she could stack her skeleton more tightly. She crossed her thin, dark wrists over her lap and gazed straight ahead, attempting the look of a duchess, impervious to their lewd chattering. Mr Tabu waved his arms and shouted at them and they sloped back to the shadowed interiors of the ticket offices. He then went off in search of the driver, Mr Peter.

But Mr Peter had taken a holiday; he had gone to see his family near Tabora. Despite this unfortunate news, Mr Tabu looked pleased with himself as he spoke to Alice. She translated: Mr Peter had been able to take this holiday because he had come into some money—a *mzungu* client who had paid him very well.

'When?'

Mr Tabu consulted the group. 'A few days ago.'

'The thirtieth?'

More discussion. 'Maybe beginning Wednesday.'

The twenty-ninth.

Strebel had left Zurich for Dar on the twenty-eighth. Today was the second of June. Koppler could still be around.

And the client? Strebel pushed to know—could Mr Tabu show them the photograph of Koppler? Mr Tabu went off with it and after a few minutes returned, tilting his head from side to side. 'They are not sure,' he said, through Alice. 'They saw him only once. They say yes, maybe. They say maybe, maybe.'

'But they don't say "No"?'

Mr Tabu concurred, 'They don't say "No."'

'Do they know anything else?' Strebel pressed. 'Where Mr Peter took this man or, when he left, did he take a bus? Or a plane? To where?'

But there was nothing more. Only envy that Mr Peter had been so lucky.

Strebel sat back and felt the sweat along his spine. He knew he'd reached a dead end—unless he traveled to this Usimba place and found Mr Peter's village. But he would not do that. This was far enough. He suddenly felt sour. He could smell himself, and he was ashamed that Alice could smell him, that she would see the smear of his sweat on the seat, the slow drip of it off his face.

At the opposite end of the bus station, a mother scolded her young child. Strebel could have no idea why she was angry, but he remembered the ways Ingrid had scolded Caroline: when she refused to hold her mother's hand crossing the road, when she wanted ice cream for supper, when she would inexplicably, inconsolably, lie on the floor and sob. Strebel had been sure that her distress was existential: an inexpressible need that therefore could not be fulfilled. It's this rage and sorrow we carry in us forever, he'd thought—I need, I need, I need—the need a craving without object, an insatiable hunger that has nothing to do with food. Or love. Or sex. These were merely surrogates. He'd imagined the giant, gaping bill of a baby bird, whom nothing would satisfy, except perhaps to swallow the universe whole.

This thought led him to Ingrid. What if she found him like this, sweating in a taxi in a town on the edge of Africa, concocting an investigation with a young Swahili girl. Concocting, yes, because it wasn't his business to be here. His work—his *duty*—stopped with a trial or an inquest; what people made of their lives after that was up to them. And sometimes, yes, he found the separation a little shocking, for he was so embedded, so intimately familiar with the emotional lives of the participants, and then it was over. He felt oddly abandoned, as if a best friend or lover had stopped returning calls. It was too abrupt, the end.

Too abrupt, always, the 'Take care of yourself.' Regardless of the softness of their skin or the curve of their dark eyebrows.

As for Pilgrim, he had failed to be objective. Professionally, he was beyond the pale. He had slept with a woman nearly half his age, a witness, vulnerable, traumatized.

If Ingrid found him, somehow, found him here, she would merely pity him. She would see the desperate machinations of a middle-aged man in need of antidepressants and a sports car. She would chide him as she had Caroline: You can't have ice cream for supper; it's not the way the world works. He would lie sobbing on the floor and Ingrid would firmly say: You can't have the pretty girl, you can't touch her and love her and have breakfast with her. It's not the way the world works.

'The hotel,' Strebel said to Mr Tabu and he was sure he felt Alice flinch. But even to smile reassuringly would be to show his yellowing wolf teeth. So he sighed and let his head fall all the way back against the seat.

At first he didn't understand the sound—that it was knocking. For it began in his dream: a suspect he'd interviewed many years ago, tapping a soda can on the table, a taunting Morse code, for he refused to speak, only to tap-tap-tap, tap-tap, and to smile. Refused to say what had happened to the child, where they might find the body, only tap-tap-tap, and that smile. Strebel opened his eyes and listened to the knocking, let it bring him into the still, hot, dark room in Tanga.

'Just a minute,' he said, and grappled with the sheet, pulling it around him. How could it be dark and so insanely hot? His first two nights he'd waited for the cool to seep in, a current of air to drift ashore. Like the cool fingers of a mother on the chest of her fevered child. But, no, the stubborn heat remained. Even on the balcony, he'd felt no relief. He'd seen a beggar down below, curled up in the open arcade of the market. The man had covered himself with a thick blanket and wore a wool hat.

Now he realized the knocking was urgent, a male voice saying, 'Mistah Strebel! Mistah Strebel!'

'Who is it?' he asked, already opening the door.

Mr Tabu stood there, his excited face coated with moonlight. 'Your friend! They have found him! The police! Come! I take you!'

Strebel's heart seized. Then he paid attention to the words. *Him.* They have found him.

They drove through the dark, quiet town. None of the street-lights worked. Kerosene lamps illuminated the interiors of bars, cafés and street-side shops. Strebel was charmed—for the darkness hid the shabbiness, made it fairytale and glimmering, and the sounds were soft: a radio, people laughing, a bicycle bell.

Even the police station was without electricity. Mr Tabu took a flashlight out of his glove compartment. It was a cheap Chinese model with the power of a child's night light, but sufficient to light their way up the cement steps. Excited voices came from the dark ahead of them. Within moments, they collided in the dark. There was a brief scuffle, a conversation in Swahili, then at last the flashlight took hold of an image. The officer wore a sharply pressed tan uniform.

'I am Chief Constable Elias Kulunju.' He held out his hand to Strebel. 'I am sorry to inform you about the death of one of your countrymen. This man—' he gestured offhandedly at Mr Tabu, 'He says you know the deceased.'

'Yes, possibly,' Strebel replied, curious as to how Mr Tabu had involved himself to such a degree as to know about dead bodies found by the police. But he had in his mind, then, an image of the drivers sitting under a tree, chatting for hours on end. Taxi drivers were like Google: they knew everything. Some of their information was reliable, but much of it was gossip, speculation, opinion disguised as fact.

Kulunju carried on down the steps. 'It is unfortunate that our mortuary is without electricity, so we have taken the deceased to the fish factory. They have a generator and have agreed to keep him in their refrigerator. Can we take your taxi? My car—' he began and then simply shrugged. 'This country.'

Mr Tabu hurried to open the Corolla's door. Kulunju glanced distastefully at the back seat before getting in. Strebel sat beside him. Carefully—because he had to check—he said, 'The body is that of a man. You're sure?'

'My knowledge of anatomy is limited. But I am fairly sure men are the same, white or black.' Strebel wasn't sure if Kulunju was smiling as he said this.

'It's just, there's a woman missing.'

'White?'

'Yes. About thirty. Dark hair.'

There was a long pause. 'You *wazungu* and your marital dramas. Do you behave this way in your own countries? Or just when you come to Africa?' He drew out *Africaaaaa* to make the point. Then added, 'No, nothing about a woman.'

The factory was on the outskirts of town. There were fewer lights and the black horizon of buildings became lower and more erratic. Then the darkness yielded suddenly to the blazing security lights that illuminated a high chain-link fence topped with razor wire. A security guard approached the taxi, and, seeing Kulunju, snapped a salute and ran to open the gate. Inside the compound, Strebel saw order: neat paths, whitewashed buildings, clipped grass. The business, Kulunju told him, was owned by an Italian and managed by a Greek.

The Greek, a polite young man, stood waiting under the light in a whirling halo of moths and flying ants. 'I'm sorry for your loss,' he said to Strebel. Strebel gave a polite nod. They went inside. There was only the faintest odor of fish—for it turned out the business was calamari and octopus for export to Europe. The Greek pointed out that the Mediterranean had been bereft of both for nearly two decades, due to overfishing. He led the way through an office and toward a set of high steel doors.

'We have done our best,' he said to Strebel. 'I hope you can appreciate the circumstances.'

The Greek switched on a light, opened the door, and they stepped inside. The cold embraced Strebel and he wanted to sigh with relief. The cold was delicious, pressing against his skin:

he could strip off his clothes and stand naked just to feel the coolness on his balls. But instead he followed Kulunju and the Greek back between the shelves of frozen squids. In the very rear of the refrigerator, Koppler lay on a metal table. He was covered to his neck with a white sheet. He was mottled, his skin pale and flaky as pastry. His eyes were covered with packing tape. They had no lids and probably no eyeballs. Strebel considered that his face bore no less expression in death than it had in life.

'Is this the man you know?' Kulunju asked.

'Yes,' Strebel said. 'Ernst Koppler. How did you know he was Swiss?'

Kulunju handed over a damp red passport. 'He was carrying this.'

Strebel studied Koppler. He had begun to rot. 'Can you tell me where—how he was found?'

Delicately, Kulunju pulled down the sheet to Koppler's waist. He had been partially eaten by things with small mouths. 'Fishermen. It's hard to say how long he had been in the water. Perhaps one day. Not much more. His eyes—small crabs...' Kulunju paused to make sure Strebel was not about to be sick. 'Small crabs and other marine animals but also the sea cause such damage.'

'Did he drown?' Strebel asked.

Kulunju shook his head, and turned Koppler's hands palm-up, revealed the deep wounds on his wrists. 'It appears he committed suicide.'

'And then jumped in the sea?'

The chief constable shrugged. 'What would you like me to say? That it is possible, impossible? Sometimes those who kill themselves wish to be found, as a punishment to their families. Others want privacy.' He replaced the sheet and stood back.

Strebel thought about what would happen now in Switzerland: the forensic team would scour every trace of the Raskazone house, of Gloria's house and Harry's house, their cars. He and his team would bring them both in for questioning. And the old boys at the bar. They'd locate Mr Peter in Usimba. The pathologist would decide if the knife wounds were indeed self-inflicted, or if there was evidence of foul play. How long the body had been in the water, and if he'd been alive or dead upon entry. The investigation would be exhaustive. And yet everyone would know from the outset that Koppler had killed himself and had reason. How his body got into the sea—by his own hand or another's—only mattered as a curiosity. No more: an exercise in efficiency. As if efficiency, like explanation, could ward off the stupid, random wanton cruelty of life.

'We have arranged for one of the fish trucks to take him to Dar,' Kulunju said.

'Thank you,' Strebel nodded. He saw then that someone had put a jar filled with frangipani blossoms on the floor near the metal leg of the sorting table. He noticed also the makeshift reverence of the room: an effort had been made to clear a place for the table away from the boxes of squid. He noticed the cleanliness of the sheet (where had it come from?). He noticed that someone had combed Koppler's hair, for it was smooth against his scalp. Care had been taken; strangers had been gentle.

Why did that surprise him so?

Lies had been told, obfuscations proffered, mysteries had dropped before him like little black stones. He would never solve them. There would be no statements. Peter the driver would never be found and no one would explain to him how Koppler ended up in the sea. Mr Tabu, the old men at the bar, the Greek manager, Kulunju—they were without malice. They accepted that life had marooned them here on the edge of the continent.

He could keep looking for Pilgrim, and he would find her—alive, he was certain. Gloria, whatever her conspiracy, had not filled him with dread. He recalled the transformation of her face when she saw the children, how she was almost beautiful.

Pilgrim was safe. Somewhere. But she had not summoned

him. Had not phoned. The letter she sent had not been to him. So Strebel rode in the front of the fish truck with the driver. Five hours later, just after dawn, they reached Dar es Salaam, and the Swiss vice-consul met them at the morgue. He offered Strebel the guest room at the Embassy and Strebel accepted. Soon, he was resting on a bed in an air-conditioned room, and if he'd been able to blot out the searing African light, he could have been in a hotel in Belgium or Reykjavik: the mustard-colored bedspread, the high speed Wi-Fi.

There would be questions. The vice-consul, his superintendent, Ingrid. He would answer, but he could not explain.

He shut his eyes. And he felt her move next to him, in her sleep, reaching out for him, with the deepest honesty of her unconscious. 'Paul,' she murmured, and he turned so that his body cupped hers. He held her lightly in his arms, 'I'm here,' he said. 'My darling, I'm here.'

HARRY

Mohemedi told him there was a boy at the gate asking for him.

'What's he want?' Harry had just ordered another beer and it was cold and slender in his hand. It fit just right. He was feeling good about now, sixth beer into the evening. Smooth, slippery. He liked to maintain this oozy sensation for as long as possible—another three or four beers. And then he stumbled downhill, drinking faster and faster, and around a sharp bend, so that he'd end up where he started: the particular feeling of sand under his skin. He'd drive home, maybe stop at the Casa Chica and dance with Sugar and things would be better for a few hours. Or maybe just drink more at home, pass out. Start all over again.

'*Mzee*, it's something to do with that American mama,' Mohemedi said. 'There is trouble.'

Vaguely, Harry connected to the words. He felt no alarm. His emotional bandwidth wasn't very wide. He really just wanted to finish his drink. And have another one. *American mama*. Gloria. What did that fat old bitch want? But floating up to him was another face. A girl, very pretty. Lillian? Oh, dear, his poor Pooh-Bear brain.

He thought about suicide a lot. The thinking was entirely satisfactory in and of itself. He couldn't be bothered to actually do it. He'd have to find a hosepipe. Maybe there was one in the boat shed? Or he could swim out into the rip tide. That would take too long and he didn't want to be afraid the way he'd certainly be in deep water. And there were sharks. Bull sharks in the bay.

Alcohol would kill him soon enough.

'The boy,' Mohemedi said. 'What shall I tell him, *Mzee*?'

What? What boy? Ah! Yes. Lillian. American. In her thirties. She was really very pretty. She reminded him of Jessica, same tall, slender build, same lethal doe eyes. Reminded him of antelopes. Jessica. Lillian. Deer in the headlights.

Something was wrong. A bad feeling. Cold spot in the room sort of thing. Cold.

Beer.

The taste of beer.

Had improved since the South Africans took over the brewery. Consistency.

Of taste and supply.

The hair on the back of his neck was prickling, bloody hell, why was it so cold? Wind off the bay? What?

But, as he was thinking, or was he saying? Was he talking to Maurice? Before the South Africans you couldn't be sure. Murky beer, the color of a diabetic's piss.

Worse sometimes: no beer. Delivery truck broke down in Mombo.

Mohemedi standing, hovering, why—

'I'll go and see her,' Harry at last remembered. He had a method for getting off the bar stool: plant both hands on the bar, move his ass horizontally right to the edge of the stool, right foot down on the floor, then the left, keep hands on the bar, straighten old knees. Dreadful creaking sound. The next part was more difficult: taking a step. He managed. One, two, one, two. A little march, ho hum. Up the steps. Fuck. Why were there so many of them? That time in Uganda. Mountains of the Moon, a wall of mud, climbing a wall of mud, every time he took a step he slid back. It rained every day, never saw the sun, never been so wet down into his bones, seldom so tired. What had he been doing there, climbing those mountains? What madness—woman or money?

The boy was waiting at the top of the steps, framed by the club gate. Illuminated by the only streetlight in Tanga that worked because the club maintained it. Boy, thin as wire, ragged white shirt many sizes too big. Something—something about him? Harry can't quite put a finger on it, too busy standing up.

And that wave of cold again. Malaria? He shivered. The cold crawled over his scalp with little cold feet.

'*Shikamoo*,' the boy said softly.

'*Marahaba*,' Harry replied. It was always pleasant, that little bit of respect even to an old soak. He had a parka in the car and put it on. Couldn't shake the cold.

They took Harry's car and he mused that the boy had probably never driven in a car before. The jerking of the clutch and the pulling of the torqued axle and the inebriation of the driver would seem normal. As they veered through the dark, following the unsteady beam of his single headlight, the boy told how he had been walking by the house and he'd heard the American mama making a strange sound. He'd been afraid to go into the house so he had looked through the window and seen the lady on the floor. She had a bag over her head.

Harry blinked the sweat from his eyes. He was feeling more sober, which made him resentful and sad and afraid. He did not like to think clearly.

A bag on her head? *Mfuko?* Maybe a hat that looked like a bag. Maybe a shower cap. No, the boy said, '*Malbolo*.'

Big blue bags with the Marlboro Man. Who made them? How did they get to Tanzania? Why? Or what?

Crikey. What was one on her head for?

Over her head, the boy clarified. Covering her head and her face.

The cold little feet were running down his arms now, down his spine. Like ants, swarming, ice ants. He drove a little faster.

Name wasn't Lillian. Funny name. Religious, but not.

Reaching the house, Harry parked under the tulip tree and got out. It was dark, no light, no *askari*. Somewhere he had a flashlight. Under the seat. But no batteries. For a moment he lost track of where he was. Then he remembered the boy. The boy was sitting very still, but he was yearning: Harry could feel it coming off him like lust. Harry got out of the car.

'Go on then,' he said to the boy and the boy slid into the driver's seat, gripped the wheel and smiled. Perfect teeth, white, straight. So many of them had perfect teeth. Half-starved, subsisting on day-old *ugali* and mangoes that fell off the trees, and teeth from a toothpaste ad. How?

Pilgrim. That was it.

The door to the little round house was open. He was about to call out but he heard it: scuffling, moaning. He went in. He and Gloria used to shag here in their brief shagging days. She'd repelled him physically in the beginning; there was so much of her, so much flesh. But every woman felt the same on the inside, every woman was soft on the inside, and he even began to like her body, how she encompassed him. And it had been nice afterward, a ciggie and a G&T. Gloria certainly had some miles on her. They could talk as equals. Laugh.

In the house now. He could just see, light from the moon. Pilgrim was on the floor. Her head was—

Bloody hell—

Her head was in a *malbolo* and it was fastened around her neck with duct tape. Her hands and feet were also tied with duct tape. She was jerking like a dying fish, the bag sucking in where her mouth must be.

Harry wasn't immediately sure if this was happening. Or a dream, a hallucination. He couldn't be sure these days.

Then he ran and ripped open the plastic.

Her wide eyes. Congo. Pro-Lumumba women put up against a wall to be shot by Mobuto's lot. CIA-backed *jambazi*. Nothing he could do to save the women or stop the men. Only keep himself alive. The women's wide-open eyes, he'd never forget: fear because they still thought they had a chance, still wanted to live, could still *think*, could still offer their bodies for rape. Their eyes changed the instant the shooting started, shutters coming down, the end of hope, the truth, a kind of relief. For him, too.

He pulled the tape off Pilgrim's mouth. She sucked in, deep, howling breaths.

'You're all right, you're all right now,' he said and held her face so that she looked at him. Her lips were blue.

If he'd stayed to finish the beer—

The boy in the white shirt—

Something—

She was coming back to him now, her breath slowing, color coming back. He cradled her head, stroked her hair. He was saying things in a soft voice like, You're all right, you're all right, it's all over now. He took the tape off her hands and rubbed her wrists. Took the tape off her ankles. Her legs were beautiful. Antelope. Jessica. It's okay now, darling. I'm here.

When she sat up she gripped him fiercely, her fingers clutching his shirt.

'There, there.' He kept stroking her hair and then lifted her onto the sofa, put a cushion under her head. 'I'll put the kettle on.'

But first he went outside. The boy was standing by the car, looking at himself in the side mirror. Harry gave him a couple of hundred shilling coins. 'Off you go now. Don't say anything about this.'

As the boy turned and trotted off, Harry saw that his white shirt was bloody and agape at the back, exposing a large wound. Even in the moonlight he could determine that the wound was large and very deep.

That it was the kind of wound made by,

say,

a propeller.

The kind of wound from which you could not recover.

Harry felt his knees give and the fearful cold rush through him. 'Hey,' he shouted after the boy. The boy turned briefly and smiled, then disappeared. Not around a corner or into the bush. Not a trick of darkness or moon. But disappeared. *Stepped back to that other place.* Absorbed. Harry steadied himself. It could just be the DTs, or some more permanent dementia.

But in his heart—that rusty old clock—Harry knew who the boy was and why he had come. For years, Harry had been waiting for him, or some other emissary. They had unfinished business.

Oh, he'd seen them before. Saw them all the time. In the shadows, in the evenings, riding bicycles, mingling with the living. Sometimes, they would glance at him, catch his eye in mutual acknowledgement, like members of a secret club. Yes, yes, their casual gaze seemed to say, We know you, you know us. But always they moved on. Their business was not with him.

He'd tried to talk about this with Gloria once and she'd laughed at him. 'Ghosts? You've been in Africa too long.'

This was true. Africa too bloody long.

But the ghosts—*shetani*, spirits—the ghosts weren't just here. He'd gone to England a few years ago, visiting his sister. They didn't get on, never had. Sandra, very conservative. Garden like Legoland, all straight edges. She lived in a modern village in the southeast, least spooky place you could imagine. But he saw a man on the bus. And a child throwing bread to a duck. They saw him, casual nods. Ghosts.

These ghosts, they came and went, back and forth. The other place and here. Maybe there were several other places, like a multi-level parking garage. The universe was an awfully big place and had to be filled with something.

From time to time, he wondered if he, too, was dead—a ghost, and this is why he could see them. But then he would get the most godawful hangover, and he was pretty sure that the dead didn't get hangovers.

Lots of things you get used to in Africa. It's the most honest place on earth. Why should the dead simply be dead? Or go to heaven? Rubbish about being reincarnated into beetles or Egyptian princesses. The dead were here, among the living. Side by side.

Harry turned and went back into the house. He found the light switch. What comfort electricity offered, to enter a cocoon of man-made light scooped out of the infinite dark. What it was like for villagers when they could afford a kerosene lamp. The reassurance, even, of a cheap Chinese flashlight.

Light.

The kitchen wasn't separate, just around the corner from the living area. He found the kettle, filled it up, turned on the stove. He noticed then that the water still seemed to be running. As if the overflow in the loo was broken. He glanced over at Pilgrim. She was curled up on the sofa. She was in shock. But she'd be okay.

Harry went into the bathroom. It was brightly tiled, the shower in the corner. And under the shower was a middle-aged white man in a raincoat. And an awful lot of blood. The blood was still oozing from his wrists, but Harry knew enough about exsanguination to know that it was very nearly over. He turned off the shower and put his fingers over the man's carotid artery. Yes, nearly over. He looked into the man's eyes.

'Don't worry,' he said. 'I'll just stay here with you until you go. Better not to be alone.'

He sat with the man, holding his hand, the blood thick and dark now, almost black like sticky tar. The kettle began to whistle and he tried the man's pulse again. There was the faintest flutter. He gave it another couple of minutes, and then, when there was nothing, got up and washed the blood from his hands. He turned off the kettle. He found some mugs and teabags. He went over to Pilgrim. She was looking at him, not his face but his shirt and shorts. The blood. As if he'd just killed a pig.

'Ah,' he said, handing her the tea. But her hand was trembling so he put it down on the floor. He took a sip of his own tea. He couldn't remember the last time he'd had tea. A beverage that was hot and bereft of alcohol.

Imagine if he'd finished his beer: she'd be dead.

'Look,' he said. 'I'm not sure what's going on. But I'm supposed to be here. I was brought here.'

He couldn't tell if she understood. *I'm supposed to be here.* Because he didn't finish the beer. Because of the boy.

She was still a little floaty, but he got her to drink a bit of the tea. He told her he'd be right back and went to the bathroom and let the water run over the dead man until it ran clear down the plug. He rinsed out his shirt. He went out to his car and got an old tarp from the wheel well. Why it was there he couldn't recall, but it had been there for years probably, taking up the space where a spare tire should have been. He wrapped the dead man in the tarp, heavy as a sack of hammers, and worried for a moment that he'd put his back out. Who'd ever heard of a knight in shining armor with a bad back?

He dragged the body out the bedroom door but when he tried to get it into the car the tarp kept falling off. The man's limbs protested as if he were still alive, catching on the door jamb, the bushes. Like a drunk who did not want to leave the bar. Who had clung to the stool in The Muthaiga Club, The Mombasa Club, The Tamarind Bar and Grill, The Juba Press Club, The Sheraton Kampala poolside bar; clung to the railing, to a tree even, as others had removed him. He recalled his fury, turning like a bright pinwheel in his chest: the unjustness of the assault! All he had wanted to do was drink.

Covering the body again, he glanced inside at Pilgrim. She lay very still, her eyes open, blinking from time to time. He wondered what she was seeing. He found his mobile phone, dialed.

'Gloria. I'm at Raskazone. Can you come?'

She'd started to give him gyp. She was expecting the kids in the morning, she was tired, it was late. He cut her off: 'I need your help. I need you.'

Twenty minutes later she drove through the gate. She got out of her car, left it running, the headlights blazing. 'What the fuck?'

He gestured down at the body. 'Help me get him into the car.'

Gloria hesitated, and he was sure she'd refuse, like a stubborn old mare. But instead she bent over, pulled the tarp back to reveal the man's face, blanched in the car lights. 'Shit,' she said. 'Oh, shit.'

'You know him?'

She made a face, as if she was chewing the inside of her cheek. 'Yes,' she said. 'Shit.'

'Who is he?'

'He's from Switzerland.'

Harry waited. Gloria took a deep breath. 'He came to see me. He was looking for Pilgrim.' She stalled again.

'Come on, old girl, out with it.'

With another breath, she obliged. 'He came to see me. He was looking for Pilgrim. She killed his child.'

'She killed his child?' Harry was incredulous. 'Pilgrim killed this man's child?'

'A car accident. Three children altogether.'

Harry was starting to understand.

'Oh, Gloria,' he said softly.

'He just, he just,' she spluttered. She was going to cry. She pulled out a cigarette, but didn't light it. 'He just, you know—'

'This is about James, isn't it?'

'Koppler knew what it was like to, to—'

'—to lose a child.'

'It makes you crazy, Harry.'

'Did he tell you why he was looking for Pilgrim?'

'No.' Then she shook her head. 'And I didn't care. I don't care. About her. People like her.'

'People like her? She's just anyone. Anyone at all.'

'You're on the outside.'

'Of what? I'm on the outside of what?'

Gloria lit the cigarette. A moment passed.

'I'm quitting.'

'Those kids have AIDS, dear. They've been abandoned by their families. It doesn't matter if you *smoke*.'

They stood there while she smoked. Finally, Gloria said, still not looking at him, grinding the butt into the sandy earth: 'You want there to be retribution. For someone to pay. Like a sacrifice, I suppose. It doesn't matter who, you can pile all your anger on anyone. He...' she bent down and pulled the tarp away from the dead man's face. 'He deserved justice.'

Harry grabbed her. He felt very sober, as if someone had pulled the plug and all the alcohol had drained right out of him. 'Listen, listen, so you get it right. Not just translated through your grief, it's like a bloody echo chamber. Will you listen?'

Gloria did not move away. So Harry said, 'She's just a person. Not a monster. She'll wake up with an image of those dead children every morning for the rest of her life.' His hand softened on her arm, almost a caress. 'I'm so very sorry for your pain, Gloria, love, with everything that is left of my heart. And I'm sorry for his. But maybe it's a mistake to go around comparing pain and trying to make it match up.'

He helped himself to one of her cigarettes, lit it and inhaled savagely. 'Only bloody thing I ever managed to accomplish.'

Gloria looked away, out at the dark sea, the star-seeded night. 'Is she all right?'

'Just a bit shaken up.'

'We'll have to clean this up. If the cops— I'll never get my kids. Oh, God, Harry, I'll never get my kids.'

'The cops? They don't need to be involved. This is a private matter.'

Suddenly, she reached out and put her hand on his gnarled old wrist. He renegotiated the movement, so that he held her hand. They held hands. Gravity is different in a place like Tanga, he thought. People fall together who normally would not. You and I, Gloria, trailing the dusty, wrecked caravans of our lives, have fallen.

Together.

'Take her, get her away from here. Take my car,' Harry said. 'I'll deal with him.'

'No.' Gloria knelt to touch the dead man. 'Let me take him. We understood each other.'

★ ★ ★

By dawn Harry and Pilgrim reached the ferry at Pangani. Harry loved how the great walled buildings crumbled under the weight of thick webs of vines. Once, centuries ago, Pangani had been a major port. Now, huts grew like shy mushrooms among the ruins.

He almost laughed out loud at the idea of progress.

There was a decent guesthouse for smugglers, because Pangani was—still, after dusk—a port; and the same goods came down the slow, dark river that always had: gems, ivory, slaves, illegally harvested hardwood. And the same goods went up it: guns. Though drugs now, too, and counterfeit electronics from Dubai.

The ferry was on the other side of the river, a small collection of cars and trucks loading up. Villagers with bicycles and children and baskets of fruit, someone with a goat. Always someone with a goat. The sun, popping above the far horizon of the ocean, illuminated the river. On contact, the surface of the water ignited in sparks. The shadowed portions rippled like yards of lavender silk. Harry marveled at how the river had come all the way from Kilimanjaro. He'd done the stretch from Boma ya Ngombe to Nyumba ya Mungu in a wooden canoe. About a thousand years ago, when he was a young man and big herds of elephant still came down to the river, back when the whole country was just animals and bush.

Now the ferry began to move out from the far bank. Only the starboard engine worked, so the boat crossed in a series of slow pirouettes. It was why he loved this country.

By late morning, he turned off the main road (such as it was) and onto a narrow sand track through a grove of palm trees. The track cut directly east, so that in a few miles they reached a small bungalow on the edge of the sea. Pilgrim got out of the car and Harry watched her walk toward the water. She had barely spoken, she was still far off. She walked to the water's edge, and then into it, deeper and deeper, like a crazed baptist.

He ran after her and pulled her back. 'Stop feeling sorry for yourself, you're not the one who's dead.' She looked at him, green-blue eyes, Jesus Christ, she was beautiful. He persevered. 'There's a basket of food in the back of the car. Go and put it in the kitchen.' As she walked up to the house, he took out the Konyagi and had a long drink. He had always been drawn to folly.

★ ★ ★

Pilgrim slept. He had given her two Valium claiming they were aspirin. He wanted her to sleep, best thing for her. But also, he needed time to acknowledge his own life was shifting. At last. To open his ears and hear the tap, tap, tapping of the past. He needed to decode the message.

They had come to him again, they had come to remind him. They did not threaten, but they were insistent.

He sat for a long time, through the hot, still afternoon and into the night, watching Pilgrim, watching the light change, drinking, though not too much.

★ ★ ★

Dreams. A long time since he'd had them. Dreams had no mercy, dreams were sons of bitches. Of course that's part of the reason he drank: to keep the dreams at bay. But he'd always drunk too much. That's why it had happened in the first place. A sober man would have made a different decision: too late to fly, go in the morning, the pussy'll still be there.

In certain dreams he turned around, banked the plane through the golden clouds and headed back to Arusha. He would wake and grasp at the golden seconds of possibility, try to suck them in like clean air. He had turned around.

But he hadn't. No. He had kept flying. He had seen the strip in the bush, a little cut in the miles of bundu, a little scratch. It was way too dark and he should have done a flyover, he always did flyovers. But he was drunk, he couldn't be bothered. He'd landed.

The sea, deep blue in the dawn light, wrinkled with wind. A little ruffle on the sand, a petticoat of surf. Incredible that the big bold sea could be so delicate. It was cheating to drink the dreams away. He should live them, he should dream them every night. His dreams should be a memorial to his shame.

Betty and Dave had had to sell the farm. They'd woken up one night, the house surrounded by villagers holding flaming torches. They'd climbed out the bathroom window, run to the Land Rover and driven off. Left everything: Betty's pugs to be killed, Dave's Steinway to be set ablaze. They moved to Iringa, managed a tea plantation. They'd stayed together. Harry had seen Betty once in Dar, maybe fifteen years ago. She was walking down the street, plumper, her hair graying, but the beauty lingered in the way she moved, the structure of her. She saw him and pretended she hadn't, ducked into a shop. He stood at the entrance to the shop, shouting, 'You can't take back a fuck.' He was at the nasty end of a bender.

You can't take back a fuck. You can't take anything back.

Now he drank the Konyagi, three big gulps, then screwed on the top. He couldn't go cold turkey, not with the girl to sort out. But he would ease off. Not too much, mind: he took another three swigs. He regarded the girl on the bed under the mosquito net. He wanted desperately to touch her, but more desperately to be the young man who he had been, when beautiful women took off their clothes for him.

Before. Before he dropped the air speed. Before he lowered the wing flaps.

Take his dreams and put them on the table. He'd sat there, listening—hearing. The propeller stopped spinning. His throat opened, his mouth had been dry.

They hadn't been able to get the living ones out until morning. A tourniquet can only do so much. So some of them died. Exsanguination.

* * *

Pilgrim made breakfast: papaya and toast, a pot of tea. 'There are eggs,' she said. But after some discussion—boiled, poached?—neither of them wanted one. She was wearing an old *kikoi* of his, she must have found it in the cupboard. It hid her breasts and hips, but this only accentuated the slim length of her arms, her lovely ankles.

'I need to know,' she said. 'About the ghosts.'

Had he told her about them? He didn't recall. He must have

been bat-faced to blather on like that. He could deny it, say it must have been the booze talking, he didn't know any ghosts.

'Need?' He was still trying to decide what he should tell her. 'Why do you *need* to know?'

'The boy,' she said.

Harry noticed the little knot of bone where her wrist joined her hand.

'The boy in the white shirt,' she continued. 'Who is he?'

Harry considered denial. What boy? 'Ah,' he said to give himself another fraction of time. He kept thinking: if I'd finished the beer, if I'd finished the beer. But I didn't. Because of the boy. So he said what was obvious, 'The boy is a ghost.'

Pilgrim laughed, an odd, contorted little laugh.

Now Harry laughed. And he caught her up in his true laugh, so that laughter flowed out of her.

'A ghost?'

'Yes, a ghost.'

'This is a ghost story?'

Later, after they'd eaten, he told her.

'It's a long time ago now. They were in the road, walking home. They'd lived near me, a young couple. One block over. I used to see them when I drove home from the club at night. For a long time I thought they were just out walking. One night, I stopped to have a chat. I realized too late the woman was crying. They've had a row, I thought.

'But the woman said to me, "We can't find our dog."

'The man put his arm around her shoulder, "He's a little terrier, a black shaggy thing, have you seen him?"

'I said I was sorry, but no, I hadn't. I'd keep a lookout.'

Harry pulled the quart bottle of Konyagi out of his pocket and took a grateful swig. He offered it to Pilgrim, and she took a taste.

'Rough.'

'Not after twenty-five years.'

She took another sip. 'The couple who were lost in the caves? Are you talking about them? I thought you said they were before your time.'

'They were. Long before.' Harry let the fact sit by itself for a moment. He'd gone over it many times, he'd checked the dates, and he was dead certain.

'The next day I drove round to their house to see if they'd had any luck and found the dog. But the house was all closed up. Had been for years. For a few days I drove home another way. And I forgot about them. The benefit of booze. Then I got home one night and found her sitting on my bed—the woman, very pretty, dark hair like you.

'"They want to know what you're going to do," she said.

'"Who?" I said. But I knew. Of course I did.

'She repeated: "What are you going to do?"

'I told her to get out. Never before, never since told a woman to get out of my bedroom.'

'Did you see her again?' Pilgrim asked.

Harry shook his head. 'Not her. Others.'

'And you're sure?'

'Sure? That she existed? Do ghosts exist?' He smiled. 'Did I make her up? Was she a projection of my poor, beleaguered conscience? Of the booze? I've thought about all that. How can I know—how can I really be sure?'

'Did you do anything?'

'What do you mean?'

'She asked you, "What are you going to do?" Have you done anything?'

'No,' he said. 'Just drink.'

Pilgrim was leaning forward now. She wasn't smiling, but her face had a kind of light. 'Anything beautiful?' she asked. 'Have you done anything beautiful?'

At first, he didn't understand what the hell she was on about.

GLORIA

At dawn she pilots the little boat out into the bay. Something not many people know about Gloria: she grew up on the water. Lake Michigan. So she can handle boats. People think she's just a fat woman. But she is a woman of great physical strength and grace, and a very able swimmer. Thirty-six years ago she was Michigan's junior state champion in breaststroke. But her real love had been butterfly: arcing up out of the water like a manta ray, the power cording like electricity through her body to her feet, and how she flew and plunged, the high arch of her strong back.

But then Milton. Soft words, such soft words, always watching from the bleachers, watching her in her swimsuit and bathing cap. Revealed. Thighs, breasts, the shape of her buttocks. She might as well have been naked. He was older and that made her feel oh so special. Don't worry, little Mary, I'll pull out. Whatever that meant she hadn't a clue. I want to be your first, Mary, little Mary, my Mary, does that feel good, Mary, I bet that feels good, god, your tasty little cherry. Technically, his impregnation of her was statutory rape. And that made the violation about age, him being forty-two and her being sixteen, and not about the bruises. He'd pinched her, hard, dozens of times, as if he was plucking a turkey, before fucking her, rudely, quickly. Then rolling over and falling asleep. What a turd blossom.

Mary never could lose the pregnancy weight. The muscle turned to fat. Her body made new fat like a morphing sci-fi creature. The upside was Milton stopped wanting to fuck her. The upside was James in her arms, on her breast, sucking fiercely. The downside was being seventeen, a high school dropout. It didn't matter how smart she was. It sure as hell didn't matter that she could swim.

The sea is still as a mirror and this makes the sound of the outboard loud. People might peer toward the noise, might see her. But then they'd have to be looking hard and with binoculars: she is wearing a kanga over her head and another over her shoulders. From a distance it would be difficult to tell she's even white. Let alone a woman. Let alone: Mama Gloria.

She sees the first buoy at the harbor entrance. The fishermen are there, dynamiting the last of the coral reefs. A lot of fishermen these days are missing an arm; they always say, Oh, a big *papa* got them. Yeah, right. A big shark with a fuse on the end that goes boom.

Out past the second buoy, the water gets choppier and the little boat thumps against the waves. Gloria wonders why she doesn't come out here more often, for how it makes her feel: like a strong, competent woman. Not a fat old hag. She bears north now, heading for a narrow gap in the mangroves. The tide's still high enough to cut through this way.

Closer in to the mangroves the water stills again. So still she could dimple it with her breath. She can see straight down, five or six feet, to the silty bottom and mangrove shoots and seagrass. She imagines the Amazon must be like this: wild green embracing the water, a low horizon, the feeling of being hidden inside. Lake Michigan was deep and murky and polluted; she could never see what was down below or how far down.

After a quarter of a mile, the channel opens up into a small bay. More of a cove, less than a quarter of a mile across. At the far sea-end is an island with an old lighthouse. She and Harry visited the lighthouse once during their lovin' days. The metal staircase, the brass fittings—everything was still there, tarnished by the elements. Herons nested in the well of the old light. She'd loved their high, forlorn cry, a sound made to carry across the water. She and Harry had a picnic and snorkeled around the coral rag. She'd been light in the water, delicate and graceful and sure. Harry hadn't noticed. He didn't want to see her pale, rubbery thighs.

Scavengers had since come to the island and taken away the metal to sell as scrap to the Chinese ships off shore. They took it to China to be recycled into buckets and shovels. And then the buckets and shovels would be imported back to Tanzania.

Machetes, too. She'd read that somewhere. Before the genocide in Rwanda. The killers had ordered half a million machetes from China. No doubt the metal had once been sourced in Africa. One thing for sure: you can count on the brutal irony of this continent. The most ironic thing that can happen, will happen.

Here she is, for example, escorting Mr Koppler to a watery grave.

In the middle of the cove Gloria turns off the motor, drifts and drops anchor. She waits a moment, checking for other boats. Then she puts her hand on the tarp and gives it a reassuring caress.

Just yesterday she'd looked out the kitchen window and seen an overweight man in a raincoat getting out of a taxi, looking around. He had no idea where he was, like he hadn't even clocked that he was in Tan-zanier—i.e. the heat and blazing sun and the totally goofy way of things, like the taxi had one wheel a different size from the other three; like he hadn't even clocked he had his raincoat on at all. He looked dazed. Mental patient dazed.

'Can I help you?' Gloria had said.

She figured out pretty much in that instant why he was there.

Not exactly why, but that it had to do with Pilgrim. She had backstory steaming off her. Husband, lover, bail bondsman— man trouble of some sort.

'I am Ernst Koppler. Excuse me to bother you.'

'No bother,' Gloria said. She'd even been excited, she was about to find out something. Part II of a miniseries.

'I am looking for an American woman.' He spoke the words mechanically. I. Am. Looking. For.

'Pilgrim,' Gloria offered.

'You know this woman?'

'Sure. Come on in. Let me get you a drink. Take off your coat, Mr Koppler.' He came in. The coat stayed on. He smelled like a tramp. But also, she'd recognized the particular stench of grief.

She made Mr Koppler coffee. He liked it black. He sat with the little cup and saucer perched on his knee. Awkward, he was, like her, plain and overweight. Back in the States people bumped into her all the time with their shopping carts or as they walked down the street chatting on their phones as if they didn't see her. She and Mr Koppler, the invisibles.

'Now, Mr Koppler, what do you want with Pilgrim?'

He said, 'She killed my daughter.'

'She killed your daughter,' Gloria repeated neutrally, but she was giving herself time to take it in. She felt so much, all at once, a great noise or strobes suddenly blasting right at her. What she wanted to say was, 'I know how you feel, I know, I know, I know. I know your heart is a hobbled beast.' She took a sip of coffee instead.

'She hit Sophie with the car,' Mr Koppler went on. 'Two other children also. All dead.'

That moment of finding out, it had been the same, surely, for Mr. Koppler. The cops at the door. 'Mrs Maynard? May we come in? It's about your son, James.'

I know, I know, rushed through Gloria's head and sort of

possessed her. She sat very still and attentive, her body squared and open. 'Now that is the most terrible thing.'

He looked up at her, his dull face, cross-hatched with spider veins. He seemed to be waiting now for her. 'It doesn't make sense, does it?' she continued. 'How objects persist, they just carry on, houses, cars, beds, other people, and your child doesn't.'

Mr Koppler started crying. He cried profusely for nearly ten minutes. Gloria let him. She didn't try to touch him or comfort him. She knew he didn't want this, she knew it did no good at all, the there, there. Then he said, 'At my shop—I have a little stationery shop—yes, I look at the pens, all the different pens— rollerballs, soft tips, dry erase markers—I look at them, and I do not understand how it is that these pens are still here, these stupid pens, and my child, my child is not here.'

Gloria sat very still, very quiet. She didn't tell him, 'Oh, it'll be all right. You'll get over it. The pain will get less and less.'

It does not.

'You closed up your shop, didn't you, Mr Koppler? And you will never go back.'

He nodded, and looked at her. Now he saw that they were the same. It was a small relief, Gloria reflected, to find a colleague in grief.

Koppler then spoke of himself in a way Gloria knew he never had with another soul. As if—and she thinks about this in the boat with his dead body—as if he was giving a testament. He wanted one other person on the face of this lonely planet to know his story. He wanted to be heard out.

Before he killed himself.

He told Gloria how his wife died of cancer. He had loved her. And—incredibly—she'd loved him. Hamida was from Uzbekistan. She'd been his cleaner at the shop. 'It was simple like a movie,' Mr Koppler had said. 'She wants a kind man and I realize I am an ugly, boring man but also kind.

'Maybe she just wants a visa when we begin. But we're happy.

Chatting, breakfast, TV, walks. And then one day she says, "I am pregnant." She thought it was not possible, after Uzbekistan. Torture, because of the books she's teaching there.' Mr Koppler beamed, suddenly, as if the sun had burst through the window with an accompaniment of violins. 'And so Sophie. Her little hands, her feet, I would look at them, touch them. Kiss. *Wunder, wunder*—you know the word, the same in English?'

'Wonder,' Gloria nodded. Yes, wonder.

Wonder rushing out of her. The way James slept, mouth open, palms open, fingers stained with ink or paint. He was so perfect she could barely breathe for loving him. Mary—she of all people, she of the awkward squad—had made perfection. Her heart blossomed, her love fell on little James like petals, softly, softly. She kissed his forehead. She lay down next to him, sheltering his small body from the world.

These old feelings stirred, and she'd fallen back with Mr Koppler to that time right after James's death. She lost the years in between, stepping through a door into another room. The past was that close, always, a door away, the walls paper-thin and she could see shadows of people moving on the other side. She could hear them, mumbled voices, but not quite determine their words.

Gloria was again raw and unraveled and unwise. She was Mary in the L.A. County morgue. 'Is this your son, James Beaumont Maynard?' She was pressing her lips against James's rough cheek. He smelled of antiseptic. He smelled of death. She beheld the hair sprouting from his ear. The shaved head. The pimple on the side of his nose. He'd killed a cashier in a convenience store hold-up in West Hollywood, a single mother of two, an innocent. And he in turn had been killed by the cops who'd stopped in to buy corn dogs.

'Yes, that's my son,' Mary had said and she threw herself on him, held on. The morgue attendant tried to pull her away from

James, it was unseemly, embracing a body. She'd told him to fuck right off, he was her son and she had a right to hold him.

She'd held James for a long time. My son, my baby boy, all I ever loved. Oh, she had wept, Mary over the body of her son. Why, why did it happen? And like a hard bead of light, the answer came: you. You, Mary Maynard, you stupid bitch, are why.

She'd apologized to her son. For being Mary Maynard, a waitress and a stupid bitch, and unable to send him to a good school when he was first getting into trouble, a bright kid, too bright and therefore bored, the teachers said. Unable to hire a good lawyer to keep him out of juvie. Shoplifting, then B&E, stealing cars. Unable to send him to college in penny loafers and an argyle sweater to study engineering or physics, because he'd been good at science. Unable to pay for his drug rehab when he was shooting up speed, smack, toothpaste. Unable to make love—all she had to offer—*enough*.

Sorry, she was sorry from the bottom of her heart, which was down there, so far, far down, right where hell must be. But James couldn't hear her saying 'sorry,' could he. Sorry was a fart in the wind.

'What do you want?' she asked Mr Koppler.

'To find her.'

Gloria knew very well that she should ask why. She knew very well, very, very well, the rage after James. She'd wanted to find the cops who shot him. She'd wanted to pluck out their teeth. She'd wanted to grind their skulls into dust. Mr Koppler did not want to sit down with Pilgrim and have a little, what was it called? Tate-a-tate.

She had to think fast. On one hand, there was sad Ernst Koppler, the father of a dead child, a compatriot in the ragged land of grief. On the other hand was Pilgrim. Gloria had first seen her in the market. Gloria, like a lovesick dyke, stared at the bead of sweat in the hollow of Pilgrim's throat. She was buying fruit, paying too much. She didn't even notice Gloria. She didn't even notice as Gloria stared at the roots of her dark hair, the strands lifting off her long, lovely neck. Her hair shimmered. Pilgrim was clean, a mountain stream, pure like a white nightgown drying on the line. Gloria stood there in the proximity of such loveliness and smelled the whiff of herself: the residue of thirty years of bacon grease. It never washed off, even with the cheapest soap.

So, on the other hand, Pilgrim. Gloria knew she could not separate the image of Pilgrim in the market from what Mr Koppler had just told her. She couldn't backtrack, could not unknow. Pilgrim is no longer beautiful, untouchable, fragrant.

'I know where she is.'

He nodded. He put down his coffee cup. 'The taxi driver, he tells me about your orphans.'

'They will be here any day now.'

'I help you,' he said.

They both waited. They were holding the same rope, moving through the dark, hand over hand.

'You understand I will not return to Switzerland.'

'Yes.'

'I have no one for my money. I am not rich. But my house, my business. I will arrange. It is enough for you. For what you need here.'

Gloria bit her lip. 'That's not necessary, Mr Koppler.' But, in truth, it was. In truth, she didn't have funds to last six months.

He held her gaze, he needed her to know him, to bear witness.

'Yes, yes, it is necessary,' he said.

It is, she silently agreed.

Money changes everything.

Gloria looks at the water, soft chiffon, the diffusion of light, a kind of magic substance. If she was Mary, plunging through it, flexing tensing arcing, if she was Mary at sixteen she'd swim away from Milton. But without Milton, she would be without James.

Far out, at the mouth of the cove, a dhow sails past: a vignette of tranquility. But if it came closer in, Gloria would see the ripped sail and the ragged fisherman with his salt-burned hands and dearth of fish. She waits, just to make sure he's not going to tack into the bay and find her. She couldn't possibly explain what she was doing with a body covered in a tarp.

She ties an old anchor to Koppler's legs. She could tie her body to his, she could fall with him into the still, green-blue sea. Companions. She could lie with him in the eelgrass and look up at the tiled surface of the water.

But instead she shuts her eyes. She says, out loud, 'James.' His name carries over the water.

She pushes Koppler out of the boat. No easy task as the little boat tips and tosses and Koppler is a heavy man. But underneath Gloria still has her swimmer's strength. There's a splash and then silence.

She watches the body sink.

Harry says she mustn't compare pain, mustn't want it to all add up. But that's a human need. The way a bill tallies, the items equal the cash. French fries are $1.99. And maybe, Gloria thinks, there is a reckoning, somewhere very far down the line, where it adds up and evens out. Profit and loss, perfectly balanced.

Harry and Pilgrim will be in Pangani now, Harry's little shack there. Where she herself had been happy, lain with him for a brief sojourn. That's when she'd told him about James, and that's when he'd begun his retreat. He couldn't bear her loss because of course—as she's come to realize—it reminded him of his crime.

She doesn't know—can't decide—if she wanted Pilgrim dead. She only knows it's immaterial to her that Pilgrim is still alive. Perhaps there's a life for her after all, who can tell. Redemption can never be ruled out.

The morning Mary went to the dentist she'd been thinking again about killing herself. It was absurd: going to fix her teeth when what she really wanted to do was stick her head in the oven. She was just so very tired. The real reason she'd picked up *National Geographic* was the cover article about suicide. The story was about the global history of suicide, the rituals and reasons, maps, charts—so much more than the plodding consequence of depression. Mary already knew her desire to die didn't come from depression, but from losing the only person she'd ever loved. The grinding loss, the meaningless years after his death had not been mental illness, only a loss she could not gain traction against.

The nurse called her name. *Doctor Babbits is ready to see you, Mary.* She turned the page and saw those dark-skinned children's faces staring out—*Africa's AIDS Orphans.* They stood half-naked in the mud, hungry, forsaken, their little hearts emptying of useless sadness and filling with violence that would keep them alive. In another issue, she'd be seeing the same faces with guns, dead eyes hidden by mirrored shades. *Africa's Child Killers.*

The most ironic thing that can happen, will happen.

Mary had touched their faces with her fingertips. Oh, her heart had said. Oh.

Mary? The nurse tapped her shoulder. *Mary? Doctor Babbits is ready to see you.* She got up, clutching the magazine. She knew it had happened, the answer to a question she hadn't known to ask.

How do you carry on?

It was like finding a crack in the earth and glimpsing the hot and certain core.

Because love endures with grief and hate. And every day, just as she feels her grief and hate, she feels her love and its great, shining purity.

She turns the boat south and west, back through the cove and the shallow channel to the blue, open harbor of Tanga's bay. She glances up in the tussling green of the land. She can almost see her little house. She can imagine herself there when the bus arrives and she will finally hold them. Oh, yes, money is everything. Her careful bribes, her persistence has paid off: the last permit has been granted. And Mr Koppler's money will be enough for quite some time.

Today, in only a few hours, in her arms, in her house, in her life, the children she has waited for, the children who have waited for her, shall be gathered safe therein.

DOROTHEA

Dorothea looked at Kessy's hands on the steering wheel. The smooth, even brown skin. He was handsome. She wanted him to know how afraid she was even though he couldn't take that fear away. But he was excited, he was confident. He glanced at her now and smiled. 'Only a few more miles.'

Her hands were flat against her thighs. She felt the sweat of her palms through her trousers. Her whole body was flooding with adrenaline. It was as if the years of loss had condensed. Sludge now filled her veins.

The old white man had come last week in this car, a Land Rover. 'Hello, I'm Harry,' he'd said and handed her the keys. 'This is for you.' Dorothea thought he must be mad; certainly he exuded the kind of manic buoyancy that marked certain kinds of mental illness. But he was insistent: the car was a gift. He refused to say from whom. He seemed to think she really wouldn't guess.

'But what will you do without your car?' she said to him.

'It's not my car,' he said, laughing. 'It's your car.'

'There is only the bus on Thursday,' she said.

'I'll walk.'

She thought he was joking. 'Can I drive you?'

'I used to walk everywhere,' he said. 'Once from Juba to Addis. Heck of a slog.'

Then he'd bought some bottled water and a loaf of bread, put them in his backpack and headed back toward Butiama on foot. A puppy with a piece of string tied too tightly around its neck followed him. He bent down, took off the string and tried once to shoo it away. But the puppy refused to leave him so he picked it up and carried it on his shoulder.

'*Simama*,' she said now to Kessy. 'Stop. I just need you to stop for a moment.'

He did as she said. She got out of the car and stood looking around her at Kenya. They were only a hundred miles from the border but the land did not look like Tanzania. Every inch of soil was cultivated and the soil itself was darker, denser. The people who passed on foot or on bicycle looked different, too, for they were Luo, big-boned with wide faces and very dark skin. They were Isaac's tribe. Hadn't she loved that about him? His otherness? That they were forging a new Africa, trans-tribe, trans-border. What the colonials had done with red pens on maps, Isaac and Dorothea were going to un-do. The borders of countries would always exist but people like them would transcend them.

Luke and Ezekiel were a mixture of her earth and Isaac's. He would rub her swelling belly and murmur to them in his language and then she would put her hand on top of his and speak to her babies in her's. Luke was born dark like his father and Ezekiel was paler like her, with a faint red tint to his hair. *Myeusi* and *Myeupe*, she would call them. Black and white, dark and light.

Far away she could just make out Lake Victoria, a thin slice of silver-blue marking the western horizon. Between here and there, small hills rolled and lifted, a quilt of *shambas* and dirt roads and villages. She had never come here with Isaac. Had he kept her from this place on purpose? Or had it simply been that they were both busy, young medical residents in Dar? He had this land in his mind, in his body, this sky, this view, his legs accustomed to its rise and fall. He knew its smells and seasons, the feel of its mud and dust under his bare feet. He'd been a poor boy, and it had taken him many extra years to finish his education, waiting for sponsors, always begging, always pushing, always scrounging.

Though she had been poor as a child, her family did well when Nyerere stepped down and the country opened itself to capitalism. It was because of their new wealth that she did not introduce them to Isaac. She'd felt instinctively that he would resent her parents' gated yard and satellite dish. She had also wanted to protect him from it so he wouldn't believe she could find a better man than him.

But the consequence had been that their families had no ties. He did not know the name of her village and she did not know the name of his.

Please, she wanted to call out. She wanted to fall on her knees on this Kenyan earth and beg God, oh please please please let me hold them let me smell them let me let me let it be okay. But you could not hope, you could not pray. And suddenly, she did not want the car, she did not want the possibility, she had grown accustomed to the hollow in herself. She did not want it carved out again, carved deeper. She was learning, slowly, to live with what had happened.

The day she'd come home, the day they had not been there— she relived this day so many times that it never became past. She'd called for them—*Ezekiel? Luke? Ezra? Luke?*—and there had been no answer. It was odd how she'd known right away, known they were not out at the market or the playground, had not gone to the beach. Her very first thought was that Isaac had taken them. She had suspected he would. In the silent apartment she felt careless, that she deserved this. But the boys did not, her small, sweet boys. And then she felt panic and she ran through the rooms. In the boys' room she saw that Isaac had forgotten Ezekiel's blanket, the one he could not sleep without. She grabbed this and ran out, down the stairs, into the street. She must find them to give Ezza his blanket. She ran along the street waving the blanket, down Mosque Street, onto Tom Mboya Avenue, she was pushing past people and in some crazy way she assumed she would catch up to them. She ran whichever way the traffic lights allowed her, as if momentum was gravity and would inevitably pull her toward her children. She was in a kind of dream and when she woke she was standing on a traffic island soaked with sweat, gasping for breath, holding a blanket. The traffic crawled past her, the *machinga* weaving in and out of cars, selling sunglasses and bottles of water and oranges and ornaments for the rearview mirror. The filthy, smog-choked air stung her eyes. People hustled past her. She sank to her knees. She wasn't crying—that would come later. She was astounded. She did not know how long she sat there before coins hit her head and clinked onto the pavement. A passing driver had thought she was a beggar.

Kessy took her hand and pulled her back toward the Land Rover. 'Come,' he said. She resisted—wanting to turn back, wanting to stay here, afraid.

'What if it's fine?' he said.

They drove on, they drove into the village, they drove to Isaac's family's house. Kessy would never tell her who he had bribed. A superior in town, a local businessman trying to get illegal goods over the border. Dozens of people. It must have cost him in favors, in money—his policeman's meager salary. He must have been persistent. He had done this for her. He had found Isaac's village for her.

'Wait here,' he said.

She watched him walk into the simple mud house. Improvements had been made—the trickle down of Isaac's success: real windows, electric lights. He could probably have built his mother a cement house, but old people didn't like change, didn't think the new was better than what had served them through seven decades of rain and drought.

A red toy car lay on its side between her and the house. Did that mean they were here? Or only that they had been here? Or only that a neighbor had children? She had a desire to run and grab the toy car and flee like a madwoman across the maize fields. Instead, she shut her eyes, she held on to the seat.

'Mama!' she heard. But she still could not open her eyes, could not move, could not bear the joke.

'Mama!'

They were there, they were getting in the car, they were swarming all over her, kissing her. She was taking them into her skin, into her body, where they had come from.

She opened her eyes and saw Kessy talking with Isaac's old mother. She couldn't hear what they were saying, only the tall manner of Kessy's posture and the stooped submission of the old woman. He was threatening her. For a moment, Dorothea wanted to call out to him to stop, because she was an old woman, she hadn't taken the boys, she probably loved them. At least Isaac had brought them here to her, instead of to his house in Nairobi or Nakuru where he no doubt had another wife.

Ezekiel was playing with the turn signals, with the light switches. 'Mama, is this your car?' As if she hadn't been gone for three years. As if she had not for a moment receded from his mind or heart. He had never doubted her and there was nothing to forgive.

But Luke. Her big boy, her *Myeusi*.

'Mama, are we going with you?' he asked. His hands were raking her arm, his voice contained all the anger and despair at her abandonment, the wild conflict between this, of his undiminished need for her, his mother.

'Yes,' she said. 'We are together now.'

STREBEL

The weather had just turned so much colder and Strebel was in the mood for soup—potato and leek or a minestrone with adequate tenor. He walked out of the station into the bright, cool October air.

It was late for lunch and the café was almost empty. He sat at a small table by the window. The waitress offered him split pea: this would do. And a beer to go with it.

He took the postcard out of his pocket. It had come with the morning's mail: an old-fashioned photo of cows drinking from a river. African cows with huge horns and humps on their shoulders. Nothing, apart from Strebel's address, was written on the back.

But he knew who it was from.

It was as if she didn't know what to say, didn't know how to describe her life. Only to let him know: I am beginning.

He closed his eyes. Imagined her. Somewhere in Africa, this dry place with cows. Her beauty would be fading. She would tidy it away. If he saw her again he would not recognize the plain, pared-down woman. He would not recognize her as she moved confidently and with certainty at the tasks she had set herself. She would have a small allocation of happiness—enough, not too much.

She was someone else now. Strebel felt a yearning of

schoolboy intensity to find her after all. To love her. To hold her and kiss her face. He began to weep, silently, his back to the empty café. There was so much sadness locked inside him. He could weep forever and not be done.

At last he stood and wiped his face and paid the bill. He walked back to the precinct the long way, beside the river. A woman with a baby was feeding the ducks. He'd arrested her a few years ago for possession of cocaine. He watched her for a long time, the baby's blonde hair in the sun, her squeals of glee. He moved on, quickly out of her sight. He met people on the worst days of their lives, and they never forgave him.

This thought made him seize up. All he did was make people sad, ruin their lives, tell them: your child has died, your husband is being held for questioning, nothing will be as it was. His efforts were merely mitigations. He didn't really put anything right, make anything better.

He pulled out his phone, dialed. He could not speak right away.

'Paul?' Ingrid said. 'Paul? Can you hear me?'

He opened his mouth, but still there were no words.

'Paul,' she said again with a touch of irritation. And that made him flinch. He almost hung up.

But then he said, 'Ingrid.' Her name like a handhold in the rock, so that he felt compelled to say it again to make sure it was real, that it held fast. 'Ingrid.'

'Yes?'

'I'll pass by the supermarket on the way home. Do we need anything?'

She did not answer right away, unsure what this unaccustomed offer meant. Never, even before they were married, had he spoken to her like this. The supermarket? He left the housekeeping to her, his socks on the floor, the bed unmade. She was almost afraid: things were as they were between them; she was not ready for change, but she had felt the shift for some time. Was he ill? Was there another woman?

'Butter,' she said with a sudden burst of courage and strange hope. 'And a dozen eggs.'

MARTIN MARTINS

Fucking Franco had insisted. He'd surprised me by being interested in the crap that passed for cultural heritage in Congo. But then, who was I to judge culture? We have some nice nuclear power plants in Ukraine. He said, 'Listen up, dickhead, there's a war on and these people are still dancing.'

'What people?' I said. 'There's no one. It's fucking creepy.'

That's how it was: no people. Not an old man sitting under a tree, not a woman with a bucket on her head, not even a fucking goat. We drove through the forest. Massive, dark trees, total silence. Some Italian journalists had gone missing right there a couple of weeks before.

The forest, man, it was not a normal forest. Not even like a jungle with monkeys and colored birds. A jungle, you feel there's life, creepy, crawly life that you definitely do not want to step on. But this forest was a bad dream; it was all wrong. There was a road, a good road, and yet no people, no one chopping down the trees. No sacks of charcoal for sale. I mean, maybe you don't know how weird that is unless you've been around the Dark Incontinent long enough.

When I was a kid I had a dream and I woke up to find everyone was gone, my mum, my pops, Uncle Mink, the whole family. I ran outside, but everyone had gone, the whole village, the birds, the cows, even the mangy dogs. And then I saw that the houses were getting up and running away. The trees were running away, their roots like legs. And I knew that whatever was coming was so terrible that all these things knew they had to get the fuck out.

That's what the forest was like.

After a dozen miles we came to a village. Again, no one.

'Franco,' I said. 'This is a bad idea. Who the fuck told you there was dancing?'

'The waiter,' Franco said. He was trying to be cool, but his lip was starting to twitch. His lip hadn't been the same, in fact Franco had not been the same, since that shit in Juba.

'The waiter?' I had to say, because I really was incredulous. We were here in the middle of a fucking war zone looking for a dance because of a waiter's say-so. A waiter in the last hotel on earth. Amazing, really, he had this starched white uniform, blinding white with fancy red and gold epaulets and shiny brass buttons. It was beautifully laundered. And then he had shorts, these old ripped-up shorts and sandals made from car tires. He spoke perfect English. Franco said he'd been a teacher before the war came and the rebels burnt down the school and all the children in it, including his own two boys.

Franco stopped the car and we got out. There were some empty buildings, most without roofs or windows. I glanced inside and saw a big splotch of red and what looked like a dress in the middle of it. But no body. Nobody at all.

The rebels had drawn on the side of the buildings. Their names—indecipherable, except for a clever scribe called REMY J. Remy J had also assembled enough letters to write 'Fuck' and 'Kill.' Sometimes people spell 'Fuck' without the 'c' or 'Kill' with only one 'l' but Remy J could spell. Perhaps the waiter had been his teacher. I don't know if Remy or one of his colleagues had drawn the guns, and what I supposed was a vagina.

Franco put up his hand, and then a finger to his lips. He

was standing very still. I listened. There it was, the very faintest sound, so you could easily confuse it with your own heartbeat. Drums.

'The natives are restless,' Franco said.

We took the safeties off our Glocks and crept toward the drums. The culture we'd come for. The beating led us like a thread through the burnt-out village. I was pining for a chicken, just to see a stupid chicken run out of a hut puck-pucking. But, man, there wasn't even a fly.

Just beyond the village, the ground fell on its knees, a sharp drop into a *korongo* where once there was a waterhole for cattle but now it was just a dry pan. A massive dust devil was hurling about, and the drumming was in the middle of it. It took us a moment to figure out that the dust came from the dancers.

They were all kitted out in masks, their feet stamping up the earth as they prowled and shook. They weren't singing, they weren't making any noise, there was just the sound of the drum. The dust cleared in brief moments so we could see the drummer in the middle, some old guy hammering hammering on a big cowskin drum with his big pink-palmed hands. And then the dust would occlude him again, and the dancers would be coming in and out of it, so we were seeing and not seeing.

I cannot deny that the sound of the drum, the pounding of it, went right into me and fucked with my heart, like the rhythm was just similar enough that my heart was all excited to have found a soulmate, but it was a seduction, because the drumbeat was just a fraction off, and it made my heartbeat change. Something was going on inside me, something was shifting about.

Also, WTF were these people doing here dancing and carrying on? Clearly, bad things had happened quite recently. And yet they were dancing.

Franco looked uncomfortable, too, shifting his weight like he had very bad indigestion, which he got after Juba. 'You happy now?' I turned back toward the village. 'Can we go?'

'No,' he said.

'Fine. I'll wait at the car.'

Everything was all wrong. I knew absolutely that everything was all wrong and would therefore get more wrong. We should not have been there, we should have turned around in the middle of that goddamn creepy forest and gone back to the hotel and had the teacher bring us beers. This wasn't our war. Any more.

I was not at all surprised to find four gentlemen standing around the car. Draping themselves like male models in Ukrainian *Vogue* over the open door, the hood, one posing in the side-view mirror. They had the mirrored shades and the camo gear, bits of it scavenged along the way, the bandanas, the AKs. I've noticed that the fashion sense of *rebels* hasn't evolved since the early nineties. They've missed the whole gangsta baggy trouser thing. But, having your trousers around your ass maybe doesn't work when you've got looting, burning and killing to do.

The leader of the foursome stepped forward and I noticed his Italian loafers right away.

'Good day. How are you?' I figured this was Remy J.

'Fine,' I said, although he wasn't really asking. 'And you?'

'I keel you. Quick if you pay. Slow if you do not.'

'Can you kill my friend first?'

Remy J laughed. They all laughed. I laughed. I love Africa, you can make a joke about anything and it will actually be funny. 'Sure,' he said. 'You like to watch?'

'Oh, definitely.'

Two of them went away and in only a few minutes came back with Franco. They were chatting and smoking cigarettes. 'So, they're going to kill us,' Franco said, offering me one.

'I didn't know you'd started smoking again,' I said, taking one.

'This pisses me off. I was enjoying the drumming.'

'Where do you want us?' I asked Remy J.

'First, you pay for quick keel.'

'Of course.' Franco and I handed him our wallets. There was

a couple of hundred dollars. He seemed satisfied. Then pointed to a wall about twenty yards away from the car. This had a number of bullet holes in it, and rust-colored smudges, like kids had been playing paintball. Only they hadn't.

Franco shook his head. 'No, no, that's not right. The light is terrible.'

Remy squinted. 'The light?'

'I was hoping you could take a photograph.'

'Of your keeling?'

'Sure,' nodded Franco. He took out his iPhone. 'Would you mind?'

Remy gestured to one of his mates. The mate took the iPhone and Franco showed him how to take a picture. We positioned ourselves against the wall close to the car, put our arms around each other and said 'Cheese!' We ended up taking a bunch of photos with Remy and the others, smiling, joking around. Remy had a real talent for posing.

But when Franco put two fingers behind Remy's head like bunny ears, he got serious. He gestured for the phone, and Franco sighed and started to hand it over.

Then, as if he wanted to be incredibly helpful to this fucking coon who was going to kill us, Franco said: 'Hey, man, I gotta unlock it for you. Disable the security code. Or you won't be able to use it.'

'Thanks,' Remy said and handed the phone back.

Franco pressed a code into the keypad.

DAH DAH DAH DAH DAH! BLAM BLAM!

Wagner. Sound of gunfire. DOOSH DOOSH. A crazy mad storm like a million bullets and people screaming AAAAHHHH with a couple of Apache choppers coming in TUKKA TUKKA and some explosions DOOSH PSSEWWWW DOOOSHH. Incoming!!! Franco and I jumped in the car while Remy and his crew dived for cover.

They were completely freaked out.

'Wahoo!' said Franco, flooring the Cruiser as we got the hell out of there.

We drove for three minutes before we started laughing. Franco reached over and squeezed my cheek. 'You are a genius!'

The recording had been my idea, sound clips scavenged from *Apocalypse Now* and a couple of episodes of *Band of Brothers*. We hadn't tried it until now.

Let me tell you, we thought we were shit-hot, so clever. And then the car started going fug-fug-fug. One of those cunts had managed to hit the carburetor.

'Shit, shit, shit.'

We were maybe fourteen miles from the hotel and in the middle of that fucking forest. We got out and started jogging. If we were lucky Remy J would give up on us. If we weren't he'd be coming after us. We hadn't seen another vehicle, but even on foot those guys were younger than us and they were pissed off. Because not everyone can take a joke.

Franco and I, we were not aging well. Smoking is terrible for lungs and all the burning tires we'd inhaled in Tripoli and tear gas in Kinshasa. Franco's guts hadn't been put back in very well in Juba; there was still a big tear in his abdominal muscles. And I still had that bullet in my lower spine.

There was not a breath of wind, not even the sound of leaves rustling. Like the trees were not real, but some kind of painted set. Something Stalin would come up with, a pretty field or village street, and then behind it piles of bodies, most of my *baburya*'s family. I kept listening and it was so crazy not to hear anything. We walked because we couldn't run any more. I was just tired, I really couldn't be bothered, like being out in the snow, that feeling you just want to lie down and go to sleep. I almost said to Franco that we should just give up, what did we really care about living?

Then we heard the bicycle bell, a bright little brriiing! We ducked into the trees. Fucking Remy was on a bicycle. They were all on bicycles, the four cyclists of the apocalypse. We stayed low and very still until they passed. But they were looking for us, they knew we weren't far, they were trying to smell us. Franco and I crept away, deeper into the forest.

We walked east, for no reason other than that it was away from the road and Remy, and we needed to pick a steady direction. We walked until it was too dark. We had to stop because the canopy of trees was so thick we couldn't see the stars. Of course, if we still had Franco's iPhone, we could have used the compass app. What a fucking genius.

After three days of walking we were not doing well at all—that fucking forest—and when that third night came we were thinking we were done. Franco, especially. But then we saw a light. Just one little point of light. And we started on, losing the light for a moment or two as we staggered on through the trees.

Finally, we came upon an old mission, a big stone house in a wide clearing. A low wall was more a landscaping feature than serious defense. The gate was open. Anyone could go in. So we went in. There were a number of kerosene lamps in the courtyard and we could therefore see the people here, families, and I wondered why we hadn't heard them further out, because it was quite a din: women cooking and talking, children crying or laughing. I listened to the other sounds, a wooden spoon on a tin plate, bare feet on straw mats, coughing. I felt like crying because my ears were aching from the lack of sound.

No one gave us a second glance. We carried on up the stone steps and into the mission. A crusty old nun came out in a bathrobe. 'Oh, dear,' she said, taking Franco's hand and leading him into a living room. 'Oh, dear, dear, dear.' As Franco sat down, she nodded to a young boy: 'You'd better get the doctor.'

To be honest, I did not remember. Certainly, when I saw her, when she walked in, she was not a woman I would recognize or even notice. I wasn't even sure she was a woman. Her hair was cut very short and she was wearing baggy clothes. And the light was very dim.

She was gentle with Franco. She felt his abdomen and took his pulse. She made him comfortable on the sofa. 'I don't have an IV,' she said. 'We're completely out.' She held a glass of water to his lips and he took a couple of sips. He looked pretty fucked up and I could see when he lay down that his belly was swollen. She plumped his pillow, then took a wet cloth and washed his face.

She turned to me. For a very brief moment her eyes met mine and I thought I saw something more than professional concern. I had no idea what it might be. She had a basin of water and began washing my face.

'No,' I pushed her away. 'I can do it.'

I woke up in the night and she was there, sitting in a chair.

'What is this place?'

'A refuge.'

The moon came through the window onto her face and I saw a certain beauty there.

'A refuge? There's a war. They'll just come here and kill you. Kill all these people. There's no refuge.'

'Do you have a cigarette?'

I sat up and gave her one.

'Sister Mary doesn't like me smoking.'

'Least of her troubles,' I said. And laughed.

'That's right,' she said.

'What? What's right?'

'Nothing.' She took another drag, but there was a smile on her lips.

I watched her. 'What are you doing here?'

'I'm a medic. I was with an MSF convoy that was attacked near the mountains. Everyone was killed except me. I ended up here.'

'When was that?'

'A year ago.'

Oh, shit, I nearly said. Because I remembered me and Franco, and it had certainly been a fuck up. The wrong coordinates, an error, really. Instead I said, 'What's the point?'

'The point?'

I noticed her hands, they were really quite lovely though worn and rough from the sun.

'Yeah, the point. The people out there, the children. I mean, you save them for how long? It's not like their lives were great even before this particular shit storm.'

'There is no point,' she said. 'It's what you make of it anyway.'

'Then why the fuck bother?'

'Listen,' she said, turning her head toward a sound. It was still far off, but closing in. The cheerful briiing of a bicycle bell.

She knew what it was, same as me, but she didn't freak out. She kept smoking.

'Pilgrim,' I said, because it came to me.

She looked at me. 'Yes, Martin.'

'I know this one. It doesn't have a good ending.'

She put out the cigarette, stood and wiped her hands on her trousers, an automatic gesture, because they were definitely not dirty. She walked into the courtyard. The sun was just coming up and the women were boiling kettles and the children, most of them were still sleeping. Pilgrim walked among them and they knew her. They offered her tea. Beyond them, under an acacia, was a Land Rover, an old 109, in pretty good shape, and so easy to hotwire.

She went out the gate. Remy J and the others were coming up the road. They stopped their bicycles and got off. Remy started talking to her, gesticulating. Though I couldn't hear his words, it was clear he was very, extremely pissed off. She stood quite still in the tall shadow of him, and as there was no point in running away, no point at all, she raised her arm to shade her face from the rising sun.

I looked again at the 109.

Instead, I said, 'Remy.' A whisper, really. Then louder, stepping toward him, because I meant it. 'Remy.'

Acknowledgements

With thanks to my agent, Kate Shaw, and to Eric Obenauf and Eliza Wood-Obenauf at Two Dollar Radio who passionately nurtured the US publication. In the UK, thank you to my champion editor, Sophie Buchan, and the team at W&N. And to Olga Gressot, Betsy Peirce and my mother who took such good care of my daughters, giving me precious time to write.

Also published by *Two Dollar Radio*

Visit TwoDollarRadio.com

THE REACTIVE A NOVEL BY MASANDE NTSHANGA

* *Sunday Times* **Barry Ronge Fiction Prize Finalist**
* **Etisalat Prize for Literature Longlist**
* **One of the Best Books of the Year** —*City Press, The Sunday Times, The Star, This is Africa, Africa's a Country, Sunday World*

"An immersive and powerful portrait." —*VICE*

THE ONLY ONES A NOVEL BY CAROLA DIBBELL

* **One of the Best Books of 2015** —*O, The Oprah Magazine, Washington Post, Flavorwire, National Post*

"Breathtaking. It's that good, and that important, and that heartbreakingly beautiful." —*NPR*

"A heart-piercing tale of love, desire, and acceptance." —*Washington Post*

SQUARE WAVE A NOVEL BY MARK DE SILVA

"Brilliant." —*3:AM Magazine*

"Enticing and enthralling, [*Square Wave*] aims to hit all the literary neurons. This might be the closest we get to David Mitchell on LSD. *Square Wave* is the perfect concoction for the thirsty mind."
—*Atticus Review*

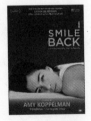

I SMILE BACK A NOVEL BY AMY KOPPELMAN

* **Now a major film starring Sarah Silverman & Josh Charles!**

"Powerful. Koppelman's instincts help her navigate these choppy waters with inventiveness and integrity." —*Los Angeles Times*

"Koppelman explores with ruthless honesty a woman come undone."
—*Bookslut*

BABY GEISHA STORIES BY TRINIE DALTON

"[The stories] feel like brilliant sexual fairy tales on drugs. Dalton writes of self-discovery and sex with a knowing humility and humor."
—*Interview Magazine*

"Dalton handles her narratives with a deft skill and a keen, distinct, confident voice that never eases up." —*The Brooklyn Rail*

THE GLACIER A NOVEL BY JEFF WOOD

"Gorgeously and urgently written." —*Library Journal* (starred)

"It seduces you slowly, the reader hypnotized from the first page."
—*Heavy Feather Review*

"An innovatively told book, a truly cinematic novel." —Largehearted Boy

THE ORANGE EATS CREEPS
A NOVEL BY GRACE KRILANOVICH

* **National Book Foundation 2010 '5 Under 35' Selection**
* **NPR Best Books of 2010**
* *The Believer* **Book Award Finalist**

"Krilanovich's work will make you believe that new ways of storytelling are still emerging from the margins." —*NPR*

HOW TO GET INTO THE TWIN PALMS
A NOVEL BY KAROLINA WACLAWIAK

"One of my favorite books this year." —Roxane Gay, *The Rumpus*

"Waclawiak's novel reinvents the immigration story."
—*New York Times Book Review*, Editors' Choice

ANCIENT OCEANS OF CENTRAL KENTUCKY
A NOVEL BY DAVID CONNERLEY NAHM

* **One of the Best Books of 2014** —NPR, *Flavorwire*

"Wonderful… Remarkable… it's impossible to stop reading until you've gone through each beautiful line, a beauty that infuses the whole novel, even in its darkest moments." —NPR

THE PEOPLE WHO WATCHED HER PASS BY
A NOVEL BY SCOTT BRADFIELD

"Challenging [and] original… A billowy adventure of a book. In a book that supplies few answers, Bradfield's lavish eloquence is the presiding constant." —*New York Times Book Review*

"Brave and unforgettable." —*Los Angeles Times*

THE VISITING SUIT A NOVEL BY XIAODA XIAO

"[Xiao] recount[s] his struggle in sometimes unexpectedly lovely detail. Against great odds, in the grimmest of settings, he manages to find good in the darkness." —*New York Times Book Review*

"These stories personify the compassion, humor, and dignity inherent not just in survival but in triumphing over despair." —*O, The Oprah Magazine*

I'M TRYING TO REACH YOU
A NOVEL BY BARBARA BROWNING

* *The Believer* Book Award Finalist

"I think I love this book so much because it contains intimations of the potential of what books can be in the future, and also because it's hilarious." —Emily Gould, *BuzzFeed*

HAINTS STAY A NOVEL BY COLIN WINNETTE

* One of the Best Books of 2015 —*Slate, Flavorwire*

"[An] astonishing portrait of American violence. The rewards of *Haints Stay* belong to the reader." —*Los Angeles Times*

"A success... *Haints Stay* turns the Western on its ear." —*Washington Post*

FREQUENCIES *A non-fiction journal of artful essays.*
"Heavy with literary weight." —*NewPages*

VOLUME 1
Essays by Blake Butler, Joshua Cohen, Tracy Rose Keaton, Scott McClanahan; interview with Anne Carson. Plus, color photographs by Morgan Kendall! Original artwork by John Gagliano.

...pporting ...lture!